BEAST

B E A S T

A Novel
of the Future World Dictator

Dan Betzer

PRESCOTT PRESS, INC.
Lafayette, LA 70505

Prescott Press, Inc.
P. O. Box 53788, Lafayette, LA 70505

Library of Congress Catalog Card Number
85-061327

ISBN Number 0-933451-02-4

Designed by Don Pierce

Printed in the United States of America

PROLOGUE

"THE MAN WHO WILL COME AFTER ME..."

I

Germany, April 28, 1945

Berlin looked like hell.

The once elegant metropolis resembled a beast-torn carcass —
but still bleeding and somehow alive.

General Constantine Rokossovsky's Second Byelorussian
Division had arrived in the northern suburbs, each troop burning
with a holy mission. The Russians, planning a dreadful revenge for
the German rape of Stalingrad, moved their malevolent machines
of annihilation ever closer to city center.

Marshal Ivan S. Konev had his First Ukrainians poised deep
within Berlin's southside. He was frustrated and angry that Stalin
had not permitted him the honor of capturing the Chancellery.
Since January 12, his troops had marched resolutely from Warsaw
with dreams of "drawing and quartering" the Nazis dancing in
their vengeful heads. Now autocratic deliberations in the councils
of war kept them from fulfilling their ultimate dreams.

Even the mighty General Georgi Zhukov, hero of Moscow and
Stalingrad, was kept waiting in the wings of the city while Stalin
decided which of his generals he would allow to make the kill. The
wait would prove fruitful for the legendary Zhukov. He was finally

given the Moscow-originated orders to rip the heart from the Third Reich by torching the Chancellery.

The Russians were aware that construction of an enormous bunker had been started beneath the Chancellery in early 1944. According to the security reports received in the communist hierarchy, had the Germans been able to complete it, there was a chance that Adolf Hitler might actually be in it!

That was all the motivation Zhukov needed and he made it plain to his staff that he wanted the Chancellery destroyed but the bunker beneath it preserved.

"Survivors! I want Nazi survivors! Especially Hitler! I want him alive so we can make him hurt for a long, long time. In fact, we will make his last hours on earth make Mussolini's death look rhapsodic by comparison," Zhukov said.

Mussolini and his mistress Clara Petacci had been captured two days earlier by Italian partisans as they tried to escape from northern Italy into Switzerland. They were summarily executed and their bodies brought to Milan on a truck. For nearly a day their bodies lay on the *piazza* until vengeance-minded Italians strung them up by their heels from lampposts. In this macabre manner, *Il Duce* and Italian Fascism disappeared from the earth.

Zhukov's premonitions regarding Hitler's whereabouts were correct. The one in whom the basic evil had spawned and erupted to kill over 50-million people still thrived in his den of hell beneath the German Chancellery. Hitler had been nowhere near fabled *Berschtesgaden* and his beloved *Berghof* when the *Obersalzberg* was bombed three days earlier. The allies had hoped that the Fuhrer had escaped to the Nazi "holy mountain" far away from crippled Berlin. At 9:30 a.m. on the 25th of April, sirens alerted the mountain people of approaching aircraft, and by 10 o'clock the inferno had begun. With throttled engines, the first wave of American bombers raced over the Kehlstein mountain range. The *Berghof*— the Hitler house — was hit, one side of it destroyed completely. The vaulted roof was torn to pieces and hung precariously in the air. The interior looked as if an earthquake had hit it. The raid was a success, but Hitler wasn't there. He had remained in Berlin in his Fuhrer-bunker. But his days were numbered! Zhukov had guessed correctly, and the Russian generals slowly closed their iron ring about the bunker.

The main commercial thoroughfare of Berlin, *Leipziger Strasse*, was now controlled totally by the Reds. Anhalter railroad station had fallen. Tempelhof airfield was in the possession of General Vassily Chuikov, who realized that the fight was still far from over. Earlier in the morning he had called Zhukov to report, "Some German SS units are still fighting like tigers."

Nearby, on the *Friedrichstrasse*, everything was burning. Fifty-seven-year-old Walter Wagner, a justice of the peace, was receiving his baptism of horror. He had just been pressed into service in a *Volkssturm* detachment. The *"Volkssturm"* was composed of civilians, too old for the regular army, pressed into last-minute duty for the final defense of Berlin. Wagner found himself surrounded by other similarly frustrated warriors who had received no training or instruction. They were only pawns, pitched into the violent maelstrom in the final hours of the war to satisfy the lingering insanity of the Fuhrer.

Hitler had decreed to his warlords: "If the war is to be lost, the nation will also perish. This fate is inevitable. There is no need to consider the basis of a most primitive existence any longer. On the contrary, it is better to destroy even that, and to destroy it ourselves. The nation will prove itself the weaker, and the future will belong exclusively to the stronger Eastern nation."

What did a few thousand more deaths mean to Hitler? The war was lost. His own death was but hours away. He would take as many as possible with him. If the great Fuhrer must die, then what right did a man named Walter Wagner have to live? Or children? Even the youngsters were pressed into the frontline service for the battle for Berlin.

Justice of the Peace Wagner was suffering vicariously for Hitler. All about him the earth split and heaved as Russian cannon fire exploded. Bright orange clouds of dust billowed as man-caused shock waves ripped buildings apart.

Not even Hitler could accuse the *Volkssturm* detachment of not trying. But fewer than 500 of them remained alive, and those fortunate few fought desperately to hold the *Friedrichstrasse* in German hands. But their attempt was made with faulty rifles and hastily-assembled grenades against Zhukov's 79th army.

Wagner heard a sudden short cry beside him and turned to see his neighbor slammed against a piling by a direct hit. Blood was smeared across the man's face, and his right eye swung across his cheek connected only by an optic nerve.

The first visible Russian tank appeared through the smoke three blocks down the street, looking like a fire-belching dragon coming through the early mist of a Bavarian valley. That was enough for Wagner. He slipped from his position in a gutted hotel and began running down the alley. Behind him the skeletal building erupted with a violent explosion. Wagner was propelled through a plate glass window but remarkably escaped with only minor cuts. Fear gripped him like it fills the heart of a deer pursued by dogs. The Justice suddenly noticed that he was crying. He wanted to go home. He knew he would die this night. His prayer was that it would happen in his own apartment.

Night was falling on the gasping city as Wagner found his front gate. In the shadows he could barely make out the outline of three men near his door. They waited silently as he cautiously mounted the steps, then one of them stepped out of the shadows and spoke to him.

"You are Wagner?" It was more a command than question.

The little man's heart began to pound and his mouth was dry. "Yes, I am Wagner. What is it you wish?"

The two non-speaking men had moved behind the frightened little man to prevent his running, while the first man continued his terse interrogation. "I am Guensche — SS Major Otto Guensche. You will come with us now, please."

Visions of a firing squad for desertion raced through Wagner's brain.

"Please, Major, you must understand. I had to run. There is no way that old people such as I can hold off Zhukov and his Russians with our homemade bombs and ancient weapons. Don't you understand, Major? We have lost the war! It is suicide on the *Friedrichstrasse*! I could not remain there and —".

"Quiet, Wagner!" Guensche had his face inches from the terrified justice. "You are in no trouble. In fact, quite the opposite. You are highly honored this day for you are wanted by the Fuhrer. He is waiting for you in his bunker at this very moment. Come!"

"The Fuhrer? He's in Berlin? But what could he possibly want with me?"

"You are a justice of the peace, are you not? Yes? Well, there is to be a wedding between the Fuhrer and Eva Braun. You have been chosen to perform it. So you will come with us now."

Wagner had heard of the existence of a Fuhrer-bunker but, like many other Germans, he did not think the story was true. Nor that Hitler was still in Berlin. Why would their leader have chosen to remain in the stricken city?

The little German dutifully followed the SS men through the maze of destruction into the heart of Berlin. He believed he was descending into hell.

Wagner was surprised to see the magnificent marble halls of the New Reich Chancellery still standing. In a far corner of the Old Chancellery garden, SS men stood guard beside an unsurfaced, dingy-colored cement block. It looked like an old beat-up pillbox hidden along the Siegfried Line. He saw a narrow doorway and small vestibule with steps leading into the bowels of the earth.

As he was escorted down the steps, Wagner became aware of two very unpleasant odors. One was the sour-sweet smell of newly poured concrete. The other odor revealed that the latrines were clogged up.

Major Guensche and the two other SS officers prodded Wagner down some 40 steps to the lower elevation of the bunker. The shaking justice of the peace could hardly believe that the Fuhrer could actually be in this hellhole with its tiny rooms — most of them three by four meters and very dimly lit.

Wagner remembered seeing Adolf Hitler at Nuremberg, standing as a god before nearly a million people. Had it really only been seven years before when Hitler spoke on that September evening, his speech brutal and bombastic, dripping with venom against the Czech state? His raving met with the delirious response of the multitudes of Nazi fanatics gathered in the huge stadium. Ah, those pageants of yesteryear, remembered in the lights of torches and screams of frenzy, seemed like distant history now.

Walking down the narrow corridor, the foursome came to the open door of a sparsely furnished room which was used as the gathering place for the officer corps. A weathered record player, hampered by a worn stylus, was valiantly attempting to reproduce the strains of a Strauss waltz. Empty liquor bottles were strewn about the room, leftovers from a frantic party the night before. Lying in a heap in the corner was the unconscious form of a party girl. Wagner could see her outstretched arm which was covered with needle tracks. One of Field Marshal Wilhelm Keitel's aides was sprawled drunkenly over a sofa, alternately weeping and giggling.

Major Guensche indicated a chair to Wagner who quickly sat down, afraid to speak.

"Stay right there until I return, Wagner. The Fuhrer and his bride will be ready in a few moments. You will be ready to officiate the wedding upon their arrival."

The justice of the peace had performed enough weddings to know what to do. But his mind could not comprehend the macabre scene about him. Was this all that was left of the mighty Third Reich? Three square blocks? And in 36 hours even that would be gone. The dream of the invincible Aryans would be consigned to dusty museums and history books.

But why? What had happened? Hitler was *Ubermensche!* Superman! Everyone knew that!

Wagner closed his weary eyes and remembered the opening lines of Nietzsche's brilliant "Thus Spake Zaranthustra."

"Behold, I teach you the Superman. The Superman is the meaning of the earth . . ."

It had been nearly seven years since Wagner had last watched his Fuhrer at a rally. Oh, what a man he had been that awesome night! Strutting across the arena, acknowledging the roar of the immense crowd with the strange tilt of his head, thrilling them with his inspired voice and powerful words! Yes, thus spake Zaranthustra, indeed! Hitler was without question, Ubermensche, sent from the gods!

"Wagner! You will come now!"

Guensche's command quickly snapped Wagner back to the real world and the stinking bunker. He followed the SS major down the narrow corridor. He was led into a small conference room where the wedding party awaited the entrance of Adolf Hitler and Eva

Braun. When the Fuhrer finally made his appearance, Wagner felt his knees grow weak. "*Mein gott!* It couldn't be . . ."

A disheveled, trembling little man was helped into the room by his valet, Heinz Linge, and led over to stand by Eva Braun, his mistress of several years — now to be his wife. Wagner thought it was an apparition. Hitler's eyes that had once dominated his arrogant and confident appearance were now a weak, watery blue. Those eyes searched Wagner's face, trying desperately to focus properly. Hitler lifted a shaking hand in a parody of greeting.

"Wagner," he began in a raspy voice, "we found you just in time. Let's get on with it. Quickly, please."

Summoning his courage and wits, the justice led Hitler and Eva Braun through the Nazi Party necessities — the bride and groom swearing that they were of complete Aryan descent and had no hereditary diseases to exclude their marriage. Even in his last hours, Hitler was the perfect German, one of the super race. On the marriage certificate he indicated that his father's name was Schicklgruber.

In her nervousness, Eva Braun, a rather pretty but shallow girl, began to sign her name "Eva Braun." Realizing her mistake, she quickly stopped, crossed out the "B" and wrote "Eva Hitler, born Braun." The two official witnesses to the ceremony were Joseph Goebbels and Martin Bormann.

The pagan ceremony ended, Wagner was released and ushered to the bunker entry where he disappeared into the exploding and terrifying night. He had lived his one moment of glory in an otherwise dreary life; and he would never be heard from again.

In the bunker below there was a wedding feast in Hitler's apartment. The Fuhrer showed little interest in the festivities and went into his bedroom to begin dictating his last will and testament. He summoned Frau Gertrude Junge, one of his faithful secretaries, and began his valedictory to the German nation and to the world which was meant also to be a last, conclusive appeal to history:

"More than thirty years have passed since I made my modest contribution as a volunteer in the First World War, which was forced upon the Reich.

"In these three decades, love and loyalty to my people alone have guided me in all my thoughts, actions and life. They gave me

*power to make the most difficult decisions which have ever con-
fronted mortal man . . . "*

Even on the final day of his life, Hitler told the big lie. He should
have written:

*"For the last thirty years, I have been owned and guided by
Lucifer himself! In my early life, I gave my very soul to him and I
am a true citizen of hell!"*

That indeed was the truth behind Hitler's unique power. By the
time he was 21 years of age, already festering with hatred and
thoughts of vengeance toward the outside world, he discovered
that he had been given supernatural capabilities. It had not been
accidental. Hitler had diligently sought for the reality of Lucifer in
his life for some time. He understood that he was the physical re-
embodiment of the spirit of Antichrist. Actively working toward
Luciferic possession, he was helped along the way by drug-in-
duced awareness. Mescalin was the agency. Aldous Huxley de-
scribed the kinds of visions Hitler must have seen:

"Heroic figures, of the kind that Blake called 'The Seraphim,'
may make their appearance alone, or in multitudes. Fabulous
animals move across the scene. Everything is novel and amazing.
Almost never does the visionary see anything that reminds him of
his own past. He is not remembering scenes, persons, or objects,
and he is not investing them; he is looking at a new creation."

There was no doubt in Hitler's mind that he had been singled out
by "the Dark One" for a spectacular career that would lead to
worldwide power. All 40 of the original members of the New
German Workers' Party were from the most powerful occult
society in the nation.

In a séance at which many of the party members were present, a
gift of the unholy spirit had operated through the mouth of Alfred
Rosenberg, a one-time refugee from Moscow, now editor of the
Nazi Party newspaper *Volkischer Beobachter.* In his supernatural utterance, Rosenberg called forth the presence of the Beast,
the spirit which all present realized had long since captured the
body, mind and soul of Adolf Hitler.

Hitler was the German messiah, the one for whom the whole
world had long waited. He himself had assured them, "I am found-
ing an order . . . from which the final stage in human mutation will

emerge — the Man-God!"

One of Hitler's confidants who defected to the West, Herman Rauschning, wrote of his former Fuhrer: "Most of all, Hitler is the reeking miasma of furtive, unnatural sexuality which fills and fouls the atmosphere around him like an evil emanation. Nothing in his environment is straightforward. Surreptitious relationships, substitutes and symbols, false sentiments and hidden lusts — nothing in this man's surroundings is natural and genuine, nothing has the openness of a natural instinct."

The world that feared Hitler would have feared him even more had they known the true source of his power. The Fuhrer believed in the legend of the "Spear of Destiny," the fable that the spear which was used to thrust Christ's side on the cross still existed, and he who owned the spear also owned supernatural abilities.

Sir Winston Churchill was aware of the Luciferic influence behind the German leader. He insisted to his aides during the war that the occultism of the Nazi Party must not be revealed to the general public under any circumstances. The English Prime Minister shuddered at the evil of the civilization that could so easily substitute a twisted cross, the swastika, for the cross of Christ.

Hitler was exhausted when he completed the dictation of his last will. He closed the document by informing the world:

"My wife and I choose to die in order to escape the shame of overthrow or capitulation. It is our wish that our bodies be burned immediately in the place where I have performed the greater part of my daily work during the twelve years of service to my people."

It was early Sunday morning — the last Sabbath of his evil life. As he went to bed, Berliners were feeling the full fury of wrath of the Allied armies. Smoke covered the capital city. Buildings exploded into fireballs as the enraged Russians pressed their relentless attack. Artillery was now being fired at pointblank range and the vanguard of several Russian divisions was now only a few hundred feet from the *Wilhelmstrasse* and the Chancellery.

Hitler rolled sleeplessly in his bed, distraught at the sad realization that he was not the *Ubermensch* of hell, yet with no thought of the 50-million people who were dead at the hands of his powerful Werhmact and Panzer divisions.

Somewhere in the deep, dark recesses of his soul there was an awareness that his life was almost over, but one would follow him whose evil would dwarf his own treachery — including the holocaust.

Somehow, somewhere, during the past two years, Lucifer had removed his hand of malevolent blessing from the Fuhrer and during that time everything had gone wrong. Whether he had been truly demented in thinking he was to be the messiah-counterfeit or whether he had been thwarted by the worldwide intercession of some unknown saints, Hitler would never know. He now had only 14 hours to live.

At three o'clock the following afternoon, the Fuhrer and his bride made their final farewells. The ceremony was brief, taking fewer than three minutes. In the silence that followed the handshaking, Hitler's valet Heinz Linge opened the door to the Fuhrer's apartment. Hitler directed his wife to enter ahead of him. Then, before disappearing from the last people ever to see him alive, Hitler turned to his old helper, the valet, and instructed, "Linge, old friend, I want you now to join the breakout group. Get out of the bunker right away."

Linge was surprised and touched by Hitler's personal interest. "Why, my Fuhrer?"

Hitler's last command was perhaps more momentous than anything else he had uttered in his years of power: "To serve the man who will come after me!"

The apartment door closed behind the Hitlers, and Major Guensche took his place guarding the entryway.

Inside the deathroom, Eva stood before a vase of roses. She knew they had not come from her husband. Such kindness would not have originated in his self-serving heart. Perhaps one of the generals had brought them. Eva was suddenly aware that her husband was speaking to her. She turned to him, embarrassed.

"Oh — I'm sorry, Adolf. What did you say?"

Hitler glared at her balefully through his pale blue eyes. "I said that all things pass away, Eva. Nothing remains. Nothing but death and the glory of my deeds."

They sat down on the blue and white sofa, several feet apart from each other.

"Eva, I truly believed that I was the one. Perhaps I really was the chosen one — at least those first few years. But something happened. I lost his touch. Somehow, somewhere I lost it."

"Adolf, whatever are you talking about? Whose touch?"

Hitler looked at Eva for a long moment, then shrugged painfully. "Nothing. It doesn't matter to me now. Here, finish this wine before . . ."

His words were interrupted by the shaking of the bunker. Shells were landing overhead, much nearer now.

"Adolf." Eva's words were tentative. "Adolf, they have come so very close. Perhaps it is time for us to —"

"Yes, Eva. It is time."

On the table in front of them were two pistols and several poison capsules. The larger of the two pistols was a standard Walther 7.65-caliber, the one Hitler had chosen for his suicide. The smaller pistol was a Walther 6.35 for Eva's use, should she need it. Hitler wrapped his gun in a tea towel.

Eva kicked off her buckskin pumps and pulled her feet up under her body. She had decided not to use her pistol. She placed it on her raspberry-colored silk scarf on the table. She put one of the capsules of poison in her mouth and, before biting into it, looked at her husband.

It was his final command to anyone and it was consistent with most of his other utterances — it brought death. "Yes, Eva, do it now. Farewell!"

He put a capsule into his mouth and raised the pistol to his temple. Eva bit into her capsule and swallowed hard. Her death was almost instantaneous. She never heard the gurgle deep within her throat and was not aware that in her death spasm she fell against her husband's shoulder. And Hitler never heard the roar of the gun that blew away the side of his head.

Outside in the hall Major Guensche was suddenly engulfed by fear. The hair was standing on the back of his hand. Although he accepted rationally that he was alone in the hallway, somehow he knew that he was really not alone — that he was in the presence of someone, or something, else. And whatever — or whomever — Guensche knew it was evil. He drew his pistol and looked about frantically. But he could see no one.

It was at that moment that Guensche smelled a dreadful odor, something that reeked even worse than the decaying flesh of long-dead cadavers. And then — then the Major heard it! The low laughter of something that was not human — a penetrating and completely terrifying sound! Guensche fired his pistol in the direction of the sound, but the mocking laughter continued, growing even louder. He now had no question at all that he was in the presence of the supernatural.

Then the subterranean hallway was permeated with a strange wind, blowing back and forth across the concrete walls, increasing in intensity like a hurricane in microcosm. The moaning of the wind, combined with the mocking laughter from the unseen intruder, was the most chilling sound Major Guensche had ever heard.

But he didn't hear it long. The faithful Nazi officer was hurled to the ground unconscious when the steel door of Hitler's apartment suddenly flew open, crushing the back of Guensche's head. Even had he retained consciousness, he could never have seen with human eyes the departure in the wind of a thousand evil spirits, led by a dark shadow — still laughing.

II

Bern, Switzerland, April 30, 1945

The late model Citroen weaved tentatively through heavy traffic going into the city along the *Thun-Strasse.* At the wheel, Dr. Mac Leman puffed anxiously on a cigarette and glanced at his watch. There was still time to get there, provided there was no unusually congested traffic delay on the *Kirchenfeld* Bridge.

Leman's mind was filled with second-guessing. He should have driven to the hospital earlier despite having the day off. He had not shaken the premonition derived upon first examination of his patient that the birth of her child would be extremely difficult. Everything about her pregnancy had been strange. She absolutely would not discuss the father — indeed, it was almost as if the child had none, that he simply did not exist on earth. When Leman had repeatedly questioned her about the man, the woman had smiled darkly and ignored him.

She had been under his care since the fourth month of carrying the baby. She was now only seven months along. Neither Dr. Leman nor any of his staff had suspected that the birth would be this premature. The call from the hospital to his home in Bern's fashionable southeast section had come as a surprise.

The Citroen had now carried him safely past the bridge. To his left, Leman could see the imposing roof lines of the Parliament building. Only a few hundred more meters to go. Perhaps he could still arrive at the ward in time.

The call from his associate had been frantic. "Mac, you must come, please. I cannot handle this situation without you. The woman's temperature has dropped alarmingly!"

Leman could see the towers of the University Hospital straight ahead of him now. Darkness was descending on the sandstone structures of the capital city — descending far too rapidly, the doctor thought to himself. Almost as if the sun were trying to leave the city.

Leman parked the Citroen in his private parking slot and ran through the "employees only" gate. The lift carried him to the ninth flour where his staff anxiously awaited him. They briskly prepared him for the delivery room.

His patient was already in heavy labor. It would be her first child — rather unusual for a woman in her mid-40s. Leman had not been able to glean any basic information from her. She volunteered only the essentials, the fundamental facts necessary to gain her admission to the hospital. Anything beyond that caused her to turn away from those who questioned her.

"Hello, doctor. I am glad you arrived in time."

Her voice was low, even for a man it would have been deep. The sound of it made a slight chill race down Leman's spine. She was not unattractive, but neither could he bear to look directly at her. She repulsed him — and excited him sensually.

"Yes, yes, I am truly sorry I was not here when you arrived, Madam. When I examined you earlier this week there was no indication that the birth would be so premature. But I am sure that your child will be all right and —"

Her laughter was genuine and sustained, although her face indicated no evidence of joy. "Oh yes, Doctor, he will be all right. His time is come!"

The birth was exceptionally difficult. The mother had lost most of her amniotic fluid. Several times attending nurses thought the child was lost. His head was low, necessitating a forceps delivery, and the instruments made a mark on the child's brow.

The mother was a good prophetess, Leman thought to himself, as he held the child in his hands. It was a boy, probably around four pounds. And he seemed to be in excellent condition.

But it was the child's eyes that got the doctor's full attention. They were looking right at him, fully focused. Aware. Intelligent. As if the baby knew everything that was going on in the room. In all his years of obstetrics, Dr. Leman had never witnessed anything like it. He could have sworn the eyes belonged to someone 40 or 50 years old.

As the staff began cleaning the child's body, they sensed a foreign, dreadful odor. It stank like something had been dead in the operating room for a long, long time. One of the nurses, quite accustomed to most bodily odors, became violently ill and ran, retching, from the room. Another attendant choked for air. It was not the normal fetid odor of the placenta. Leman himself had never experienced such stench in his life and he felt as if he were being asphyxiated.

Then came the sounds, the last series of sonance their ears would ever hear. One of the noises was the mournful crying of a wind that seemed to come from the central elevator shaft, growing louder and louder. They could hear it whipping down the corridor toward the delivery room, knocking aside everything in its path. The doors to the room crashed open and the wind instantly enveloped them all, striking everything to the floor except the gurney where the mother and child lay. They seemed to be in a quiet cocoon.

In that terrifying moment, Dr. Leman heard a sound he would never have forgotten, had he lived. It was not a human sound — a low mocking laughter. It was grotesque and strangled. Leman was thrown against the wall by the swirling wind and he tried vainly to cover his ears to keep out that terrible, insane laughter, now growing louder and louder. Everyone in the room heard it and yet there seemed to be no source of its origin.

Leman picked himself up so he could check on the patient on the table. Incredibly, she seemed to be sleeping — that same dark and sinister smile on her face, like a malevolent Mona Lisa. Then Leman saw the baby, looking directly at him. Those eyes! Oh, God, those terrible eyes! They were a pale, watery blue and they stared at him balefully, cruelly. Leman saw the unmistakable look of sheer evil in them. And he felt a hand inside his chest close over his heart and crush it to pulp.

All five bridges leading away from the downtown area were jammed as weary workers began their tedious drive home. A thick fog hovered over the Aare River, adding to the confusion and frustration of traffic. And it had grown quite dark several hours before the normal time.

The brightest light in the city was a most unusual one. Most of the drivers noticed it immediately. The light hovered over the downtown hospital. It was intensely bright — like a star.

1

In the stifling August heat, the 22-square miles of Manhattan, New York City's centerpiece, looked like a shimmering fortress of concrete. Its three million citizens and workers were bigger than most of earth's armies; yet, for the most part, each citizen felt and looked alone — and lonely.

A speeding yellow taxi thundered its way through the cement and steel canyons. One wheel hit a hidden chuckhole, sending the driver into a paroxysm of rage and its passenger nearly to the floor.

The rider, 48-year-old Clayton Daniels, gingerly righted himself in the worn seat, glared at the driver who was completely impervious to anything so mundane as creature comfort, and applied his glowing lighter to a Merit menthol. He leaned painfully against the torn armrest and shook his head gently as he thought to himself of the 12-thousand or so similar cabs clogging the streets of the Big Apple. "The ultimate weapon," he mused silently. "We will not be destroyed by missiles and bombs, but by these lousy cabs and their insane drivers!"

As President of IBC (International Broadcasting Company)

Television News, the ruddy, slightly overweight passenger was not all that accustomed to such a primitive mode of transportation. Usually he drove his Audi 5000 or rode in the company limousine which carried him to the destinations of his choice. But he had wisely decided against the opulent luxury of the latter conveyance in order to keep his destination discreet. The person who had summoned him had made that specification very clear.

Daniels inhaled deeply on the quickly disappearing cigarette and indulged in his peculiar habit of allowing the smoke to escape from the gap between his upper front teeth. Some office wag had once proclaimed (although not in Daniels' hearing, of course) that God had created the mouths of Clayton Daniels and David Letterman from the same mold. Someone else had pitched in the name of Alfred E. Newman.

Watching the smoke seep through the slightly open window, the news executive considered the telephone call that had set him off on this chase through Manhattan. It could not have come at a more inopportune time. He had to solve several in-house computer problems and all hell was breaking loose at the United Nations again.

At about 10 o'clock that morning, Daniels' secretary Ivy Browning had buzzed his intercom with the terse message that he was wanted on the phone. Daniels had cursed silently to himself and informed Miss Browning that he wanted all calls held for at least another hour. But the patient secretary responded, "I think you will want to take this call, sir; it's Jacque Catroux."

Daniels could not have been more stunned had she said the caller was Jesus Christ. Jacque Catroux, "the man-about-town" — the town being London, Paris, Rome, Brussels, Geneva or Berlin. Catroux was the newly elected "czar" of Europe — not his official title, of course (the official moniker was Chairman of the European Economic Commission). But for all intents and purposes Catroux ran the whole show on the Continent. He had been chosen by every parliament and legislature in Europe, which had enlarged upon and improved the pre-World War I German concept of regional monarchies, each with a crowned head, but under the centralized leadership of a military strongman, who at that time had been the Kaiser. Catroux was not the Kaiser, nor was he a military strongman. But politically he had clout. He was, in fact, a powerhouse. It was his political and economic acumen that had turned Europe from its meandering social and economic drift to the dynamo with which Japan and the United States now had to contend. Despite his decided European leanings, Catroux was strongly pro-United States; and so on both sides of the Atlantic he was everyone's "favorite man."

Daniels felt somewhat embarrassed when he realized that he did not even know the European was in the country. How had someone of that magnitude slipped into the United States without the media knowing? And why would Catroux personally call him? He apparently did not have an underling even dial the telephone; he called himself. Daniels could not imagine the President of the United States doing such a thing. And no one considered the president of the stature of Catroux! What was this all about, anyway?

The newsman had grilled his secretary, "Ivy, are you positive it's Catroux?"

"Well, sir, I can only tell you that he so identified himself. And I must say that his voice has that remarkable resonance and peculiar accent."

Daniels had paused. "This is rather unbelievable. I'm trying to get my bearings here, Ivy. Did he say why he was calling?"

"No, sir, he did not. I don't mean to presume, sir, but Mr. Catroux is waiting on hold."

"What? Oh, yes, I'm sorry. Please put him through. Mr. Catroux? Clay Daniels here."

The melodious, resonant, baritone tones glided into Daniels' ear. "Ah, Mr. Daniels! How gracious of you to receive my call!"

"Not at all, sir, not at all. Please excuse my delay in responding, but to be very frank with you, I was flabbergasted when my secretary identified you as the caller. It is not every day that one receives a phone call from such a distinguished statesman. I am highly honored."

The magnificent voice chuckled quietly. "Small wonder you're the president of America's finest news operation. You certainly know how to turn on the charm. Well, this may surprise you, Mr.

Daniels, but this call has nothing to do with any current news story. At least, not for the time being. But I would like the pleasure of your company at a very private tea this afternoon in my hotel suite. One of my associates will be present, and we would like very much to speak to you about a private matter."

The invitation to a private conference with the European Czar stunned Daniels. Catroux was the hardest man on earth to reach for an interview. Why would this renowned statesman want a personal and private time with him?

"Sir, I am flattered by the invitation. Stunned would be a better word. May I ask what this concerns?"

After a brief pause, Catroux's voice changed just slightly — a harder edge to the velvety tones.

"Mr. Daniels, I am very sorry that I do not give details over the telephone. One might be listening, you know. You can understand my care in such matters, I am sure. But let me assure you that it will be more than worth your while to accept my invitation. Please follow my directions carefully: no one, not even your secretary, is to know where you are going. Do not mention my name to anyone. In fact, please instruct your cordial Miss Browning to forget that I called today. It is essential that no one knows I am in your country."

"Yes, sir, that will be taken care of. And where may I find you, sir?"

"Ah, I will look for you in my hotel suite at one this afternoon. I am staying at the Helmsley Palace on Madison Avenue. Suite 22-A."

Daniels did not respond for a moment. The only sound was the soft hiss of the phone receiver. The news executive was attempting to digest this remarkable invitation. When he finally collected his wits, he said, "I shall be honored to be there, Mr. Catroux. Needless to say, I am intrigued by your call. But despite my tight schedule, I will do some reshuffling and be at your suite as you have requested. And I thank you for calling."

It had not been at all easy to change his afternoon schedule, nor to avoid the softly probing questions of his longtime secretary. A meeting with Sandra Marchetti, his vice president in charge of personnel, had to be postponed, much to the vocal dismay of Ms.

Marchetti. But finally Daniels had been able to extricate himself from the IBC Building and head for the Helmsley Palace.

The cabbie was a homely little man with mousey hair that receded sharply. He was wearing his dark, horn-rimmed glasses perched far down his generous nose. The blunt stub of a long-since-burned-out cigar escaped the right side of his twisted mouth.

"Here we are, mister — the Helmsley. That'll be 12 bucks."

Daniels took the bills, including a good tip, from his wallet and placed it in the waiting hand. As he expected, the driver did not even grunt a "thanks" and pulled away from the curb. With his black eel attache' case, Daniels entered the sumptuous lobby of the Helmsley Palace.

"Mr. Daniels?"

The voice startled the news executive and he turned to stare into the face of a huge, uniformed man.

"Yes?"

"Excuse me, Mr. Daniels, but I am to escort you to the suite where your host is waiting. Would you follow me, please?"

The guard's words were kind, but the voice was not. Daniels wondered what would have happened had he refused to follow. Rather than provoke the fellow, Daniels got in step without a word, carefully looking over the hulk in front of him. A slight protrusion near the man's armpit indicated the presence of a gun.

But it was the uniform itself that caught Daniels' eye. He knew he had seen a similar one somewhere, but he could not remember where.

An expensive, carved mahogany door opened and the two men walked into the vestibule of the finest suite in the Helmsley Palace. The guard tapped on the inner chamber door and it was opened by a small, smartly tailored gentleman who welcomed Daniels, excusing the guard who disappeared quickly. The little fellow offered a tepid hand.

"Mr. Daniels, I am Warren Edmundson, legal counsel for Mr. Catroux. Thank you for coming. You are very prompt. Mr. Catroux will appreciate that. He will join us momentarily."

Daniels entered the lavish room. "Well, thank you very much. I suspect my media background accounts for my time awareness. My goodness, this place is really 'uptown,' isn't it?"

"Mr. Catroux likes it very much here. May I fix you a drink?"

"Yes, thank you. Vodka martini, please."

Daniels sat in a high-backed chair next to the stone-sculptured fireplace. He appreciated the support of the chair; he had suffered various back ailments since he was hurt playing football in prep school. Doctors had put off surgery as long as possible.

But it wasn't his back that was bothering him so much now. It was a nervous stomach. Daniels could not really figure out why. He had met world hotshots before but, he had to admit to himself, never one like Catroux.

"Mr. Edmundson, I am naturally quite curious about receiving this summons here today. May I ask, sir, what's going on?"

The counsel continued fixing the drink at the wet bar across the room, his back to Daniels. When he had completed his task, he turned and walked slowly across the marble floor to the news executive, placing the drink and a linen napkin on the inlaid coffee table.

"Well, Mr. Daniels, I think we should leave the explanations to Mr. Catroux. This is his party. I think you will be somewhat surprised — and perhaps gratified."

"I'm already surprised," Daniels muttered half to himself.

The stiff atmosphere was broken when the bedroom door opened and the Czar of Europe, Jacque Catroux, entered. Daniels, his drink halfway to his face, stopped as if frozen. Even Edmundson stood riveted. The man in the doorway did that to you. Daniels had seen him in person several times, but only at a substantial distance. Even then the presence of the man was overpowering. In the small confines of the drawing room here, his presence was asphyxiating.

Catroux was tall, better than 6 feet 3 inches. His golden hair was worn fashionably short, barely touching his ears and collar. He was very slim. His tanned complexion and excellent physical condition made it difficult to estimate his age. His clothes were conservative, but of the finest fabric and cut. He wore no jewelry. Nothing about his person detracted another's gaze away from his most prominent feature — his pale blue eyes. They were a shade of blue that Daniels had never seen before. They radiated many passions and intensity. And they were kind!

Catroux's face was finely chiseled, with a Roman nose above his expressive lips. He wore no facial hair. His sinfully-expensive linen sport shirt was open at the neck. Daniels could not take his eyes off him. Although he cared very little for the homosexual lifestyle, he thought to himself that he was looking at the most beautiful man in the entire world!

Suddenly Catroux was walking toward him, hand out-thrust.

"Mr. Daniels, thank you for coming on such short notice. And for being so prompt. A rare virtue these days, I'm afraid." His handshake was firm and strong.

Now on his feet and feeling very much alive, the newsman responded.

"Sir, it is my privilege. In fact, it is a thrill to these old radio ears of mine to hear your voice. I daresay there's not another voice to equal it anywhere, and God knows I have heard thousands of them in my lifetime."

Catroux uttered a genuine laugh of excitement. "Well, aren't you kind? And coming from such a media expert, I take it as a marvelous compliment. I thank you, sir. Oh, but please — be seated, won't you?"

Daniels was taken by the seeming naturalness of the man. There was none of the affected pomp of so many government people he had met. He had once heard Catroux address a national political convention and was captivated then by the man's ease of speech and his winning gentleness. And here, in the closeness of the sitting room, he exhibited the same qualities. Apparently his charm was not just for the television cameras.

Catroux leaned against a wall and addressed his legal counsel, "Warren, would you freshen Mr. Daniels' drink, please? Ah, thank you. Now, let's get down to business."

Daniels reached for his attaché case, but his host stopped him gently.

"No, Mr. Daniels, please — you won't need any notes. I promise you that you will not forget anything I say." Again he laughed gently.

"I shall get right to the point, my friend. I want to hire you!"

The wide look in Daniels' eyes indicated his shock. "You want to WHAT, sir?"

"I am going to offer you a job of such magnitude that I daresay you cannot begin to grasp it today. Yes, I know that you are already a television news executive, and you are the best of four such executives in America. And I know that your salary and bonuses exceed a half-million dollars annually. So, on the surface, it would seem foolish to offer you this position, as some of my aides back on the Continent have suggested. But please hear me out. I think you may be more interested than you could ever imagine."

With a shaking hand, Daniels fumbled in the breast pocket of his sports coat for the nearly-empty pack of Merits. A drop of sweat glistened on his cheek in the glow of his lighter. "Mr. Catroux, I am flattered beyond all measure, but —"

Catroux continued speaking as if he had not been interrupted.

"A newsman should have all the facts, Mr. Daniels. I have barely begun. Please bear with me."

The tall figure moved a high-backed chair toward him and sat down, casually putting one stylish leather boot on the marble top of the coffee table. His blue eyes penetrated his guest.

"You are aware of the rather miraculous transformation of Europe." It was not a question, but a statement of fact. "For a number of years I have believed that our western democracies, especially on the European continent, were in danger of extinction. Let me tell you why. Everyone spoke about centralization of power and commerce, but, in truth, every nation did its own thing. We were shotgunning our future, rather than sighting a rifle barrel right on the target.

"But early 1981 was a marked time for Europe. Do you remember it, my friend, when Greece joined the Common Market?"

Daniels nodded affirmatively, because he remembered the auspicious occasion very well. In fact, earlier in his news career as a field reporter for NBC, he had been stationed in Athens.

Between the end of World War II and the Colonels' military dictatorship which came into power in 1967, no fewer than 41 governments whirled in and out of office. The military government stopped the political merry-go-round, but the consolidation of government under the army was repressive and brutal. For seven years the Greeks suffered under a roughshod tyranny that threatened to remove them to the dark ages. One well-known motion picture star shocked the world with her stories of tyranny in her country of Greece. However, renewed conflict with Turkey, sparked when the Colonels tried to seize Cyprus by engineering a coup against Archbishop Makarios, the island's president, caused the Greek citizenry to dump their ruling junta and ruthless despotism.

Constantine Karamanlis, who had once been prime minister in a time of relative tranquility, was returned to head a government of national unity and was swept into victory at the polls.

Daniels could still remember the magnificent speech in which Karamanlis warned the Americans of their time-worn fickleness. He had told his people: "In our day there are no messiahs; and if by chance we think we have found one, it will not be long before we turn on him. So we Greeks have been since ancient times. We are skillful at making idols, not that we may worship them, but that we may have the pleasure of destroying them."

Catroux's voice broke into Daniels' reverie. "You will remember that it was the courageous insistance of Karamanlis that caused the Greeks to make the important decision to return to the NATO alliance and hence to the Common Market."

"Yes, I remember," Daniels responded. "And the inclusion of Greece brought the Common Market nations to 10."

"Correct!" said Catroux, leaning forward. "And for the first time since the fall of Hitler the Europeans began to think in terms of the entire continent instead of nationally. We had 10 big names in the fold, Mr. Daniels. Ten of them! Germany, France, Italy, the Netherlands, Belgium, Luxembourg, the United Kingdom, Ireland, Denmark and Greece. A rather imposing list of nations — the European Economic Community."

Daniels stubbed his cigarette in the ashtray and looked at his host skeptically. "But as I recall, Mr. Catroux, the EEC never really had enough clout to call the economic shots. And then in the early '80s under Reagan, when the US dollar soared, your European currency virtually disappeared. And your gains were minimized."

The European laughed in delight. "Precisely sir, precisely so. You are observant! And do you know why Europe could never catch up to even Japan economically? I shall tell you! We never learned the lesson of centralization of power. Even though we boasted a common banner, that of the EEC and even NATO, each nation still had its own axes to grind. Yes, the EEC helped substantially, but not enough! Europe was still weak and under constant military threat from the Soviets. Had the United States pulled its quarter-million troops out of Europe, Russia would have come in within 24 hours. You know that, don't you?"

"Yes, sir, I do remember. That's why the Russians did all their saber rattling when the United States installed new missiles in Europe, and particularly in Germany and Belgium."

Catroux leaned back and looked at Warren Edmundson. The attorney had remained standing all this time. "Counselor, do be a good chap and fix me a drink, will you? There's a bottle of Remy Martin on my dresser." The diminutive legal counsel disappeared quickly and obediently, Daniels noted. Maybe almost too obediently.

"Now," continued Catroux, as he accepted the drink from Edmundson, "let's get down to the bare pavement here. What has caused Europe's rather remarkable recovery? What brought about this transformation whereby individual national goals were sacrificed to the consortium of international unity?"

Daniels felt obliged to answer the obvious. "Mr. Catroux, the consensus of opinion in our judgment is that you alone brought about the change. You, more than Napoleon, certainly more than Hitler, were the catalyst of Europe. The change was not because of some issue, but because of a person. You were that person! You single-handedly changed the continent! Some observers called you a 'miracle-worker.' " In the presence of Catroux, Daniels felt almost like a supplicant, a worshipper.

Catroux sipped at his drink, hardly consuming any of the alcohol. He looked wryly at Edmundson who stood at the other side of the room as mute as rock. "Well now, Mr. Daniels, at the risk of sounding self-serving, much of what you say is essentially correct. The fact is that I did change the face of Europe in both business and politics. In those matters we are now on a virtual even footing with your own nation and Japan. And, may I say, sir, that we have only just begun. And you will see vital changes in the military picture as well. I believe you will see Europe arm faster than Germany did under Hitler."

Daniels felt a sinister uneasiness. "But, Mr. Catroux, surely you do not equate yourself with the Fuhrer?"

The blue eyes pierced Daniels like twin lances. The chuckle was utterly without humor. "Only in the positive virtues the man had. And let's face it, my friend, the German did have some virtues, didn't he?"

Clay wanted to get away from that subject as quickly as possible. "Sir, excuse me, but getting back to my potential involvement with you — what did you have in mind? I am more than a little curious."

Catroux sat silently for a moment, put his drink on the coffee table, and stood up. Hands on hips, he looked straight at the nervous news executive. "All right. Moment of truth — at least partial truth. I don't want you to be shocked at what I am about to tell you. But events in the next few days will end civilization as we know it."

The shock etched on the American's face would have been funny had it not been so serious. Daniels fought to catch his voice. "Mr. Catroux, what are you saying here? Is this a joke?"

The tall man with the golden hair glided to the desk and leaned on the edge of it, arms folded, his eyes never leaving his guest. "Mr. Daniels, I cannot give you any details. But it is my opinion that an event is about to happen that will demand all of the world's free nations to band together."

Daniels blurted out, "Are you talking of war, here, sir? Is Europe about to be attacked? What are you saying?"

"No, there will not be war. Not just yet. However, such a military holocaust is possible within a few months in the Middle East. I am not sure myself, Daniels, of the actual event that is about to transpire. I only know that because of it, your United States of America will be forced into a treaty with our own EEC. Not just an economic treaty, but military. We will be bound together forever, my friend."

Daniels moved to get up. "Well, of course, we are allies with our NATO friends. We always stand at their side to —"

The transformation in Catroux was sudden. His blue eyes flashed fire. "Daniels, you do not understand. Please just listen! What I am saying to you is that the governments of Europe and your own United States will very soon be forced to merge into one vast western entity. One government. One army. One money system. One leader. The two entities will be known as Euroamerica. And when that happens, Mr. Daniels— and it's going to happen no later than the end of the year, just months from now — I shall need your assistance most assuredly."

Daniels was now more angry than frightened. "Sir, I do not discount your knowledge, nor do I violate your hospitality here. But such a thing as you have stated cannot happen. It will not happen. The United States would never agree to such an amalgamation of nations or —"

The fire in Catroux's eyes had disappeared. They turned to a hateful, baleful, dead blue. "Believe me, Mr. Daniels! Believe me that it will happen. I repeat — by year's end. Euroamerica will be formed, and it will last for 1,000 years or more."

A stale and sickening scent had somehow wafted into the room. Daniels seemed to be the only member of the triad who was aware of it. The smell made him nauseous. He desperately wanted to vomit his martini and breakfast all over the exotic oriental carpets. He fought for self-control and stared at Catroux, still leaning against the desk, arms folded. In a thick voice, the European spoke again.

"Mr. Daniels, I am — I repeat this, I AM — going to lead all of the western nations. Not just Europe, but the United States as well. As shocking as this is to you, and I cannot expect you to believe it yet, I have told you the absolute truth. I want you to join me as my personal aide, my speech writer and press secretary. No one on planet Earth is your equal in these skills. Your half-million dollar salary is peanuts compared to what I can offer you. You may have anything you have ever desired. I guarantee it!"

Daniels felt sheer panic in his gut. "Sir, I must really protest this whole conversation. At the risk of being a rude guest, your words are subversive. I cannot believe that you are uttering them. You are not going to lead my nation, nor am I about to serve you. And furthermore I should like to leave this room at this instant."

Daniels walked shakily to the door as Catroux pushed himself away from the desk and stood directly in front of him. He was smiling broadly, but it was not a pleasant smile. It was more like the grin of a bully.

"Oh, Daniels, my boy, my dear, dear boy! I am going to do exactly what I have just told you I would do."

Daniels was very frightened, very angry. His words were heated. "I'll tell you what I am going to do, sir. I am going to leave this room and your presence for good. And may I say to you that any future coverage you receive from IBC television may not be in your best interest. I shall instruct my people to research you from your birth until now. You have blown a marvelous contact, my misguided friend. Now let me out of here!"

Daniels reached out a hand as if to brush away the tall figure before him. But his actions were not necessary. Still smiling, but gently now, Catroux stepped aside. "As you wish, my son. As you wish. You are angry, and I apologize for that. But new ideas are sometimes painful, are they not?"

The newsman scoffed. "New ideas? Hitler had those ideas. Napoleon before him. Alexander dreamed the same mad schemes. No, Mr. Catroux, treason and treachery are not new ideas. They are as old as man."

The man with the golden hair looked down at him as a patient father would observe a child. "Treason? Treachery? Strong words, those. And so unnecessary. Was your George Washington a traitor when he threw off the tyranny of England? The king thought so, but your colonists did not. No, it all depends upon whose ox is being gored, doesn't it. This is a new age, a new kingdom, Clayton. And you are a part of it with me. I have so declared it, and so it shall be. You and I, Clayton Daniels! You and I!"

The very thought chilled Daniels' bones. Raging emotions constricted his throat and his words came out tight and thin. "Mr. Catroux, for the last time I say to you that I am leaving this room. Don't try to stop me!"

Catroux threw back his handsome head and laughed. "Try to stop you? Why would I do such a thing? Why, this is a free country. I will contact you again in a few days when you have had the chance to think through the matters I have confided in you. Warren, bring the guard and have him take Mr. Daniels to the cab stand."

Clayton glared hard at the tall man and snapped, "That won't be necessary. I know New York like the back of my hand. I don't need your help or the assistance of trained goons."

The blue eyes leveled on him. His voice was steady and hard. "Mr. Daniels, I said the guard would take you back. Thank you for coming. I will contact you within the week."

As the huge uniformed escort guided him to the foyer of the hotel, Daniels could hear Catroux still laughing. But it didn't sound like just one voice. Or even two. It sounded like a choir of voices, very strange ones too. And their laughter was almost other-worldly.

It was not until he was nearly back at the IBC Building that Daniels remembered another detail. Suddenly it popped into his mind. The guard's uniform! The buttons near the collar! The insignia on them was comprised of two lightning bolts.

Then Daniels put it together. That had been the official insignia of Hitler's SS men!

2

Daniels was in a dark mood when he arrived at the IBC Building. Ivy Browning watched him intently, wondering what had happened to her usually amiable boss. She did not press him for any details as she knew he would tell her everything he wanted her to know. Ivy's loyalty to Daniels was a legend in the television facility and she exhibited it fully that afternoon, determining to undergird him anyway she could.

Daniels went about his duties perfunctorily, thankful there were no committee meetings, watched his anchor Harlan O'Brien's 5:30 newscast, and drove home. As he manipulated the Audi through the traffic he mused that O'Brien had unknowingly missed the chief news story of the day, that of Jacque Catroux's boast of taking over the United States government. There was no way O'Brien could have had the story as only three men were privy to it: himself, Catroux and Edmundson, the shadowy legal counsel. None of the three was about to reveal what he knew to anyone, each for different reasons: Catroux, because it would have been an indictment against his apparent integrity; Edmundson, because Catroux would demand his silence and loyalty in any matter in question; and Daniels himself, because he wasn't completely confident that the nightmarish afternoon had truly occurred exactly as he remembered it.

Daniels parked the silver Audi in the parking garage and entered the elevator. His tastes were admittedly snobbish. He had not begun life with such a list of classy tastes. It is, in fact, difficult to be a social *arriviste* in Council Bluffs, Iowa, the river town where he had received his introduction to the news business years ago.

But those common midcontinent days were a thing of the past and far away. He now ruled over New York's television news kingdom. In weaker moments he would have admitted feelings of insecurity about the situation. He had never had the dashing appearance of most on-camera people, and even though he seldom appeared on the screen anymore, his 5 feet 10 inch frame, slightly on the pudgy side, didn't help build his self-esteem. Nor did his constant battle with hair loss. So he made up for much of that with fulfillment of lavish wants. He could have what he wanted. And what he wanted was old and luxurious.

Daniels' home was the entire top floor of the Hotel Marguery, a palatial edifice of yesteryear that occupied the west side of Park Avenue between Forty-seventh and Forty-eighth Streets. The place cost him a bundle since the rent was based on a per room per annum basis. He could have cared less. He would have paid the tab had it meant starving. Never again would he live in a clapboard house near the banks of the Missouri River.

Few streets in the world boast the concentrated wealth of Park Avenue. Paradoxically, its architecture is schmaltzy and dull, every building is boring, resembling the others. But inside they are different. "Yes," mused the newsman, "inside is where heaven begins." Rare marbles, imported stones, matched woods and nickel-bronzes were used to marvelous effect.

Then, speaking of fine architecture, there was Marsha Lavin, his live-in girlfriend — warm, gorgeous, ultra-feminine and very, very pregnant. Divorce proceedings with his wife Arvella were still in the messy stage. At stake was a bundle of money and visitation rights to five-year-old Robert.

Marsha met him at the door with a warm embrace. He stepped back and admired her with a grateful grin. Despite her five-month pregnancy she was still incredibly sexy and Daniels blessed the day he had met her.

After a quiet meal, the two watched a video film on their large projection screen and then the girl slipped off to bed. She could no longer keep the long night hours with her lover. Daniels spent the remaining hours of the day musing over the activities of the afternoon.

Numerous questions plagued him. First, Catroux had predicted some cataclysmic event that would change the course of history. Was he just talking or did he really know something? After all, this was not a crackpot off the street with a wine-induced prophecy. But what could the European know about American affairs that he, the president of the nation's largest news department, did not? Still, one of the first things a good reporter understands is that he or she does not know everything. Omniscience is a power reserved for the gods. But surely something so big as to attack the U.S. government itself would have some portents. Yet he could not uncover a clue.

Second, what made Catroux believe the current U.S. administration, as conservative as mom and apple pie, would sit still for a merger with Europe? Or the general population, for that matter. Even talk of such a historic union would probably foment rebellion in much of the land. Calls for impeachment of the president would ring from coast-to-coast, with IBC leading the uproar. No, Catroux was not very knowledgeable at that point, Daniels was sure.

Third, what would it be like to work for such a powerful figure as the European, to just snap your fingers and move mountains? While inwardly Daniels was repulsed by the whole treacherous concept, he realized he had inner stirrings about the possibilities and potential. He cursed himself silently and tried to get the thing out of his mind.

As midnight approached, the newsman, still wide-awake and upset, stood silhouetted in the western window of the bedroom dressing room. He was flanked by draperies designed by Sarp and Mattheus. The only light that actually originated in the room was the soft glow of the cigarette cradled loosely in his fingers. He smoked like a steam engine, knew it was probably going to kill him someday, and had no intention of giving up the habit. He looked out from his eagle's nest perspective on the several blocks that insulated him from traffic along the Hudson River. The lights of a lonely boat headed north as Daniels considered the pageant of nightlife all around his tower home. He knew from experience that the over-populated island of Manhattan would that very night evoke the best and worst of human existence. In an alley near Broadway, a mugger might be ripping off the body of his victim while just a couple of blocks away a flashy new musical would premiere to a jewelled crowd. It occurred to him that life and death mingled in those dark streets below, so evenly perhaps that it was difficult to know which was light and which was mere shadow. God help the wretch who made the wrong judgment.

Daniels' penthouse, high above Park Avenue, was a welcome sanctuary from the mayhem and pressures of national television. During those brief hours between midnight and four a.m. there was a fragmentary lull in the city tempo. Peace and quiet at last. Daniels suffered from insomnia and if he were to get any sleep at all, it would have to be in that brief nocturnal cocoon. He turned from the window and crawled into the bed by the warm Marsha already asleep.

Muted lights from the great city seeped through the open drapes revealing highlights of the large bedroom. Marsha had decorated it impressively around an excellent copy of one of the famous Odalisque series by Henri Matisse. Two of the walls were covered by hand-carved oak, the other walls by madly expensive wallpaper. The carpet was the type that creeps around your ankles, pure extravagance underfoot. The furniture, Mediterranean and massive, was covered with framed photographs. Many of the figures in them were well-known in politics and the entertainment world. Most were autographed. Daniels himself appeared in many of the pictures, cavorting with the great and near-great.

One photo stood apart from the others. It was a five-year-old boy with rudy complexion and a hint of dependence in his eyes. He bore an uncanny resemblance to the news executive.

The elegant jazz of Bob James escaped the two Klipsch Century speakers on the far side of the room. The cassette deck was automatic, playing and repeating the "Heads and Tails" album through the night softly, ever so softly.

The subdued light revealed two figures lying close together in bed. Even in sleep, Marsha was stunning, her ash-blonde hair spread across her pillow. Her soft breathing, coupled with the delicate music, lulled Daniels into a ragged and intermittent sleep.

In recent years it had become harder and harder for him to rest well. The tension of his job made it difficult to ever completely unwind. Even the downers prescribed to him by the company physician no longer made much impact on his sleeping ability and he was not about to increase the dosage. It was one thing not to sleep; quite another to become addicted to pills. Too many of his compatriots had fallen into that well-intentioned manhole.

Daniels mumbled in his sleep, not words that could be understood — only mutters, disjointed and fragmented sentences and half-called names. And predominent this night was the debonair Catroux.

Often Daniels had the recurring dream that the world he had long since covered for various news bureaus was shrinking to the size of a basketball. Everyone knew everything about everybody — shirt size, food preference, make of deodorant, and even the deep secrets that never escape the bathroom and bedroom walls. Nothing was sacred any longer, nothing was private. Only another newsman could appreciate the horror. Each time he wrote a story millions of people screamed back at him, "We've already heard that! Tell us something new. We are bored to death with IBC news!"

Daniels rolled in his sleep during those nightmares, his back aching and his sub-conscious mind weeping in the night: "Oh, please don't be bored! Anything but that. Be angry, be disgusted, sue us, fight us — but don't be bored! Boredom cuts the audience and that cuts the rating points which cuts the sales potential, which is the name of the game! That means no work, no more Hotel Marguery, no more Marsha! Back to the banks of the Missouri River and Council Bluffs! Please don't be bored!"

These feelings of insecurity hovered over him like a moth. Thoughts of losing the big-city opulence haunted him, fleetingly in the daytime when he could do something about it, and continuously at night when he was victim to his inner demons. But at last the twin nightmares of unemployment and Jacque Catroux passed, and Daniels relaxed against Marsha's warm body, perspiration dampening his pillow.

Recent days in the news department would have tried the sanity of even the most placid of men, which Daniels surely was not. His daily dosages of Tenormin and Dyazide for high blood pressure were evident of that. His job was a love-hate relationship. He was pouring his life into the mechanism of IBC news. Little else mattered to him except Marsha. There was a similarity in his passion for the department and his frenzied coupling with her. He loved it all! Everything about it, the words, the incessant flow of words, the sounds of clacking machines, clicking word-processing keyboards and softly whirring cameras. He loved the brainstorming sessions in executive counseling chambers, attended by white-coated waiters. He was stimulated by the fact, or was it the fantasy, of human beings temporarily merged in the ecstasy of top-flight television production. To paraphrase Patrick Henry, "Give me IBC or give me death!" he often thought.

Of course, there was the counter-balancing pressure that could make your eyes feel as if they would explode. Pressure that could make the veins and arteries constrict and cause you to believe that one day there just had to be a blowout.

Pressure like two days ago when IBC missed the biggest story of the day to CBS. It was only pure stupid luck (luck for CBS — hell for the reporter) that CBS's Bill Marlow was having a televised luncheon interview with Iranian President Sadegh Kavir in Teheran, tape to be used in a *Sixty Minutes* story. So no other newsmen were around when the bomb went off. Marlow had screamed in agony, the CBS camera capturing the whole savage mess, as he had seen his arm float away in seeming slow-motion from his body. Viewers saw Marlow's bulging eyes trying to comprehend the devastation around him as Kavir's body just disintegrated — tiny, wet fragments of it sticking to the wallpaper.

A horror story! Of course that's what it was! But CBS got the whole thing on videotape. And it was just sheer luck, that's all. That was the only reason a competitor had the scoop on the biggest story from Iran since the hostage crisis under President Jimmy Carter. The assassination of the Iranian president with the CBS camera gleefully recording every bit of it. Oh yes, IBC had all the details 40 minutes later with the caption "Video courtesy of CBS" supered over it. Sheer, stupid luck, that was all. But try to tell that to the sales department when the ratings came out. The sales people didn't understand the nuances of Lady Luck. There was no column for "luck" in the Arbitrons. Only points. Only success. Too many flukes like that one yesterday could destroy the credibility of an entire news department. The public was fickle. Skill was not enough, scheduling was not enough. Somewhere along the way you had to have luck!

Maybe that's what had happened today with Catroux! Maybe luck was smiling on Daniels now. But, no, that could not be for Catroux was offering treachery against the United States government.

Daniels stirred again fitfully. The soft woman beside him opened her eyes for a moment to watch him. She moved forward to kiss him gently on his eyes. He instinctively placed his arm snugly about her full body, subconsciously aware of her hair that smelled like jasmine. The combination of her warmth and the security of her close body temporarily drove the tormenting demons from his mind, and he finally lapsed into a deep sleep.

He dreamed of childhood days, of tossing a hooked worm into the shallows of Half Moon Lake and yelling in delight as a bullhead smacked the bait. He dreamed of gentle breezes blowing across the plains from the Missouri River and of laughter at the family table. It was a million years ago.

On the nightstand, next to the sleeping couple, was a small brass alarm clock. A green glow reflected from the hands, revealing the time to be 3:12 a.m. It was to be the last moment of sleep for Clayton B. Daniels for a long, long time.

3

A series of piercing bells began a racket in Daniels' brain. He tried desperately to sort them out. No, it wasn't the AP or UPI machine — someone had jerked the plug from the wall. Ah, it must be that firetruck racing down Park Avenue — no, the firemen were clearly pointing out to him that the bell had been removed. The ringing grew louder, more insistent, persuading the newsman to reluctantly open his eyes.

The telephone! Of course, that blasted phone!

Daniels cursed, turned over painfully and fumbled for the receiver. His brain finally figured out a way to get it to his ear.

"Yes?"

"Clayton? That you, Clayton?"

It took Daniels some time to recognize the voice. It belonged to Chris Sergeant, night editor of IBC who wrote most of the news copy for the network's 6 a.m. *Wake Up News.*

Daniels breathed in deeply, trying desperately to come to life.

"Yeah, Chris, it's me. Do you have any idea what time it is?"

"Clay, I'm sorry, really I am. I know it's just after three o'clock, but I thought you ought to know about this development before we do anything with it on the air."

Daniels' mind had finally started to function. If Chris were calling him at this hour, then it had to be important, like gang-busters important. His night editor was a crank and a royal pain in the neck, but he never cried "Wolf!"

Daniels reached for the lamp near the bed, flipped it on, and sat up, his feet sinking into the yielding carpet.

"OK, Chris, I'm awake, I think. What's happening down there? They catch Kavir's killer?" Stories of the previous week's assassination and all its world-shaking implications began parading through his head.

"No, Clay, I wish we were that lucky. I wish this were about Iran or the Middle East or anything that made any sense at all. This is a brand new story and I'm telling you that it is without question the biggest story I have ever touched. I'm scared to death, Clay, and I need you down here. Now!"

Daniels had never heard that stage of panic in his steady night-man's voice before. "Chris, what in the world is going on there?" He was now wide awake!

There was a brief pause on the line as Sergeant collected his thoughts.

"Clay, it's the most bizarre thing I have ever heard. I have checked out the early reports and their sources and I swear that what I am going to tell you is legitimate. It seems that a substantial segment of the New York population has just — just — vanished!"

Daniels exploded. It was too early for games. "What do you mean 'substantial'? Fifty people? A hundred? And what do you mean — 'just vanished'? Come on, Chris, f'r cryin' out loud, man, it's three in the morning!"

Sergeant continued as if Daniels had never spoken. "Not just New York, either. Other cities are apparently experiencing the same thing. People are vanishing— zap— right off the planet. And I mean they are disappearing in droves. I got word of it about 45 minutes ago when the local police scanner started going nuts. You know, Clay, that we don't pay a whole lot of attention to the local stuff. But these reports were so wild that I started listening. People were calling the New York police and highway patrol to report missing family members. I mean families by the thousands! The callers say they have looked everywhere. Wouldn't have been much if there were just one or two families, but, my God, Clay, they're calling in and jamming the lines. Calling us here too. It's a madhouse down here. And there have been many accidents too — bad ones. Police have reported that the cause of the accidents was — uh — was —"

"Was what, Chris?"

"Was because there — uh — there were no drivers in the cars!"

Daniels leaned back in bed, grinning. "All right, Chris, very funny. You really had me going. Scarti put you up to this, right?" Lawrence Scarti, Vice President of IBC News Special Coverage, was an inveterate practical joker. "You tell Scarti I'm gonna be on him like —"

"No, hear me out, Clay! This is not a joke! And you haven't heard anything yet. It gets more weird than this. You know, it's just a little after midnight in Los Angeles, so there are still a lot of people up out there and they already are aware of what's happening. Thousands still sitting up watching *The Tonight Show* and *Letterman*. So they've been told. In fact, so many people have disappeared in some states that the governors have already declared martial law!"

"Chris —"

"I'm telling you, sir, there are millions of people missing in this country. And we're getting some preliminary indications that tell us this thing may be international. Our London guys are going bananas, Clay. We need you here. I've already called some of the other execs, but, man, we gotta have you here."

"Chris, is this a rib? Is this the old Orson Welles' *War of the Worlds* thing? 'Cause if it is —"

"Clay, c'mon! You know me better than that! I wouldn't horse you around like that. I'm not into jokes, and you know it."

Daniels ran his fingers through his sandy, receding hair. "OK, Chris. I'm sorry. You're right. You wouldn't do something like that. But, dear God! Millions missing? You sure you got the story right?"

The nightman's voice shook with fright. "No, Clay, I'm not sure about anything, to be perfectly frank about it. But I think we are probably experiencing the biggest story in history. In fact, Kay Banes has already notified the affiliates that they are to remain on the air all night." She was Vice President of the IBC Affiliate News and Satellite network.

That news shocked Daniels into momentary silence. In all his years in the business only a few things had caused the networks to stay on the air all night — elections, assassinations and other world-shaking news. His night editor must be right if Kay Banes had contacted the affiliates. It must be an incredible story.

"All right, Chris, why don't you send a car for me?"

"It's already on the way, Clay."

"Thanks. Do you have any idea just how many people are supposed to have disappeared?"

"Well, there's no way to tell at this point. But I am guessing that in New York City alone there must be well over a hundred thousand. Not *that* many calls have been logged yet, of course, but the lines are jammed. And worldwide? I don't know — maybe millions."

Daniels slumped against the headboard, his hands shaking. Marsha was wide awake, watching him in alarm. "Well, Chris, I'll get dressed and be down there in a half-hour or so. And thanks for having the foresight to send the car for me."

He hung up the receiver and reached into the nightstand for a cigarette and his lighter. As he drew in the pungent smoke, he saw he was shaking. He could not remember being so frightened, twice in one day, but this time he didn't even know why.

Marsha sat up, pulling the sheets under her chin.

"Clayton?" The one word formed a complete question.

He turned toward her. Even in the crisis of the moment he could not help noticing her beauty. Under nearly any circumstance she could thrill him. Even her ever-expanding abdomen did not detract from her allurement. Her face was fine-featured, marred only marginally by a slightly wide set between her dark blue-violet eyes. And those eyes showed fright tonight.

Marsha clutched his wrist. "Tell me about that call, Clay. Please! What is happening?"

"I'm not sure, sweetheart. Chris tells me there is something going on at the studios. I'm not really sure what to tell you. But

Chris was truly shaken. Could you hear what he said at all?"

She shook her head just slightly. "No."

"Well, he was talking very fast; it's no wonder you couldn't catch any of it. Marsha, he told me that apparently some people, a whole lot of people, have just suddenly disappeared. There is a lot of panic in the city as well as in other major population centers of the country."

"Disappeared? But how? Why?"

"I haven't a clue. But I have to find out."

Marsha reached for him protectively. "Oh, Clay, you don't have to leave at this hour, surely."

"Yes, I'm afraid I do. I don't know how long I'll be gone. Chris has already called Kay and the affiliates are going to be on the air all night. Our flagship here is already giving the news."

"But it's not even 3:30 in the morning! Let one of your people handle it."

Clay looked at her kindly. "Dear, I didn't get to be the president of this outfit by sluffing off on the workers. You know that. Now I don't know when I'll get back, but I think you should flip on the TV and try to follow what's happening."

She put her arms around him and caressed his ear with her lips. "Hey, this sounds a little scary. Like a bad horror movie."

"Well, the thing that concerns me is that we don't know why the people have disappeared. But I'll tell you this — I have never heard Chris Sergeant sound so scared before. I have an instinctive feeling that this is something — well, something that doesn't make any rational sense. And that bothers me terribly."

Those words were hardly out of his mouth when he remembered the prophecy of Jacque Catroux just 14 hours earlier: ". . . events in the next few days will end civilization as we know it . . ." The memory of the statement haunted him.

"Darling, are you all right?" Marsha's embrace tightened.

Daniels gently disengaged her arms and padded over to the closet. He slipped into a pair of jeans and a pullover sweater. Then he sat on the edge of the bed to put on his socks and his tight Italian-made boots.

"Marsha, I'll call you as soon as I know something. OK? You just rest easy here. And don't worry! Please!"

She raised up from the bed and moved toward him, the sheet falling on the carpet. Pressing against his body, her kiss was passionate.

"Please be careful, darling. I don't like you on these city streets at this hour."

"Everything is going to be fine. I'm not a hero. And the studio limo should be waiting for me by the time I get downstairs. I will be in constant touch with you. OK?"

"OK."

They stood together. He kissed her tenderly and moved away. Glancing back at her with obvious affection and a touch of desire, he quickly left the room.

The elevator dropped him to the ground floor and he entered the garage lobby level. It was deserted. Before leaving the apartment he had pushed the button that would alert the night watchman that he was coming. Old Fred Garner had patrolled the lower floors and garage of the hotel since anyone could remember and Daniels always enjoyed seeing the vintage watchman on those occasions when he came in late or left unusually early. Fred was well past retirement age, but the tenants of the Marguery had appreciated him so much that he stayed on the job. Their appreciation was born of the fact that he was a truly competent watchman and vandalism and theft had been virtually nil there.

But when Daniels got to the garage, Fred was nowhere around. He called out several times but there was no response. The limo had not yet arrived, so Daniels stepped to the tiny booth Fred laughingly called an office. The lights were on, and a pencil was resting on a note pad where the officer had obviously been filling out a report. Apparently he abruptly stopped writing in the middle of a sentence as if he had just suddenly been called from the room.

Daniels felt a slight tremor creep down his spine. Suppose it was all true! Suppose all those people had vanished! Suppose old Fred was one of them. There was little question that he was gone, nowhere to be seen on the premises. That was not like him. He had always been on the job. Consistency was his chief virtue. Now he had obviously disappeared somewhere. Maybe like the others — all the others.

Daniels heard the limo horn sound and walked into the warm night air. Muggy. Sticky. He often asked himself why he didn't chuck his nerve-jangling job and work in some little hick TV station in the desert. Better to fight lizards and snakes than this terrible humidity.

He quickly greeted the driver, whom he had never seen, and slipped into the roomy rear compartment. A cup of hot coffee was waiting for him along with *The Wall Street Journal, The New York Times* and *USA Today*. It was only a couple of miles to the IBC Building but Daniels never wanted to waste a moment.

The papers, however, went untouched. It was far too early for anything about the disappearances to be in these editions, and the disappearance was the big story. Possible solutions to the mystery appeared in his probing brain. He tried to sort them out in some rational, analytical manner. Was it some new Russian neutron weapon, leaving buildings but destroying life? Couldn't be. Otherwise, why would he and Marsha and this driver, whoever he was, still be here?

Was it the encroachment of some new time or space dimension? He felt like Rod Serling inviting the public into *The Twilight Zone*. How in the world could millions of people just disappear? It made no sense. That bothered him terribly. He was only comfortable when things made sense.

It would be a long time before anything made sense to Clayton Daniels again.

4

Chris Sergeant listened to Daniels' promise to come to the IBC Building, hung up the telephone and leaned back in his worn swivel chair. The ancient, rickety piece of furniture would have been thrown away a long time ago had the night editor not screamed long and loud. He had thrust his rather generous nose into the maintenance director's face and yelled, "Listen, mister, it has taken me 12 years to break that chair in so it fits properly. So take your diseased hands off my property!"

Similar outbursts against other IBC personnel had created a floor-by-floor dislike for Sergeant. It meant nothing to him. He wasn't running for any public office.

He leaned against the desk and put his face in the palms of his hands, using his fingers to massage his hurting temples. All in all, he conceded, Daniels had accepted his morning message of doom with some equanimity. He had debated for several minutes whether he should call the department's chief executive. It was admittedly a rotten time to wake up someone who put in as many hours as Daniels did. 12- to 14-hour days were normal for the man, and his staff tried not to bother him at home unless it was an emergency.

Sergeant had been positive that this was an emergency. Everything in his news past, his finely honed instincts, told him that this was a big, big story. After replacing the receiver, he had felt relieved that he had obeyed his usually reliable intuition and that Daniels was on his way to the studio.

It was not unusual for important stories to break on the graveyard shift. For while it was about 3:30 a.m. in New York, it was 9:30 a.m. in most of Western Europe. It was still an hour later in the Middle East. A lot could happen during the EST night shift.

The old night editor was a cunning reporter. And he knew it. There was nothing smug about his knowledge of his competence, just solid comprehension that he could handle most situations as well as or better than most. He was not overly modest about his acumen. More than once he had informed newcomers and upstarts of his experience and competence when they had dared question his judgment. Twenty-eight years had molded his sixth sense concerning news values and sharpened his writing abilities.

However, such experience had cost him. Like many others in the media, his career had been at the expense of his marriage. He had not become involved with another woman and was not a heavy drinker, the bane of many a good newsman. His whole life was wrapped up in IBC and the morning news. His surroundings were his gods. With his seniority he could have requested other assignments and probably got them. But he did not really want other assignments. There was just something about the night — and the night people — that possessed him. Normal husbands were home with their wives and children, if they had any, but not Sergeant. His wife Sandy had begged him to ask for daytime work but he refused. Then a man came along who was happy to acquiesce to Sandy's wishes and desires, and she left Chris a crisp farewell note and split. There had been no children to their union, so the breakup had not been overly complicated. Sergeant mused that it was rather odd that he had not been too upset about her leaving. On the contrary, he was somewhat relieved. Nor did he look for another woman. He was wedded to IBC and the nocturnal hours. The strange little man was one of those who would quickly die following mandatory retirement.

Sergeant often glanced around the newsroom, his eyes taking in the numerous desks, computers, typewriters and wire service machines. He would begin his ritual litany — a sigh and the thought that this room was the nearest thing to home he would ever have.

However, being completely honest with himself, Sergeant knew his strange melancholy had even deeper roots. The desks he scanned were, for the most part, vacant. The night crew was a skeletal one, far reduced from the daylight hours mayhem. The night shift was quiet, *sans* warm bodies. He liked that. People meant clutter, noise, involvement and unnecessary confusion. The truth was that Sergeant genuinely disliked most people. He did not "suffer fools" as the old poet wrote. Oh, he craved writing about them — their pitfalls, breakdowns, indiscretions, achievements. He just didn't personally like them. He could never have been a feature writer, but few men could equal his researching and writing skill as a night editor.

It was he who had painstakingly uncovered the story behind a prominent United States senator and his liaison with a page boy. The senator's name had frequently been mentioned as a presidential candidate. Sergeant's vigilance had taken months. He ignored the slammed doors, denials and threats. No one could shake his resolve to know the truth. When his story was released, no one could deny the facts he had uncovered. Not even the disgraced senator who had fallen from power and had lost his family. Other news people respected the diligence it had taken Sergeant to dig out the story, but nobody liked him for it. That was pretty much the story of his life. His contemporaries considered him a professional, even admitting that he was very good; they just didn't like him.

It took something highly out of the ordinary to shake Sergeant's cool. Only a few times in his long career had he been sucked into a story emotionally. But tonight he was emotional! He was shaken by the reports of all the disappearances around the world.

It had started about 1:30 that morning when the first call came in. Sally Wright, an assistant researcher, had answered, grimaced and transferred the caller immediately to Sergeant. "I can't handle this person — you had better talk to her."

Taking unneeded phone calls was his least-favorite activity. He swore under his breath, gave the girl a withering glance, and picked up his extension. He heard a young woman's voice, nearing hysteria, crying on the line.

"Hello, ma'am. This is Chris Sergeant, night editor. What's the problem?"

Torrents of rapid-fire gibberish tore at his ear.

"Slow down, lady, I can't understand a word you're saying."

The caller had attempted to compose herself and start over. She was able to communicate something of her anguish.

"My babies! My babies are gone! I just went into their bedroom to check on them and they're both gone!"

This was not a call for a network newsroom, but rather for local police. Sergeant again shot an annoyed look at Sally Wright, and tried to explain. "Well, lady, I am sorry to hear that, but you have called the wrong people. There is nothing we can do to help you. This is the IBC news bureau. You need your local police department. They can help you."

But the woman would not be put off.

"Sir, I have already called the police and their dispatcher took my number and said he would call me back as soon as he could. He said they were swamped with calls just like mine, that a lot of people were gone. Vanished! He said there must have been several hundred disappearances reported tonight in their precinct alone."

Warning buzzers exploded in Sergeant's brain. He cupped his hand over the receiver and called across the room to the girl. "Turn on the police scanner." He turned back to his caller.

"Go ahead, lady."

"Then I called the sheriff's office and got the same response. Same thing at the state patrol. I don't know who else to call, mister. Can you understand this? My children are missing — and so are a lot of other people!"

Sergeant was nonplused. It was the first he had heard about any mass disappearance. His source at NYPD was falling down on the job. Or maybe this thing had happened so fast that his informant hadn't had a chance to call. Or this lady was just a little crocked. Too much partying the night before. That had to be it.

"Lady, maybe your kids just walked outside or something. Have you looked out the door?"

The woman cursed. "Look, you don't understand! My youngest child is only five-months-old, and the other is just two-years-old.

They can't open our bolted doors and go cruising in and out of this place!"

"Well, what about your husband? Has he looked around the —"

"My husband took off when my last child was born. I don't know where he is."

"How about the windows? Are their any open windows?" Sergeant was thinking about the possibility of kidnapping, although he didn't want to tell that to the distraught woman.

"No!" She was growing hysterical again. "All the windows are closed and locked. I'm not stupid, mister. That's the first thing I checked was the windows. I thought maybe some pervert had broken in here and taken my babies. But no one has been inside this house! I swear to you! The doors are still locked and bolted and not one window has been touched."

Sergeant's sense of logic was now offended and he didn't have enough tact to keep it from showing.

"Ah, c'mon lady! If nobody got in and nobody got out, then your kids aren't gone, are they?"

"Yes, they are! I am telling you that my babies are gone! I have looked in every room, under every piece of furniture, in —"

"Were their bedclothes or covers disturbed? Were the beds rumpled?"

"No, and that's rather strange. It looks as if someone just lifted them out of bed— gently. And I've called and called them and they don't answer. Please, mister, send someone over here to help me!" She went into total hysteria, then slammed down the receiver.

That had been the first irrational call. Similar calls now filled every incoming line. All of the people are off the wall, thought Sergeant. One big nut house.

A customer in an all-night restaurant suffered serious burns when the waitress was pouring him a cup of fresh coffee. Suddenly she vanished and the pot fell against the man's face, severely scalding him. Witnesses said the waitress just disappeared!

Then there was the report of people raiding a gasoline station on the off ramp of Interstate 684 near New Rochelle. The attendant had disappeared and fuel was being stolen by the hundreds of gallons with no one to stop it.

A sobbing man tried to tell Sergeant that he and his wife were embracing in bed and ZAP, she was gone.

When the calls started, Sergeant's mind replayed Orson Welles' *War of the Worlds*, the radio show that caused havoc across America. Surely something like that must be happening now, he thought. The whole thing is some kind of radio or television promotion — or a film hype.

But he chucked that idea as soon as it hit him. If the disappearances — or whatever they were — had been connected to a media event, then why wouldn't he have known about it beforehand? After all, he was working in the center of the biggest television news conglomerate in the world.

But the story that had really unnerved him and made him determined to call Clayton Daniels was the one he had received from a reliable source at Kennedy International Airport. Through the years, Sergeant had developed informants in key areas across the nation and, indeed, in some foreign lands. Some of these people were paid, some were given "tips" by Sergeant on a purely piecemeal basis, while others just wanted to see their leads on the morning news. But for whatever reason the "moles" informed him, they had been of extreme value to the network. Sergeant was justifiably proud of his tipsters.

His Kennedy source was a fellow named Jack Wilingham, nearing retirement as a member of the night cleanup operations in the international flight buildings. This job gave Wilingham access to virtually every airline that originated from that particular complex. He had given Sergeant a few good leads through the years and the newsman had tried to make the calls worth the custodian's time. The Kennedy source was one of the first callers in the bizarre series.

"Chris, this is Jack at Kennedy."

"Yeah, Jack, how ya doin'? Thought maybe you had died or something. Been sometime since I talked to you."

"Naw, it was just that I didn't have nothin' to give you. Until tonight. Man, I got something brewin' here now that sounds like science fiction."

Sergeant tensed, flicking a record switch that would automatically feed the telephone conversation to a dictating machine.

"Great, Jack, let me have it as quickly as you can. These phones are ringing off the hook. What's going down out there?"

"OK, it's a missing flight."

"A what? A missing international?"

"You got it, Chris. It's Royal Jordanian Flight 793, coming in from Amman by way of Vienna. Should have landed four hours ago. Last RJ flight due in today."

Sergeant's patience was ebbing. "Well, so what, Jack? Maybe it's weathered in somewhere. Some of those RJ flights refuel in Amsterdam, you know."

"Not this one, Mac! It ain't in — and what's more, it ain't gonna get in. The last message from 793 was received while the plane was still over Newfoundland. It was nearly home, man!"

"Well, had it left Amman and Vienna on schedule?"

"Oh, yeah! It left Amman about 11 yesterday morning and stopped for passengers in Vienna. That's a short stop, Chris — they don't even let the New York passengers leave the plane. So it was right on schedule when it cleared Austria. The last thing we heard from the flight crew was that everything was OK, that they were flying automatic control until they neared the Canadian coastline. And that's the last they called in — or the last we could rouse anyone."

"So how long has it been since that last contact?"

"Over four hours ago! And here's the thing, I mean, here's the story! The tower officials still have the thing tracked on their radar!"

Sergeant leaned back in his chair. Jack's lead had the makings of a big story.

"So where is the plane now and how come you know so much about it?"

"Chris, you can't keep a story like this quiet around the airport. Too many people have access to too much information. For one thing, there's a bunch of people outside of customs who have been waiting for friends or family members, and they're yelling like crazy, they know something is wrong. Besides that, you got all the guys in customs, baggage people, plane service crew — here's all these guys hanging around for the 747 to get in so they can finish their work and get outta here. OK, the plane doesn't show and they wanna know why. They ask questions. You know what I mean? So I got a good friend who works in the tower who gave me this information about 15 minutes ago. He knows the whole deal. The plane didn't land, and it didn't crash. It's still flyin' by itself, on automatic pilot, somewhere. Some story, huh?"

Sergeant tried to concentrate on what he had just heard. More questions popped into his mind.

"Now let me get this absolutely right, Jack. You're telling me that there's a 747 flying around somewhere over this country, it's full of people, and no one's flying it as far as you know."

"You got it, Chris. Radar has the plane tracked somewhere over southwest Indiana. Fuel is critical now. And there's 297 people on board."

Sergeant sensed a painful tightening in his gut, the same sensation he always had on the eve of a solid story.

"Indiana? How in the world can the plane be in Indiana? What happened to the flight crew — the, the pilot and the navigator and —"

"Who knows? The guys in the tower just simply don't know what happened to 'em. One of the fellas said that the entire flight deck apparently just — just vanished! I mean, they all just flat disappeared!"

Sergeant's temper came through. "Disappear? Aw, come on, Jack! How in the world could a couple of pilots and navigators get off a 747 somewhere over the Atlantic? They just go for a stroll on the wing maybe?"

There was a chuckle at the end of the line.

"Very good, newsman! Maybe that's what they did. How should I know? All I know is that the plane is hours the other side of New York City and still goin' like a bat out of hell. At least it's goin' until the fuel's gone which should be about anytime. Then there's gonna be one big crash. So unless that crew reappears real fast and makes it over to Lambert Field in St. Louis, well, a lot of people are gonna buy a farm tonight."

Sergeant's mind raced over the new information. Thousands had disappeared in New York and apparently in other places as well. Now a 747 was flying itself over Indiana and would probably dig a massive grave for everyone in it somewhere in Kentucky or

Indiana — maybe Missouri. Panic on the West Coast where people were still up and aware of friends who had vanished. Terror in London and Paris where it was past breakfast time and millions hadn't shown up to eat.

"Thanks, Jack. I'll get back to you and if this thing is what you say, I owe you a big one. I promise."

Sergeant hung up and glanced over the large newsroom. Everyone on duty was bent over a phone, writing feverishly and casting worried glances at him. One of his associates had called in other workers who were now arriving, unshaven, with uncombed hair, and questions in their eyes. It was all like some kind of Andy Warhol painting; nothing made any sense, just a jumble of color with no connecting lines or points.

Chris glanced at the wire service machines. AP, UPI, the regionals and locals were all clanging robots of doom, belching out reams of copy that spread awareness of an illogical disaster in the making.

Sergeant knew he needed help and so he had called Clay Daniels.

5

Manhattan at four a.m. is relatively quiet and restful, and spectacularly beautiful in a melancholy sort of way. The ugly coils of serpentine access roads and expressways lie hidden in the folds of darkness and millions of lights of myriad color and size spotlight men's efforts to rise as gods to the heavens.

Most of the city's fabled nightspots had already closed as Clayton Daniels' driver threaded the limo through the sleepy streets. The IBC news building recently had been constructed close to the Time/Life Building near West 48th and Fifth Avenue. It far surpassed the Rockefeller Center home of NBC. Its creators had displayed the brilliance of engineering minds in designing this 20th century colossus for dispersing news. By use of now-common satellites, conventional electronics and a few *Star Wars* gadgets pioneered by the network, Daniels' crews had near-immediate audio and video contact with any point on the globe, not to mention distant canyons of space.

A whiff of the warm night air brushed Daniels' cheek as he lowered the back-seat window to let his cigarette smoke escape. His mind was so busy that it did not register the sights that usually gave him such delight enroute to the office — the stately line of old mansions, now-dark exclusive clubs, historic churches with their penetrating steeples, art galleries, antique shops and museums.

Daniels' thoughts returned to Sergeant's call. Then some open door of the reasoning process propelled him much farther back in his life following his graduation from Ohio State University in Columbus. For a time he had served as an assistant newsman at WMAN, a small radio station in nearby Mansfield, Ohio, where he also doubled as a play-by-play announcer for the tough Buckeye Conference football association. When his immediate boss moved to greener pastures, Clayton was elevated to the news director's job. He quit the sports scene entirely and devoted all of his energies into becoming a good reporter. There wasn't much pay. He felt like the man who cleaned up after elephants in the circus. Someone asked him why he didn't quit. "What?" he cried, "and give up show business?" Despite the lousy pay and equally pathetic working conditions, Daniels experienced the real world of minor league journalism — and he learned it well. He also served as area news source, or "stringer," for the *Toledo Blade* newspaper and WEWS, Channel 5 (the ABC affiliate), in Cleveland. His contact with the pros at both the *Blade* and the TV station helped him gain expertise and also stimulated his drive to excel beyond his current common status.

His superiors in Cleveland soon recognized that he had abilities and it was only a matter of time before he made the jump to television news. Channel 5's major thrust was local news, featuring the commentaries of the legendary Dorothy Fuldheim, who in her 80s was still the city's highest-rated TV personality — and a frequent guest on NBC's *Tonight Show*. News was far and away the best moneymaker of all local programming in Cleveland. The station was owned by the Scripps-Howard Company which had invested megabucks in the news department. The investment paid off when Channel 5 became the number one news station in Ohio, a ranking it held for most of the decade.

Daniels' initial days there were at the bottom of the pecking order. He was not much more than a glorified "gopher." But he didn't seriously mind for he was fulfilling his dream by working in one of the most productive training grounds any young newsman could have. He soon became aware of the fact, as did his supervisors, that his forte was more in the field of production and administration than being on camera. He was not overly handsome, did not have that toothy, sleek appearance of many anchormen and could not make himself manufacture the "canned jolliness" required of local news personnel. Daniels hated that whole approach to news reporting (". . . and highway patrol officers said that nine persons died in the fiery wreck. Well, Jack, how did your weekend go? How was the party?") To Daniels, news substance and clarity of reporting were of greater importance than the reporter's latest golf score or the shenanigans of his new baby.

It also was not in Daniels' favor that he was stocky and sandy-haired, two features that did not make him look too good on camera. Even good makeup did not equalize this important shortcoming. What he did have was a fast and accurate mind when it came to systematizing facts and concepts. No one else at the station could equal him.

By the time he was 31-years-old, much to the dismay of many who had waited in line for the job, Daniels was promoted to news director, the youngest ever at WEWS. His salary jumped to the near six-figure level, more than he had ever dreamed of earning. It was during that heady time that he met Arvella and the two were married within a year. A few years later he was invited to the IBC network in New York.

The young executive enjoyed network news far more than the local variety. At Cleveland, as in other cities big and small, news production had become more and more personality-oriented, using the "happy talk" approach to garner those all-vital rating points and hence the big bucks. While "being there first" was still important, it was equally valid that your "how to present it" was flashy and glitzy. Daniels had learned all the tricks; indeed, he had invented some. He knew how to use more spectacular video footage than a news story actually warranted (even though this procedure often failed to give a true picture of the actual happening) and spicing up the verbal give and takes among the reporters on-camera. Daniels had done it, despite finding the efforts distasteful. He often told anyone who would listen that the station was allowing the "how" of presentation to overshadow the "what" of content. It had taken some of the edge off his enthusiasm for local news, but the dollars had held his attention.

At the network though, the "story" was the whole bit. Facts were as sacred as a grotto in Israel. Gradually, budgets, technical gadgets, union negotiations and programming became his life. And he loved it. He could not remember the last story he had actually covered as a working reporter and, to his delight, he could care less.

But he still would get excited over a breaking story, especially one of international merit, and Sergeant's early morning phone call had brought him to life. He knew the information the night editor had disclosed made absolutely no sense — the possibility of men and women vanishing off the earth in wholesale quantity.

He reached forward to the console in front of him, ignoring the built-in bar and coffeemaker, and flipped the dial of the radio to a 24-hour news station. Daniels thought the reporters sounded strained as they began reading news bulletins that had begun streaming in via wire machines and from their own men on the streets. He sat back and sucked in cigarette smoke as he heard one incredible story after another.

"And in Honolulu at this moment, there is a TV studio full of spectators who are wondering how it was done — that is, how the special guest on the talk show disappeared right before their eyes.

"Dr. William Howard, one of America's best-known ministers, was appearing on the *Philip Jacks Show*, live. He had been invited to tell of his recent appearances in the People's Republic of China, the first such public religious meeting allowed since the revolution. As Dr. Howard answered the pointed, and at times caustic, questions, to everyone's shock — he vanished. One moment he was chatting amiably, the next moment his seat was vacated. Viewers at home suspected trick camera work. But host Philip Jacks was sitting fewer than three feet from him. Two of the cameramen were only 15 feet away. The 260 persons in the studio audience realized that it was not a special effects trick. They have been unanimous in reporting what they saw — the minister simply vanished. At this hour, no one knows where he is or what happened to him. Now, here is another report from —"

The radio voice turned to static as the limo driver turned off the main thoroughfare into the parking garage beneath the IBC Building. Daniels turned the radio off. His mind, so accustomed to logic, was trying desperately to put it all together. No local television programmer would be so stupid as to try to make a man disappear on live television. And, even if he were, a man of the ministerial integrity of Dr. Howard would not go along with it. Daniels did not believe in organized religion, but this fellow Howard had never betrayed his dignity or values. No, obviously it was not a planned trick. But what was it? What force had taken effect to temporarily suspend the law of gravity for some people, yet not for others? Why had some disappeared and others, like himself and Marsha and Chris, were still around?

According to preliminary reports, the missing persons must now total in excess of a million worldwide. Where did they go? What had broken down in the time and space dimensions to permit such a mass disappearance? It appeared to be a worldwide Bermuda Triangle, only one without water and pirates.

Daniels stepped out of the limo, thanked the driver and walked to the private entrance door at the rear of the new building. The only thing he knew for sure was that no TV station or newspaper syndicate could claim an exclusive story tonight. Everyone knew what had happened, they just didn't know why. Every hick radio and TV station and weekly news gazette in the country by now would have their sleepy-eyed staffs reporting for duty.

His task now was to get his crew to find out why all this bizarre activity had occurred. That would be the story, the exclusive. Daniels was determined that IBC would somehow be that fortunate and enterprising network.

6

Daniels was in his office less than five minutes when he called an emergency staff meeting to begin promptly at 4:30 a.m. in the executive conference room. Everyone was expected to be there. Telephone calls had gone out to the entire production crew to arrive at that same time, without exception and without excuse. Daniels had personally called his vice presidents: Lawrence Scarti of Special Coverage; Ben Matthews of Political Coverage (just in case leading American politicians were among the "evacuated"); Kay Banes of Affiliate News and Satellite and Sandra Marchetti of Personnel.

The request was not as unreasonable to some as it would appear, for under normal working conditions the regular morning production staff and on-camera personnel arrived by five a.m. to prepare for the 6:30 news. That was followed by the seven a.m. *Wake Up the Nation* show, now number two among the big four network morning news shows. So no one really complained much about the early call. Daniels rarely made impossible demands on his people (although he had gotten a bit tyrannical when Arvella left him), and the staff and crew knew that if he had called an emergency meeting it would indeed be an emergency.

But the normal camaraderie and morning humor was noticeably lacking as the key participants found their places at the table. Along with Daniels and his executive officers were:

Peter Doyle, host of the *Wake Up* show, a 22-year veteran of TV news, rather plain-appearing but gifted with gracious warmth and charisma, features somehow magnified by the cameras;

Jackie Quinland, co-host, hired for beauty and not for brains (Sergeant had once said — not in her hearing, of course — that everything of value she had ever uttered could be printed in pamphlet form);

Janssen Hennings, the morning newsman who, if offered the choice between his life and his job, would have to think it over;

Marilyn Garrett, creative producer of the morning 7-9 show, several times divorced by men who could not equal her ability and drive;

Writers John Saks and Raymond McClure, who had the ability to make almost any on-camera entity believable if they could read cue cards with some degree of realism;

Then there was night editor Chris Sergeant and his assistant Sally Wright.

Most of the *Wake Up* staff and crew had been together for the duration of the morning show and, by and large, there was genuine feeling for one another. Positive feeling, except for the thoughts some had about Chris Sergeant. He would never have been their first choice to bring to a social function, however, they realized his dependability in news gathering.

The one thing everyone in the room had in common was a sincere affection for Clayton Daniels. In a business known for questionable hiring ethics and sometimes brutal firing procedures, Daniels was a fair man. He had an understanding of the needs of his employees and could motivate them without their feeling manipulated, a rare characteristic in that business. Daniels really wanted his workers to be successful, not only at IBC but also at home — something at which he himself had not been of championship material.

He had the capacity to make those under him look good. For one thing, he was not threatened by them. He had no apparent fear of losing his job to them, although he was not all that positive about outside interlopers. He was superior at delegating authority and getting proper accounting from those he trusted.

He would have been the first to admit that he had a loyal staff. Each one, from the vice presidents down, had been helpful in his or her own way during those fragmented years when Daniels' marriage had crumbled. His effectiveness at IBC would have been undermined had he not been undergirded by them. He knew that for a fact and repeatedly showed his appreciation.

He had deeply loved his wife Arvella, and he still did. She was not as physically beautiful as Marsha, nor as sensual. But there was something about her demeanor, her personality, her bearing that Daniels knew he would never be able to forget.

Their relatively short marriage had been difficult for both of them. The farther Daniels advanced in the industry, the farther apart they grew. He was taken up with the television business and world affairs, frequently traveling around the world. She was content, in fact, adamant, about staying home with their son Robert. She also had a growing attachment to a world that Daniels thought was crazy. For while he was consumed by what he thought of as the real world, she had turned her attention to religion.

Clayton had never believed in such things. He was not even sure he believed in the existence of a God. Arvella's dedication to her religious exercises was a turn off to him. They could not communicate about it without arguing and so the tension between them increased until they could no longer merely discuss the problem; they yelled about it.

Neither of them would have cited religion as the final culprit that destroyed their marriage, because each knew that that subject was only the tip of a monumental and hidden iceberg. There were other matters, social and physical, that entered into it. But regardless of the reason, the separation had hurt him deeply. His weekly visits with Robert, which he fulfilled with resolute faithfulness and joy, always hurt him more than he would have admitted to anyone.

He thought he had truly attempted to understand his wife's concept of life. Perhaps if she had been only nominally committed to her religious endeavors he could have lived with that. Other people attended church without slipping into fanaticism. It was one thing to attend church services if that's what one really wanted to do; but it was quite another to make religion your whole life, which is exactly what Daniels thought Arvella had done.

At times he introduced her to his friends as the new Billy Graham. After all, she preached almost all the time. Arvella had bought the whole ecclesiastical jargon; hook, line and sinker. She actually believed the medieval ideas and teachings. Daniels would never buy such preposterous concepts and so the rift between them increased to the breaking point.

Daniels never talked about it to anyone. His staff, and especially Ivy Browning, his secretary, believed that he probably loved Arvella as much as ever and would never be as giving and open to any other woman. They also believed he would never marry Marsha, despite her pregnancy. They understood that as much as he cherished Arvella, he would not, he could not, sublimate his sense of logic and reasoning for her superstitions and tradition.

Daniels reclined in his chair at the head of the conference table and looked at the staff, hopefully for some answers. His whole perception of reality was being sorely tried by the insane news of the mass disappearances. He had tried to sort out facts — but what facts? It was a fairy tale intrusion into the very real world of détente, missiles, famine and politics. Those stories all had some understandable qualities. But this?

One of the white-coated company waiters brought in fresh coffee, hot tea and some not-so-fresh doughnuts from the commissary and the emergency meeting was underway.

Daniels leaned across the table to the craggy-faced star of the *Wake Up* show. "Peter, help me here — what was the special thrust for this morning's show? What did you have planned?"

Doyle raised his eyes toward Marilyn Garrett, the producer. "I think you'd better get the answer to that from her, Clay. She has the whole format handy."

Marilyn paused, coffee in mid-air. "Well, it would have been a rather normal day, Clay. The news stories are — or were — rather routine. Jackie is scheduled to interview Lauren Bacall about her new show on Broadway. Uh, Miss Bacall will arrive during the second hour for her part. Then we have several good taped interviews, one on that Iranian assassination the other day — the CIA has a couple of interesting theories about it. It looks like more Russian interference on the Iranian border and we're guessing it's tied in with the assassination. Turkey may be involved. But we don't have any definite or substantial interviews that just have to — uh — to go on. What I am saying is that everything is definitely secondary to the big story of the morning, which is the disappearances."

"Yeah, she's right, Clay." The affirmative came from Doyle. "This series of missing people is right out of science fiction. But I think we're going to have to spend both hours on it. I doubt if people who have had family members vanish are going to be interested in anything else. And, Janssen, your film crews should have some pretty good video tape by airtime, don't you think?"

Hennings nodded in mute agreement.

Daniels leaned back, nursing a cooling cup of black coffee. "OK. I'm going to be right here with you all day — or however many days this thing takes. Marilyn, you better have someone call Miss Bacall and tell her that her segment may get cut — that is, if she hasn't disappeared too. Kay, let's start feeding the affiliates immediately. Give them whatever we have."

The director of Affiliate News and Satellite Service was ready. "Sir, quite a few of the stations are already on the air — or have been on all night. They will be taking our feeds as they can, putting in their local news as well. From our early reports, almost the entire network has been alerted and is either ready or already broadcasting."

Daniels smiled an acknowledgement. "Thanks, Kay. Now, Janssen, you ought to start feeding within the next 15 minutes. Any problem with that?"

Janssen Hennings could have gone on the air at that very moment, but technically the cameras and crew were not quite ready.

"No problem, Clay. Fifteen minutes should be fine. We won't have all the video we would like, of course, but there is a constant feed now from all the affiliates."

Daniels nodded. "Yeah, OK. Well, I wish we knew more about this nutty thing, but we need to put it in gear. I'll not leave the building until we have solved the mystery and everything's back to some semblance of normal."

The staff stood to leave.

"Hold it a minute." Marilyn Garrett's voice sounded urgent, stopping their exodus. "I have looked for Manny Dow all over this place today. I can't find him. Any of you seen him?"

Sally, who had been there most of the night with Sergeant, volunteered: "Well, I called him, along with the rest of the staff, when Chris told me to begin rounding you up for this meeting. That was sometime before four o'clock. But there was no answer at the Dow home when I called, so I figured he must have already left to come in early."

"You mean his wife didn't answer the phone?" asked Marilyn.

"Nope. I let it ring 20 times at least. But no response."

"That's strange," said Janssen. "Why wouldn't his wife answer? She wouldn't be coming in with him would she? Unless one of their cars broke down and she needed to drive somewhere today."

"Maybe she's on a trip or something," offered Saks.

"Don't think so," responded Marilyn. "Manny usually tells us everything that's going on in his family, and he hasn't mentioned her being away. What do you think, Clay?"

Daniels had listened to their conversation about the popular little floor director with more than just passing interest. There was something nagging at his mind, trying to open a door of light or reasoning, but he couldn't quite get hold of it. Too early to think. He turned to Sally.

"Are you sure Manny's phone was working properly? Check with an operator about it?"

Sally chuckled. "Now, sir, that's something you drummed into my head when I first came here — check all possibilities. Yes, I checked on their phone. There was nothing wrong. Manny and his wife just weren't there, that's all. Maybe they're on their way in. Or dead."

She meant the last part as a joke. But nobody laughed.

It was Raymond McClure who voiced what the others were afraid to. "Do you suppose that he and his wife are among those who have disappeared?"

"Yeah, that's a good question, Ray," said Daniels, chewing on the edge of his Styrofoam coffee cup. "But why in blue blazes would they vanish? Why would Manny and his wife disappear and not, say, John or Ray or you, Chris? I think that's the real story here. Obviously some people are not where they're supposed to be. Maybe they really have vanished. But why them? That's the answer we need!"

Daniels words grew more heated as he spoke because he could not bear illogical sequence of facts.

McClure answered him. "Well, Clay, you're right. That's the issue, to be sure. I think Manny will show up. We don't want to jump to conclusions here like a bunch of cub reporters. Send one of our people over to their apartment to see if he can rouse anyone. Have him check with the manager of the complex. But somehow get Manny here. We are going to need him desperately."

Daniels sighed loudly and looked around at the solemn faces of his staff. "This is weird, isn't it? Well, good luck. I want everything you can pack into our first feed this morning."

The room emptied in seconds, the crew leaving behind nearly empty coffee cups and cigarette stubs on the long-since scarred table top. Daniels watched them go with mixed feelings — appreciation for their proficiency and a haunting premonition that the days of normal life in his business were over.

One thing he knew for sure. This was a day unlike any other he had ever experienced. And, early in the morning or not, he felt like he needed a drink.

7

The faint, yellowing front lights of the rickety '64 Mercury barely lit the dirt road that led from Kentucky Route 62 to the mangy-looking farm shack beyond the rise. Piles of rock and assorted collections of trash, accumulated through the years, lined both sides of the drive. An unusually severe winter for western Kentucky a few months ago had combined a series of snows and ice storms, gouging out huge chuckholes in the path of the car.

"Someday," said the driver Ed Miller to himself, "someday I'll borrow Charlie Filmer's tractor and bulldoze this road." But "someday" to this old man never arrived.

Broken springs in the car's suspension system and the absence of anything faintly resembling shock absorbers made the ride even more unbearable. The driver's body felt each impact and, with each bump, his soft curses filled the stagnant cab of the car.

Miller felt lousy. He had stopped hours earlier at his favorite watering hole in western Paducah. A clapboard building, barely hanging together, served as the lounge for the county's chief wine sippers, most notorious of whom was Miller. He had not expected to stay very long — maybe just a couple of beers and be on his way home to rural Camelia. But then Jim and Mike and several of their buddies had come in, and the pinball tournament was underway.

When the raucous rivalry had ended, and the empty cans of booze were stacking up, a lively and drunken discussion on state politics had ensued.

Mike had started it. He usually did. He allowed that Governor Armand Creeden was the biggest crook in state political history. That was all Miller needed — those were fighting words. Only the concerted efforts of the less-inebriated kept them from fighting.

Later both men, the alcohol fully in effect, tearfully apologized and chose to forgive each other over a drink. And that one led to another and another.

There were not many hours of night left when the party broke up. Miller's head felt like it had been crammed into the Mercury with a shoehorn. Every little bump in the road was like ball bats against the side of his temples. He felt deathly sick to his stomach.

The vintage vehicle now crawled along the dirt side road just north of Camelia. Even in his inebriated condition, Miller noticed that the airport searchlight was stabbing the skies at nearby Barkley Field. He had never noticed the lights on there after midnight. But the incident made a fleeting impression and was then drowned in the alcohol.

A rabbit darted in front of the flickering headlights and Miller swerved violently to avoid the animal. It was that lurch that did it. In his drunken state, Miller's foot kicked against the brake, the Mercury skidded sideways on the loose dirt and hit a huge hole. His chin slammed against the steering wheel. He opened the door and crawled out. There in the rocks and garbage the old man made an offering to the gods of the earth of all that he had consumed that night.

The ceremony ended, he leaned against the fender, gulped in the fresh Kentucky night air and looked around. He wiped his chin with a dirty sleeve and promised himself for the several hundredth time that he would stop drinking. That repentent litany over, the old man laughed silently to himself. Who was he kidding, anyhow? What else on earth was more worthwhile than those hours he spent in the clapboard shack, drinking with his buddies?

He worked part time as a watchman in one of the manufacturing plants on Paducah's southside. He didn't make much money, but then he didn't have to. His house was not worth the $2,500 he had paid for it, with its bare wires, broken windows, leaking roof and outhouse. He wasn't about to fix it. Let it crash to the ground for all he cared. He still had the Merc. It would probably go on forever, he allowed, despite its constant groanings.

No, Miller thought, he didn't have it too bad, really. Not too much work, no responsibilities, good buddies to drink and fight with, and a faithful old car. What more could any man want? Unless it was a new head — one that wasn't about to explode.

He would feel better tomorrow, he hoped. Then he would just take the day off. Take his rifle and get some rabbits up on the ridge. The thought made him feel much better.

Miller had just opened the car door when he heard the first sound of disaster. It was a low whining noise coming from the woods to the east, rapidly growing louder. But it was so dark in the woods, with very little moonlight, that he could not see anything. He knew something was coming! The approaching sound grew louder.

He had never heard anything so weird, so haunting. He could not describe it exactly — kind of a shrill moaning, a whistling. And very frightening!

The sound came closer. Miller could now see that it was something in the sky. Blinking lights became visible, lights that blinked several hundred feet apart, slipping lower and lower to the earth. One of the lights was somewhat higher than the other as if the huge object were descending at a severe angle.

It was the most horrifying moment in the old man's life when it dawned on him that the approaching monster was an enormous airplane, bigger than any that he had ever seen land at Barkley Field. But then this plane wasn't going to the local airport either; it was going to hit the ground somewhere between him and his shack. Miller figured the situation very quickly, even in his stupor. He knew there was no runway or anything resembling flatland in the immediate area. There was simply nowhere to set down any kind of an airplane, even a little one, here. The 296-foot craft was going to land in rugged hills and even the sotted Miller perceived that airplanes could not do that.

The plane was now less than a mile away and appeared to be just skimming the surface of the earth. Just ahead of it, a hill, covered by woods, rose sharply. The plane hit the incline at over 400 miles per hour. Miller felt the ground shake. His ears were assasulted by the screeching, jarring sound of thousands of tons of metal crashing to the ground.

Fire shot into the sky as one explosion followed another. In the eerie light of the flames the old man could see dark objects being propelled from the plane structure — or what was left of it. The objects were charred bodies. There were no screams. The impact had killed them instantly.

The horrified old man didn't know it but he was watching the final dance of death of Royal Jordanian Flight 793. Broken electrical cables had now begun to spew fire and ruptured lines belched out hydraulic fluid. The bright electrical lights flickered once, twice, then were extinguished forever. Now only the burning remnants of the plane and bodies made visibility possible.

The 747 tumbled nose over tail, smashing trees like they were made of papier-mache'. The great engines had sucked in huge quantities of debris and Miller could hear them spool down. Several wheels exploded from their hidden compartment and sailed through the air like lethal Frisbees. The old man could hear them whooshing through the night air.

The tail section blew into a million fragments, some of the pieces burying deeply into already dead bodies of passengers. One of the fragments pinged against the Mercury, causing Miller to automatically duck his head. What had once been a magnificent chamber of flying comfort was now a fire tunnel with many bodies still strapped into seats and burning with the plane.

A large fragment of some part of the plane whistled over Miller's head and smashed into the rocks behind him. The smell of the raging fire and burning flesh and the horror of what he had just witnessed set off another eruption in the old man's stomach, and he leaned over the front of the car and vomited.

His thin, veined legs shook violently and his abdomen continued in dry spasms as he climbed behind the wheel of the old Mercury and drove toward the inferno. But the dirt road ended abruptly where huge scoops of earth and gravel had been torn away by a piece of the doomed plane.

Miller shut off the car, leaving the faint lights on to help him see. Summoning up some resolve he didn't know he possessed, he walked toward the wreckage, the lights behind him casting strange shadows in his pathway.

Pieces of the 747 were strewn nearly a mile through the woods. Some of the older, dead trees had caught fire and created a macabre lighted walkway for him, each tree a torch in the night.

The only sounds were the crackling fire and a slight breeze that fanned the flames. Small bursts of firelight danced across the death ridge. Images were forming a mental picture in the drunken man's mind, images that he would never be able to erase, no, not with all the alcohol he could consume.

A dark form lay in his path. Miller wondered if it was a small deer that had been struck by some part of the plane. He leaned down to examine it closer. His cry was a piercing wail in the night. The form was not a deer at all, but rather a human body, one leg and most of the head missing. The clothes had been burned off and the body was so mutilated that Miller could not tell if it had been a man or a woman.

He didn't need to see any more. He stumbled back to the Mercury, hoping that he would not trip over any more obscene corpses and praying that the battery of his old machine would still turn over the engine. The front lights were perceptibly dimmer now. But Miller's luck held and the engine fired. He found a spot where he could turn the car around and began backtracking to the little town of Camelia. He would find a telephone there. Someone had to know about the crash. Someone had to share this night of terror with him.

The old man's body was wracked with spasms of fear and pain as the Mercury bobbed and dipped down the ridge to the intersection of Route 62. Miller turned back east on the paved road, wiping tears from his eyes as he drove, making everything ahead just a blur.

His muffled sobs mingled with the throb of the antique engine. What had happened here this night? What gods had spewed this corruption on his homeland? He had no comprehension of how many bodies lay dead over the ridge where he had for so many years tracked rabbits.

Behind him, the 747 continued to burn, spreading to some of the dead trees nearby. Miller's little hut was the last thing to ignite.

The old man tried to watch it through his shaking rearview mirror. It looked like the entrance to hell.

8

Chris Sergeant received the call from Paducah, Kentucky, that RJ 793 had crashed and there were no survivors.

The news crew at Paducah's Channel 12 was already on the scene and that meant that IBC momentarily would get its first video feed, featured by an interview with some old man who had witnessed the crash. It was a big news story and Sergeant remembered he needed to thank Jack Wilingham at Kennedy for the earlier tip.

It was the first crash of a 747 in years. The usually reliable planes had compiled the most remarkable safety record of any airplane. And 793 should have made it safely as well, thought Sergeant. But not even the Boeing Company could make an airplane land safely without a crew. Unfortunately this Amman-based crew seemed to have disappeared somewhere over the Atlantic.

Sergeant swore silently to himself. What kind of thought progression was that — "the flight crew had disappeared" —

Everything about the story, about the whole night, was unreal, unearthly. A series of incredible non sequiturs, each defying the art of logic.

He and Peter Doyle had already conferred with Marilyn Garrett and decided that most of the *Wake Up* show would be news-oriented. The Bacall interview was cancelled as were other planned features. Two main stories had to be covered fully — the disappearances of millions of people and the crash of the 747, which were directly related.

Meanwhile, Daniels, fully apprised of each new development, closed himself off in his comfortable private office. Ivy Browning had by now arrived to assist him. Someone in maintenance had the foresight and courtesy to light a fire in the small corner fireplace. No one else in the building would have wanted a fire in August, but Daniels kept his office temperature in the constant 60s, and a small fire was therapy to him. The hissing and crackling of the logs were soothing to his deteriorating state of mind.

He leaned back in the soft leather chair, his fingers massaging his pounding temples. He remembered that he must take his morning Dyazide. If only he could get his brain clicking. There had to be an answer to the mystery of the missing millions. "What a book title that would be," he grinned mirthlessly to himself: "The Mystery of the Missing Millions!"

He glanced at his desk and caught sight of the picture there — Marsha! How beautiful she was! Her silken hair was tossed back, revealing the oval face that featured violet eyes and full lips. Daniels wanted to call her to see if she was all right. The baby was due in several months, and Marsha had felt her body severely changing. But there was not time to call her just yet — perhaps later.

The intercom on his desk buzzed, breaking into his thoughts. He pushed the button. "Yes?"

"Clay, this is Chris."

"What's happening? Any solutions?"

"Naw, Clay — just more problems. It looks as if we're going to have to give some time today to coverage of the Iranian situation. The military there claims it caught the guy who blew up President Sadegh Kavir. They're interrogating the poor devil right now. Whether he actually did it or not, they'll say he did and probably put on a public execution. The fact is, Clay, that with Kavir's death, the Iranian government lost its last touch with the real world

— certainly with the West. And we are getting reports now of Russian infiltration on the Afghan-Iranian border."

Daniels nodded wearily and breathed a soft profanity into the receiver. "Chris, I have a feeling we're going to be on the air forever. Well, all right, I think you're right about the coverage. Tell our man in Iran — uh, Russell Sorenson — to stay on the stick and —"

"Clay —"

"— and what, Chris?"

There was a pause as if Sergeant could not bring himself to tell his boss the latest development. The silence ended the last of Daniels' fragile patience.

"And what, Chris?"

"Well, I hate like everything to tell you this, but Sorenson doesn't seem to be in Iran!"

"He what? What are you talking about? Of course he's there. He fed us stories all day yesterday and, in fact, I talked to him on the phone around noon our time."

"Yeah? Well, he might have been in Teheran last night, but he's not there now. In fact, I don't think he's anyplace right now. Nobody's seen him in Teheran for at least six hours. Our crew has called his room, checked the Swiss Embassy, checked the mobile unit and even talked to some of the more rational and friendly Iranians in the news bureau there. I'm telling you, Clay — he's not there. Russell Sorenson has — has disappeared!"

Daniels was quiet.

"Chris, how about a girlfriend there? Have you checked that?"

The veteran news editor snorted. "You kiddin', Clay? This is Sorenson we're talking about here. Straight, old-fashioned Russell J. Sorenson! You know he wouldn't step out on his wife. And our guys wouldn't do it in Iran if they were so inclined. Man, that's a quick way to be stoned to death by those Moslem nuts."

"Yeah, yeah, you're right, of course. I'm not thinking very clearly yet. Well, how about his wife then? Where is it they live — uh, Buffalo? Yeah, that's it — Buffalo. Did you call her there?"

"C'mon, boss, give me some credit here. Sure I called his wife. Daniece, that's her name. At least I tried to call her. She's not around either. Apparently she is among the missing too."

Daniels felt like he was about to have a coronary. His chest muscles had tightened perceptibly. His stomach was on fire. He needed to vomit. He answered his news editor softly. "You think Sorenson and his wife have really just vanished along with all the others? You really think that?"

"That's the way it looks, Clay. Just like all the others."

Daniels' mind suddenly clicked. Maybe there were some pieces of the puzzle that could be locked together here, giving at least part of the overall picture.

"Chris, now think this through with me. We have at least two IBC people gone in this, this — whatever it is. Manny Dow and Russell Sorenson. Their wives too, apparently. Now maybe there's some common connection between them, some common denominator. And that connection might just be a tip-off on why they've vanished. Check the computer file on our personnel — or better yet, get Sandra Marchetti on it. See if there is any kind of outside connection, no matter how fragile, no matter how bizarre. And get me the answer as quickly as possible. It shouldn't be any trouble with the computer index."

Sergeant had no time to answer. Daniels hung up the phone, opened his desk drawer and took out a cigarette. His fingers were shaking as he lit it. He drew the acrid smoke into his lungs and leaned back in his chair to think.

Sorenson was a fairly new man on the staff. Not a bad reporter. A hard worker, a real digger. Not too hot on the air, but a good reporter all in all. He would persist in following leads when others would quit in defeat. Daniels liked that. Sorenson had been fairly well-accepted in Iran, at least by the Iranians whose dip sticks reached the oil. They gave him room to work, let him stay at the Swiss Embassy and in general left him alone. No one seemed to have any problems with him. But he was kind of a loner. Didn't drink, which helped him in Iran. Those screwball Moslems wouldn't even let you do that. How did they expect you to live in that wretched city and not drink?

So, all in all, Sorenson was a good employee. Never be an anchorman, but he had no desire to be. No real weaknesses of character that were known. So much for any hidden shadows there.

Now about Manny Dow. Been on the staff a long time — 10 or

11 years. Little guy. Funny as he could be. Kept the staff laughing with his impressions and dialect jokes. He could imitate the president perfectly. Dow was a hard worker and there weren't many slip-ups when he was on the floor. The on-the-air people loved him, felt confident with his direction.

How about vices? Daniels laughed to himself. He couldn't think of any vices the little director had. Idiosyncrasies, yes! But vices, no. Loved his wife and daughter. Kept his nose clean.

Both of these men, Sorenson and Dow, were good men. They were dependable workers, although not overly creative. Decent fellows. Maybe that was the connection — maybe all the really good workers in the world were disappearing. Just like Ayn Rand's plot in *Atlas Shrugged*. All the good minds, the producers, the workers — just vanishing to some lost colony or valley in the mountains.

Ah, rubbish! Daniels flattened his cigarette in the ashtray. No answer in that line of fairy-tale logic. He had a whole bevy of super workers in the building right now. No one worked at IBC unless they were productive in their given field. If some invisible "John Galt" were raiding the talented workers of the world, there would be few at his network. In fact, he mused ruefully, he himself would be gone. Daniels knew there weren't many executives as hard-working as he.

No, there had to be some other connection between Sorenson and Manny Dow. Something no one could figure out. Something hidden. And, if so, it would probably connect them with the rest of the vanished people as well, although for now it seemed pretty far-fetched to truly believe that theory.

Daniels glanced at his watch, stood up and began pacing the floor. He was getting antsy for some kind of computer readout on the employees. It might not offer the solution to the mystery but he had to start somewhere. There was some logical answer to this thing and he planned to find it today.

Millions gone!

Just vanished in a split second.

Dear God in heaven, why?

9

Everything was awry in the elaborate manse of Bishop Gerald Simonson. The celebrated religious leader was in a dark mood as he turned the telephone over and flipped off the switch that controlled the bell. One more telephone call, he knew, would be the proverbial straw on the old camel's back.

He was usually an early riser, greeting the sun at five a.m. with calisthenics and jogging around the spacious fenced-in yard. But there had been no such physical delights today. The first call had jangled him awake at three o'clock and even the gregarious bishop was not all that gracious at that hour. Unless, of course, it was some parishioner in distress of spirit, one who was very rich and very generous.

The prelate groaned softly and touched his splitting head. When would he ever learn that he couldn't handle drinking? One martini — maybe two. Why did those people expect him to drink with them when they knew he couldn't handle it? But then, who was he kidding? He would have had the booze had he been alone on an ocean island.

He strolled out to the front gate to get *The New York Times.* For the first time in his memory, it was not in the driveway. He wondered what had happened to his faithful paper boy.

A soft breeze rustled through the bushes and, to Simonson's aching head, it sounded like the percussion section of the city symphony. He cursed softly and went back into the house. Perhaps *The Times* could have given him a clue to his congregation suddenly gone berserk.

Closing the massive hand-carved door behind him, he wondered what had possessed the normally sane members of his flock. Ordinarily pretty solid citizens, they must have all sipped of the fruit of the vine the night before — or at least the ones who kept calling him all morning. What gibberish! They had some cockeyed story about missing friends and family members and wanted him to find them.

Well, he had news for *them*. The bishop-founding-father of the Church of America wasn't about to go stumbling through the streets of New York City searching for lost sheep.

A sudden thought occurred to him and he leaned against the doorway to the kitchen, giggling like a schoolboy. Of course! Why hadn't he thought of it before? Bishop Henry in New Jersey was behind this little charade! Certainly, that had to be it. How that man of the cloth loved his practical jokes. Simonson had been the brunt of more than one of them, but nothing this elaborate. Henry must have contacted several dozen people to call him at three or four a.m. with this cock-'n-bull story. People vanishing into thin air! Where is Batman when you need him?

Simonson could imagine his ecclesiastical comrade horse-laughing at this very moment. Set him up, would he? Well, two reverends could play that game.

He picked up the telephone, readjusting the switch, and dialed the familiar New Jersey number. One ring. Two. And it was answered. "Strange," Simonson thought. "I thought he would be sound asleep."

Henry's voice seemed strange and far-removed from any reality. "Hello, hello. This is Henry here."

"Well, well, reverend! Good morning to you. Really thought you had me, didn't you? Yes, pretty funny. Ha-ha. I am laughing myself to death over here. But I'll get you back, Henry, you know that! 'Vengeance is mine,' saith the Manhattan minister. 'I will repay'!"

"Huh? Oh, morning, Gerald. What in the world are you rambling about? What's happening there?"

Simonson chortled. "As if you didn't know? Come on, about 20 or 30 of your cronies have called me already. Some mass disappearance, hey? Well, it was all very clever, but I'm wise to you now and . . ."

"Gerald —"

". . . about the only thing that disappeared at their houses, and yours, I'll wager, was a bit of brandy, eh? Well, no matter. I will get you back. It may take me a bit of time to think of something quite as Orwellian as your plot, but I will concoct some grand scheme!"

"My God, Simonson! Listen to me! I haven't had *anybody* call you!"

Simonson had to laugh, even though his head was screaming. "Sure, sure. Good show. What a great actor you are! Even when caught in the act!"

His friend sounded hysterical. "I am leveling with you, Gerald! This is no joke! My telephone has been ringing constantly for several hours. Something quite terrible has happened, I'm afraid — I mean, really horrible! People are missing, Gerald, they are missing!"

The joke had worn thin. Simonson was getting angry. He swore softly and slammed down the receiver, remembering again to turn off the bell.

The bishop went to the kitchen to put on a pot of coffee. He thought he needed some rather badly. "The whole world is nuts," he mumbled.

Gerald Simonson was the most respected churchman in the Big Apple. Now nearing retirement, he revelled in adulation. The walls of his manse, where he had lived alone since Esther's death 12 years earlier, were covered with honors of every kind; certificates, academic degrees, keys to various cities, the Lions' Club award for "Outstanding Citizen," and many others. He had served as pastor of the prestigious Fourth Avenue Church for 22 years before receiving the title of "His Excellency, Bishop and Patriarch of the Church of America" — the flagship church of the denomination. "Bishop for life!" Simonson smiled a congratulation to himself as he prepared the coffee pot.

He was noted nationally, as well, for his newspaper column, "The Person You Want To Be!" His three books had not been whopping best sellers, but they had generated additional income to his already full personal coffer. By every standard of ecclesiastical excellence he knew about, he, Bishop Gerald S. Simonson, was a success."

He plugged in the pot, waited for the first gurgle, and switched on the radio to station WOR. Always had been his favorite. The news department was a no-nonsense operation. He liked that. You could count on their coverage!

The radio voice shocked the aging minister. It was that of Victor Mellaine, the top newsman at the station. He was normally heard only in prime drive time, which surely wasn't five a.m. "Something urgent must be up," the bishop noted.

"Uh, ladies and gentlemen, good morning. But then again — it may not be so good after all.

"In the strangest night perhaps in all Manhattan's history, police, sheriff's deputies, state patrolmen, and other law enforcement officials have been joined by the Red Cross and the National Guard. They are all trying to solve the riddle of the missing persons."

Simonson felt a cold chill split his shoulder blades.

"All of these departments have been swamped by reports of missing persons. It is still too early to make an estimate of the number, although preliminary reports indicate the figure could exceed one hundred thousand in New York City alone."

The bishop eased into a kitchen chair, his face chalky white. "My God, those calls were legitimate! What has happened?"

"Law officers have no real answer to the mystery. The common report is that it is as if the earth opened and just swallowed them. There are few, if any, clues.

"The Thirty-First Avenue subway is the latest in a series of bizarre disasters apparently related to the disappearances. The train reportedly went out of control, speeding through the tunnel for several miles before striking another subway train which had stopped. Five persons were killed on impact, and still others were reported dead in the panic and trampling of bodies that followed. Police are baffled by the accident. So far they have not been able to locate the operator of the run-away subway. WOR news has learned that the operator was Jack Timmons, a part-time employee of the transit system. One officer said that the front of the train was so severely damaged that Timmons was probably killed; however, his body has not been found at this report. Nor is there any indication of blood in the control area.

"Another disaster is being investigated this morning at the Bekin Warehouse unit on Fifty-Second Street where . . ."

Simonson stood shakily and opened a cupboard where he kept the coffee cups. The empty cup rattled like a tambourine in the shaking saucer. He felt a painful tightening in his chest and his robe was soaked through with sweat, even though it was chilly in the manse.

Even more disturbing than Mellaine's newscast was the logical progression of thought forming in his mind. Simonson had an inkling of the ultimate conclusion of the matter at hand, and the concept filled him with terror. "Surely, it could not be! Not this! Not now!" All the rationale he possessed was trying to assure him that the stupid early morning phone calls, his friend Henry's report from New Jersey, the WOR newscast — all of it was nothing more than incredible coincidence. Nothing more than a pull of a passing comet. Perhaps a dream. He rubbed his aching head with a trembling hand. "Nothing more," he murmured. "Nothing more!"

The coffee pot ceased gurgling and he poured the hot black liquid into the cup. Then he opened another cupboard where he stored one of the city's finest liquor supplies and liberally laced the coffee with expensive alcohol. He forced down a scalding gulp as the voice of doom continued on WOR:

"Mayor William Garnn is already in his office at this early hour and, as we have previously reported, requested that the governor send in the National Guard. The governor has complied with the request. We have the mayor on our hot line. Good morning, Mayor."

"Yes, Victor, hello. I'm not so sure about its being a good morning. We will have to see about that."

"Mayor Garnn, first of all, can you confirm this rash of missing persons reports?''

"Well, yes I can. The simple fact is that we are being swamped with such reports. Of course, everything now is pretty sketchy, you understand. We don't know what has happened. But it does indeed appear that there must be literally thousands upon thousands of New Yorkers missing.''

"In other words, sir, you are telling us that a multitude of our citizens has vanished.''

"Uh, no, Victor, that's not what I am saying. We have reports of missing people. We don't know that they have vanished. That's what we are trying to find out. We actually got our first report of a missing person about 1:30 this morning. So, as far as we know, all the disappearances have taken place since then — well, really, all in the same basic time period. So whatever it was that caused the situation must have happened sometime after 1 a.m.''

Simonson poured himself another cup of loaded coffee and hunched over the radio on the counter, his face a mask of torment and fear. He listened for every nuance.

"Mayor, there is no question then that all this is really happening and not a repeat of *War of the Worlds*?''

"Victor, I wish it *were* a joke! I wish Orson Welles was repeating his gigantic hoax of many years ago. But every indication at this point is that the disappearances are real. Something has happened here. And, apparently, all over the world.''

"Then, Mayor, the big question is, how? Where did they go and how did they get there? Why did they leave? How can that many people suddenly just disappear from the earth?''

The mayor hesitated. "I cannot really answer you. I am leveling with you. I don't have a clue as to what happened. But this just well may be the biggest news story in the history of man!''

Simonson reached over to shut off the radio. He gripped the coffee cup tightly and wept. Tears made uneven rivulets down his unshaven face. Every nerve in his body was on fire. His heart was thudding dully in his chest and he realized that his pulse rate was dangerously high.

The thing that he had told people never would — never could happen, had come to pass! "Irrational,'' he had thundered. "Impossible!'' He had even written a book on the subject. It had sold well — the best of the three — especially on campuses. *Goblins, Spooks and Pulpits*. What a title! How people had laughed when they saw it! The bishop had a Mercedes 500 in his garage, purchased with the royalties from that effort. He had written of the superstitions, fears and myths believed by many people. At this moment, he would have gladly returned the car and everything else he possessed if only he had not written that book.

He made his way through the manse to his study, trying to get control of himself. The walls of the room were lined with ceiling-to-floor bookshelves, each shelf in the lower half pulled out on piano hinges, revealing even more book space behind. Many of his volumes were the original leather-bound editions. Many others were collectors' items, worth thousands of dollars. Each volume was indexed and Simonson could put his finger on any paragraph, line or word he needed in a moment of time. He also had the help of his complicated computer and six word-processing software programs. His library had always been the envy of his colleagues.

He pulled back the velvet drape from the window and looked across the park to the sea where the sun was beginning to rise. Its first rays illuminated the green mansard roof of the elegant Hotel Westin.

He noticed a piece of paper being propelled by a soft breeze. It landed on a park bench several hundred feet from his window. Simonson felt a communion with that pathetic piece of waste paper; he too was now to be blown by the winds of fate wherever they wished. It was all as scary as hell, he thought.

He reached into his pocket for a Kleenex and gently wiped his face and perspiring forehead. He must tell someone what had happened. He knew! He knew! There was not a question about it in his anxious mind! He had the answer to the great mystery.

He walked to the spacious mahogany desk and sat down in his chair, reaching into the middle drawer for his reading glasses. With some difficulty, his shaking fingers adjusted the spectacles to his ears. Opening his personal phone directory, he looked up the special number he had for IBC News and his friend Clay Daniels.

He carefully dialed the number and listened to the constant, strident ringing on the other end of the line. It would be a few moments, he knew, before he could get through. While he waited he opened the bottom drawer of his desk, moved aside several hanging file folders, and placed his quaking hand over the black .38-caliber revolver concealed below.

10

The first video picture transmitted by satellite from Paducah, Kentucky, was technically good but the sights were ghastly. It was still dark in the western part of the state, so inadequate artificial light had to be used. Viewers could make out where the plunging 747 had sheared the tops of trees for nearly three-quarters of a mile. Then, dropping even lower, it had crushed a stand of pines before reaching its grave on the hillside.

Some brave, or ghoulish, cameraman had taken close-ups of some of the bodies, mangled and burned, looking more like charred hunks of beef than human beings. At least the technicians had not perfected the transmission of odor so viewers were spared that horror.

Marilyn Garrett had been adamant when she first saw the transmissions. The morning-show producer barked, "I don't care what the other nets do. We are not showing those body close-ups. It is not necessary and it's exploitative." There was enough legitimate footage to more than depict the narrative.

It had been the interview with eyewitness Ed Miller that made the clips come alive. Now brutally sober and somehow eloquent in his description, the old man told of watching the crash unfold. He gave chilling details of the sounds, the heat, the flying debris, of finding the body in the path.

Daniels watched it with a practiced eye. He moved over to his producer. "Well, Marilyn, what are you and Janssen going to do with that?"

She looked over her shoulder at him and responded, "We're going to edit out the unnecessary carnage and then play the heck out of it. The Paducah news crew did an outstanding job under the circumstances, Clay. We need to send them our congratulations."

"Yeah, you're right. I'll tell Ivy to draft a letter this morning. What else has come in on the disasters?"

"Well, the subway wreck has been tougher to get. It's confined to that shaft and there are a lot of crews present. Our guys tried to get a consensus of all the nets using one crew, but there's so much panic everywhere, and the police are getting so paranoid that it's impossible even to get a hearing on the matter. So every person is fighting for shooting space."

The pair watched the continuing clips unfold on the studio monitors. One particularly sad tape showed startled and silent crowds huddling in the early morning streets of Manhattan. Their faces reflected questions that had no answers. Amazingly, much of the city was still sleeping — the lucky ones who were still unaware of the horror story that had given the earth a death-kiss during the night. "But they'll find out soon enough," Daniels mused.

A sudden thought crossed his mind. "Anyone hear from Manny, yet? Know where he is?" No answer. The staff was still searching for the floor manager but with no success. "We need him, people! We need him right away. Keep on it."

Writer John Saks stuck his head in the control room. "Clay, a phone call for you. Sounds urgent."

Daniels snorted. "Well, what isn't urgent around here today? I can't take it now, John. Get the number and I'll call back."

"Uh, this guy's pretty persistent. Says you know him. Says he's a bishop of something or other."

The executive looked up sharply.

"Was his name Simonson? Bishop Gerald Simonson? From a church here in New York?"

"Yeah, that's the guy, Clay. He said it is vital that he talk to you right away."

"Come, come! What does he want?"

Saks' answer dropped like a bomb.

"Well, he says he knows where all the people are — why they've all disappeared. He says he can prove it to you."

Everyone in the room stood as if on cue. Daniels ran to the nearest telephone and punched up the line. He had known Bishop Simonson for years and considered him a pretty straight fellow, even if he was too far left in his political views for Daniels' taste. But, better to be a little off on political issues, he thought, than like some of the rest of the preachers who spouted their theological gibberish from behind pulpits. To his analytical mind, most preachers were witch doctors. Nothing more.

"Bishop Simonson? Daniels here. Glad you called. What's happening? John said you had some vital information for me."

The bishop tried to speak but his voice sounded tight, almost strangled, as if it were coming out of a choker chain. Daniels would have sworn the prelate was crying.

"Bishop? Are you okay? Can you hear me?"

"Yes, yes, Mr. Daniels, I can hear you. Have you figured out yet what has happened here today?"

"Uh, no, we haven't, sir. Not a clue, as a matter of fact. All hell — excuse me — is breaking loose, not only in the city but apparently all over the world. And we don't have any idea why. Do you?"

The bishop hesitated, then replied.

"Yes, Mr. Daniels, yes. Please take down this information. It will hold your answers."

The executive grabbed a pencil from a technician and prepared to write on a memo pad. "I'm ready, Bishop. Go ahead."

"Very well. Please write down these words precisely as I give them to you. Are you ready?"

Daniels was growing impatient. "Yes, yes, go!"

"Write down: First Thessalonians four, thirteen through eighteen. Got that one?"

Clay wrote furiously. What kind of nonsense code was this? "Is that it, Bishop?"

The voice continued in its steady cadence. "And then this one:

Matthew twenty-four, thirty-six through forty-four. Did you get both of them, Mr. Daniels?"

Daniels was in no mood for this game. "Of course, I got down what you said, Bishop. I'll repeat it for you. First Thessalonians four, thirteen through eighteen and Matthew twenty-four, thirty-six through forty-four. But so what? I mean, this doesn't give me any answers to —"

Daniels never finished his statement. His ear seemed to explode with the impact from the receiver. It was as if a cherry bomb had gone off at the side of his head.

Several of the crew had gathered around him, waiting anxiously for some clue from the clergyman. Daniels pulled the receiver from his ear and rubbed it with his free hand.

When he was able he spoke into the receiver: "My god, Bishop, what was that?"

There was no answer.

"Simonson? Bishop Simonson?" There was no reply, but Clay could hear a soft gurgling sound on the other end of the line, a tiny delay in which he heard nothing, then a crashing sound.

Daniels knew what had happened. The bishop had just blown his brains all over some of his highly prized books.

He punched a different line and quickly dialed the familiar number of the New York Police Department.

"Officer, this is Clay Daniels at IBC. Listen, I know you're swamped. But when you can, send an ambulance and car over to the manse of the Church of America. Huh? Right. Fourth Avenue. You're going to have to break in the door. I'm afraid the bishop has just killed himself."

11

The shock of the bishop's suicide made an impact on the IBC staff. Daniels looked at his people with pain in his eyes. Although he had been friendly with Simonson, he really didn't know him that well. A few banquets here, a civic ceremony there. But the clergyman had been a nice man and Daniels liked him a lot.

Before the sound of the shot on the telephone, Daniels would have said that his sense of logic could not be further violated on this bleak morning. But he would have been wrong. He felt even a deeper hurt stab his heart and pierce his brain.

He picked up the memo and walked down the hall to his office. After pouring another cup of coffee, he sprawled in his chair and looked at the piece of paper. What he had written at the bishop's request looked like some kind of code.

"First Thessalonians four, thirteen through eighteen and Matthew twenty-four, thirty-six through forty-four," he read to himself. "What does it all mean? Whatever it is, it must have meant something to Simonson. These were the last words he ever spoke before he pulled the trigger."

Daniels called Ivy and told her to bring the writers into his office.

Saks and McClure appeared within moments, along with Ivy.

"Simonson thought he knew something. He gave me these words to write down. Then he died. No explanation, no clue — nothing. Just these words. But the bishop really believed they meant something that would explain the mystery of the disappearances to us. Got any ideas?"

Saks shook his head. He had watched Daniels write the message down while he was talking on the phone with the bishop. Yet the words were foreign to him.

McClure rubbed his brow and looked carefully at the message, hoping it would reveal something — anything.

"I don't know," McClure replied. "I mean, I know what the words are and where they come from but I don't know what they mean, exactly."

"Go ahead, tell us anything you do know," Daniels urged.

"Well, I think the name 'Matthew' here may be a character in the Bible. In fact, I think there is a part of the book that bears his name. So the word 'Matthew' here may mean that portion of the scripture. And I would guess that the numbers are the chapters or lines or something. I really don't know much about it, but I think it may be some kind of reference system to find specific words. And this 'Thessalonians,' I don't think is a person. It may be another part of the book."

McClure looked at Daniels and the others and added, "Well, does that make any sense to you?"

John Saks responded first. "I don't know, Ray. It appears that you know a whole lot more than any of the rest of us. Clay?"

"Well, sure, that makes some sense," Daniels answered. "After all, Simonson was a man of the cloth. So, reciting some scripture reference would not be out of character for him. Anybody here got a Bible?"

Although there was heavy tension in the room, everyone smiled. It was a stupid question and they all knew it.

"Why sure, Clay, I have one in my briefcase all the time," Saks said. "Right next to the original of Mona Lisa and a 1948 Studebaker. Are you kidding? Never read one in all my life, I don't think."

McClure was not so flippant. "Uh, no, Clay, I don't have one, either. But there's one person on this staff who does — old Manny Dow kept one right on his desk. I remember we used to kid him about it when he first came to work here. Every day, I guess. There still may be one on his desk."

Daniels asked Ivy to check the missing floor manager's desk to see if such a book indeed was there. If so, he wanted it as soon as she could get it to him.

He turned to McClure and asked, "Ray, did you happen to notice your verb tense? You said, '. . . Manny . . . kept one on his desk . . .' As if he's no longer around. You think he's gone, don't you? With the others."

McClure looked at Daniels and spoke with words that had no tone. "Don't you, Clay?"

"I hope not. I would miss him terribly, I think."

Ivy returned with the book in her hand. "You were right, Raymond. It was there, just as you said."

Several white-coated waiters followed Ivy into the inner office bringing fresh doughnuts and coffee.

Daniels took the black-covered book from his secretary and opened it. He started looking for the general index.

"Did you ever read one of these things?" he asked. "I haven't since I was a kid."

Saks shook his head. "No, Clay, I'm afraid that's part of my education that I have neglected."

"Me, too," Daniels said. "There are a lot of sections in this book — must be well over 50 of them. Let's see, Genesis, Exodus . . ." He stopped reading aloud. The names sounded foreign to him as his finger traced through the column of books.

"Here it is! Matthew! Page 885," he said, jubilantly.

"What about that other reference?" McClure asked.

"Uh, Thessalonians — first Thessalonians, the bishop said. Let's see." He continued tracing the list. "Acts, Romans, first Corinthians . . . uh . . . Philippians, Colossians . . . yeah! Here it is! There's a first and second Thessalonians. Page 1122 is what we want. Let me try to find both of them."

Ivy and the two writers watched intently as their boss tried to find the two vital references. "Well, the first one the bishop quoted me was first Thessalonians. Let's look at it first. Perhaps there is a reason he gave them to me in a specific order. OK, here, the numbers are four, thirteen through eighteen."

"What do the numbers mean?" Saks asked.

"Well, I suspect the first number, the four, is the chapter in question and then the other numbers, thirteen through eighteen, are paragraphs or something. Yes, that's it! Here it is. I found it."

"Read it, please, out loud!" McClure said.

Daniels could not remember ever having read a scripture either to himself or to anyone else for that matter. He began slowly.

"But I would not have you to be ignorant, brethren, concerning them which are asleep . . ."

"Now what do you suppose that means? 'Asleep'?" Saks interrupted.

"Let him read, John, for cryin' out loud!" McClure said.

But Daniels decided to answer the question. "Well, there's a little asterisk kind of explanation by that line, John. By 'asleep' the writer here meant, uh, dead. So this must have someting to do with being aware of people who have died. OK?"

"Sorry, Clay. Didn't mean to butt in," Saks said. "Please continue reading."

Daniels looked down at the book again and read, ". . . which are asleep, that ye sorrow not, even as others which have no hope. For if we believe that Jesus died and rose again . . ."

Daniels cursed, remembering his arguments with Arvella. She had actually believed this stuff, he thought.

". . . even so them also which sleep in Jesus will God bring with him. For this we say unto you by the word of the Lord, that we which are alive and remain unto the coming of the Lord shall not prevent them which are asleep. For the Lord himself shall descend from heaven with a shout, with the voice of the archangel, and with the trump of God: and the dead in Christ shall rise first . . ."

Daniels looked up from the book and stared at the three staff members. Their eyes questioned him, betraying the fact that they did not comprehend what he had read.

Daniels looked back at the book ". . . Then we which are alive and remain shall be caught up together with them in the clouds, to meet the Lord in the air: and so shall we ever be with the Lord.

Wherefore comfort one another with these words."

He completed reading the passage, raised his eyes, and said, "Well?"

"I guess the old bishop threw us a curve," McClure said. "I was really hoping we had latched onto something to show us how millions of people just zipped off. Instead we got some mythology."

"Mr. Daniels," Ivy broke in "wasn't there another reference the reverend gave you? Perhaps it would be helpful to read it too."

Daniels looked at her with a rueful grin. "Ivy, dear Ivy. Always so cool and detached. Well, maybe you're right. I don't think you are, but — maybe."

"Matthew, sir — and the reference there was chapter twenty-four with verses thirty-six through forty-four," she reminded him.

"Thanks." Daniels muttered as he began searching through the book.

"First, let me throw you a real curve," Saks said. "Do you suppose there's any way we could find a common denominator among all these people? How about blood-type? Or personality similarities? Or some other broad general category — something that would link them together in the disappearance and not, not us or, uh, the bishop?"

Still checking the pages, Daniels answered, "I'm afraid it would take too much time, if we're trying to beat the other networks on this thing. It could take years to do that kind of research."

Looking down at the floor, scuffing the carpet nap with one toe, Saks said, "Perhaps you're right. Unless we got very, very lucky."

"OK, I've found the other place here. Let me read it."

While the others poured coffee and reached for doughnuts, Daniels continued reading.

"But of that day and hour knoweth no man, no, not the angels of heaven, but my Father only. But as the days of Noah were, so shall also the coming of the Son of man be. For as in the days that were before the flood they were eating and drinking, marrying and giving in marriage, until the day that Noah entered into the ark, And knew not until the flood came, and took them all away; so shall also the coming of the Son of man be. Then shall two be in the field; the one shall be taken, and the other left . . ."

The air in Daniels' office had suddenly become electric. The four people seated around the table looked at each other with genuine alarm. And a little fear.

". . . Two women shall be grinding at the mill: the one shall be taken, and the other left. Watch therefore: for ye know not what hour your Lord doth come. But know this, that if the good man of the house had known in what watch the thief would come, he would have watched, and would not have suffered his house to be broken up. Therefore be ye also ready: for in such an hour as ye think not the Son of Man cometh."

Daniels completed reading and closed the book. After a lengthy silence, he said, "Well, so much for my friend, the bishop. His mind must have already been gone before he pulled the trigger. I can remember when old Simonson used to laugh at passages such as these. Told me quite a few times that no one in the church believed fairy tales like these any more."

"I'm not so sure you're right about that, Clay," McClure said. "Perhaps the clergyman had just found out that he had been wrong all this time. That the missing people were captured by some deity."

Daniels glared at the writer and fumbled in his shirt pocket for a cigarette. He flicked his lighter and leaned back. "I think you're nuts. And if Bishop Simonson believed that nonsense, then he was nuts."

McClure persisted. "Now hear me out, Clay. None of us has come up with anything better. I have a gut feeling that we may be on to something here. John, you mentioned a moment ago that perhaps there is some common denominator among all these missing people. Right?"

"Yeah. So?"

"So — what if we discover that all of these missing people were fanatics or believers, or whatever you want to call them. Suppose that each one of them really believed what Clay just read about one person taken and the other left behind. Suppose that they are all involved in some nutty organization. And they have all disappeared. If that were true, what looks like a cock-'n-bull story sudden takes on a whale of a lot of credibility. At least it does to this old news writer. Huh?"

Saks jumped up angrily. "No! No, I won't buy that. If you're saying that all the religious people have made a mass exodus from this planet, then why didn't Clay's friend, the good bishop, disappear too?"

"Well, I think I can answer that," responded Daniels. "First, I don't believe what you have offered as a possible conclusion. But if it were true, it would not have involved Bishop Simonson. See, he was a churchman, to be sure. But he never believed in all that supernatural nonsense. In fact, he gave me a book he wrote a few years ago, that knocked all that stuff right into a cocked hat. Arvella filled me with this bull almost every night. And I got sick of it. So I asked the bishop for some advice. That's when he gave me his book. He didn't believe any of this nonsense. No, he wouldn't have fit in with a religious crowd at all."

McClure looked at his boss with a steady gaze. His answer was chilling.

"Right, Clay. And he didn't disappear either, did he? In fact, I think when he woke up this morning and learned about all the people who had vanished and he investigated it, putting two and two together and getting a solid old four, I think he flipped! I think he went into a depression, got himself a little stoned and to salvage his conscience maybe, he calls you and gives you this information. He tipped you off, Clay, that's what I think. Then he was so shook he didn't have the courtesy to let you hang up before he blew his brains all over his study."

"Baloney!" Clay exploded. "Simonson told me one time that all those idiots believed that little children would be taken in the exodus. You know, kids who were not old enough to make moral decisions. Innocents. So, Ray, if your theory is valid, then all the little children of the world will have vanished with them."

McClure's face mirrored genuine alarm. "My God, Clay, what do you think most of these telephone calls have been about? Children! They have disappeared like the morning mist in the sun. Missing by the thousands!"

Saks came to the defense of his boss, not out of loyalty alone, but because he desperately hoped Daniels was right. "Ah, Ray, you're jumping to some faulty conclusions. Those words Clay just read are folk stories, superstitions. You can't just suspend the laws of physics and vanish off the earth. Now I grant you some people are missing. But I believe we're going to find a perfectly rational explanation for this phenomenon."

McClure stared at his co-worker. "OK, John. Suppose you come up with that 'practical explanation.' Where did all the millions go? Kidnapped? Big picnic somewhere? Did they all decide in the middle of the night to go visit relatives? Come on, John, give us some plausible rationale for these amazing disappearances."

"Hold it, you two," Clay broke in. "Let's stay off each other's backs. Now it's past five o'clock, Janssen is already on the air giving facts we know. No other network has come up with any answers, either. Most of the nation is either up by now, or will be shortly. We need some answers."

McClure was not finished. "Let me give you something else to chew on. Manny Dow is apparently one of those who has disappeared. At least we can't seem to find him anywhere. Now we all know that Manny was into religion pretty strong. He believed in life hereafter, healing, heaven — even hell, I think. I used to tease him about it a little. Never could ruffle him though. Anyhow, Manny may be gone. And he believed all those things you just read to us, Clay. He talked about them a lot. Now let's check out some of these other people who have gone. If they were like Manny — if they believed the same stuff — then maybe we have come up with a common denominator. And if this checks out every time, we just may have the biggest story in the history of man!"

Clay's mind was racing. "Say, what about Russell Sorenson, our man in Teheran?"

"What about him?" asked Saks.

"Well, he apparently vanished as well. Now do either of you guys know him personally? Or know anything about him at all? Was he into this religious thing?"

McClure looked like a prisoner who had just received the death sentence. "Clay, I didn't know Russell was gone. First I have heard about it. We are — were — good friends. Went to college together. Yes, Clay, I'm afraid that Russell was one of those religious guys too. Totally involved in it. And it looks like he has disappeared."

There was a silence in the room. Four people sat looking at one another. Clay Daniels, a shaken news executive; John Saks and

Raymond McClure, news writers who were facing a possible solution that defied logic; and Ivy Browning, who was too frightened to talk.

Daniels stood. "All right, now listen. I admit that this religious factor is interesting. But I really think it's a series of coincidences. I don't buy it as the solution, not at this point. But it's the only solid lead we have. Ray, get a list of missing people and try to run a preliminary check on each one. See if any of this is a factor in their lives."

The writers stood to leave.

"Wait a minute, John. I want you to do something. The bishop once told me that children would be involved in this thing. All we have to do to discredit this whole theory is to find one child. That's all — one child, say, under the age of six or seven. Find me just one child, John! Please!"

The last word was spoken as a prayer.

The writer was still a little angry. "It's stupid, Clay. You know that. This theory is crazy. I think it's wrong."

"So do I, John," Daniels responded. "But we have to check it out."

The three men were pale. Ivy picked up her notes and left the room, followed by the two writers who were intent upon disproving a ghastly fairy tale.

12

By six-thirty a.m., it looked as if the fairy tale might be true after all.

When Ivy Browning and the two writers left Clay Daniels' office, he was alone to nurse a nearly finished cigarette and a cup of stale coffee. Something far back in his aching head told him there was an answer to the mystery. However, it was nearly six-forty-five a.m. when he felt the first stab of premonition that the disaster did indeed have an answer and that it had struck very close to home. Robert! Of course, Robert, his own son! How in the world could he have forgotten to check on his own flesh and blood? Five-year-old Robert! One simple phone call to his son would disprove the bishop's theory. It would prove that all the children had not vanished.

Clayton closed the door to his office. His heart was jumping and his chest felt as if it were on fire. He reached in the middle drawer of his desk for a bottle of "downers" and gulped two of them with his lukewarm coffee. The concoction caused him to gag.

He lifted the telephone receiver to his ear, punched the out-of-house nine-digit and quickly dialed the familiar number. Thankfully, when he and Arvella had separated, she had moved to upstate New York and was not terribly far away. It had made his regular visits to Robert much easier.

Daniels concluded dialing, opened a fresh pack of cigarettes and sat back with one unlit between his lips.

One ring. Two rings.

His son was growing so fast. Looked like his dad, Daniels proudly thought. Despite the tension of the situation, he grinned appreciatively. He had reason to think the boy would grow up with a fairly normal outlook on life, despite their rocky start together.

Three rings. Four.

"Come on, come on," he growled into the mouthpiece. "Answer the phone, Arvella."

Clay knew she would have already risen for the day. She had always been an early riser. In fact, one of the delights of his marriage to Arvella had been the breakfasts she could whip up so easily. Morning after morning, she consistently favored him with breakfasts fit for royalty. He felt sure that their separation had not changed her early morning patterns.

Five rings. Six. Seven.

Daniels allowed the rings to torment him until there was no doubt that there would be no answer. He gently lowered the receiver to the hook, a veil of perspiration beading his upper lip. "OK, Clay," he muttered to himself, "don't jump to conclusions. Think this through carefully. Arvella and the boy must be visiting somewhere. But where? That's the question!"

He ran his stubby fingers through his rumpled, sandy hair, poured a fresh cup of coffee and lit the cigarette. The smoke rose slowly to form an ethereal haze around his face, accented by the glare from his desk light.

Suddenly he pounded the desk with one balled fist. Of course! Janice Watkins! Arvella's good friend. She would know where she was. Yes, good old Janice, he thought with some dark amusement. He could never stand having her around but maybe now she would make up for all the boredom she had caused him.

He looked up the phone number and quickly dialed it. This time there were only two rings.

"Hello." He could tell he had awakened her.

"Janice?"

"Yeah. Who's this?"

"It's Clay, Janice, Clayton Daniels."

"Yeah? Really? Clay, this is great! You know Arvella and I were talking about you just last night."

"Well, that's nice to hear, Janice, but —"

"You know, she still thinks you're pretty neat, Clay."

The newsman held his cigarette between his first and second fingers and massaged his eye with his thumb. "You talked to Arvella last night? Is she still there in your apartment?"

A perplexed little laugh greeted his question. "Oh, no. She wasn't here then, Clay. I was over there — at her place with her and Robert. I left about 11 o'clock and Arvella said she was going to bed. We had tucked Robby in hours before. So I suppose she is still at her place. Call there, Clay. I'm going back to sleep."

"No! Wait a minute, Janice! Please! I already called over there and she didn't answer. She's not home. Nor is Robert. Now, Janice, they have gone somewhere and I've got to find them. Do you have any idea where they could be?"

"Nah, Clay — I think you're wrong. Let the phone ring a little. Don't you know it's still dark outside?"

"Janice, first of all it's daylight, and more important than that, I let the phone ring at least 20 times. Believe me, she's not there. Now did she say that she might go somewhere today?"

"Don't remember that she did. No, I'm sure she didn't. In fact, we're supposed to meet for coffee at lunchtime today. So she's certainly around somewhere."

There was a pause.

"Janice, you haven't heard the news yet today, have you?"

She laughed. "C'mon, Clay! Are you kidding? I was out like a light when you called. I haven't heard a thing. Why?"

"I'm already at work — have been for quite a while. The world's gone nuts, Janice. Millions of people have just disappeared. A lot of them were from New York."

The girl was confused by this new information.

"Clay, are you drunk or something? You don't sound like yourself."

"Didn't you hear what I said, Janice? Millions of people have just vanished. There's no other word for it — vanished! And I think maybe Arvella and Robert are among them."

"What?"

"Now listen to me. Did Arvella ever mention anything to you about the possibility of — of someone taking away a lot of people from the earth?"

Her shrill laughter pierced his ear.

"Are you nuts, Clay?"

His loud curse instantly stopped her laughing.

"Listen to me, woman! Just shut up and listen! I am leveling with you that large numbers of people are no longer apparently on this planet. Something happened right after midnight. These people are gone. The only clue we have is that the few we have been able to check out so far all had one common denominator. They, uh, they believed that someone was going to take them away from here. Now I think Arvella and Robert are gone. So answer my question — did she ever talk about things like that?"

The laughter had stopped and Clay heard a faint sniffling at the other end of the line.

"Clay, I'm sorry, I didn't know. I mean what you said sounded so stupid coming from you. Let me think a minute. We were together last night, as I said, but then we're together a lot. And, yes, Arvella did occasionally mention some of those things to me. In fact, she usually got in her two cents' worth about it in the course of an evening."

"Like what, Janice? What would she say?"

"Well, you know — the stuff you hear preachers say. Weird stuff, Clay! I'm telling you! I would just sort of — you know, brush it off. I mean, my god, nobody's believed that stuff for generations."

After a brief silence, she added, "Clay, you still there?"

"Yes, still here. But I'll tell you something. I'm not just real sure that the story is so far-fetched. I think she is really gone, Janice. And so is Robert and —"

The voice turned pouty. "Clay, you're not really serious. There is some other explanation, surely!"

"Well, would you like to come up with one," he bit off savagely. And hung up.

Daniels groaned softly and leaned back in his chair. He ground out the cigarette and felt a faint sting of tears in his eyes. He felt an ache now, not only in his head, but in his heart.

Smoke from the defunct cigarette curled to some point of darkness above his head. He stared mutely at the closed door ahead of him. His gaze fell on Manny Dow's book — still perched on his desk where Raymond McClure had left it. The note on which he had jotted down the bishop's babblings was lying beside it. He picked up the heavy black book and looked at it curiously. It was supposed to be the all-time best seller, yet he didn't know a single soul who ever read it much, if at all. Except maybe Arvella. She read it every day of her life. She used to ask if she could read it out loud to him. He never had allowed it.

Daniels leafed through the pages. He had no idea there were so many of them. What strange names! Obadiah . . . Nehemiah . . . Zechariah. He wondered idly who they were.

Remembering the part of the book McClure had read to him — Matthew something or other — Clay tried to find the reference to study it again. The paper reminded him. With a little trouble he found the reference once again. He read it and then read it again.

Chills crept up and down his spine. The pieces were coming together, not with a click, but with a dull thud. There was the dreaded phrase: ". . . I will come again. . ." Like some MacArthur of yesteryear, this strange Jew had promised his followers of a return from the grave. How could that be?

It revolted his sense of logic. He fought it intensely. It could not have happened; absolutely could NOT have taken place! But the arguments on the other side of the issue could not be denied.

"All right then, where *are* all the people?"

His hands clasped behind his neck, pulling his head forward, Daniels groaned softly.

"Are you all right, sir?"

The words jolted him and he sat upright in his chair. It was Ivy, standing in front of the desk.

"Oh, Ivy, I didn't hear you come in. Sorry. What is it?"

"Marilyn wanted me to remind you that it's nearly time for the *Wake Up* show, and she thought you would probably want to watch it. The team would appreciate it if you would come down to the control room. I think they're really edgy about this whole thing, and your presence would mean a lot to them."

"OK. Thanks Ivy. And by the way, thanks also for coming in at this awful hour of the day."

"You're welcome, sir. Anything for the company. And anything for you," she added softly.

Daniels nodded slightly in gratitude.

The two walked out to the hallway.

13

Daniels' back was beginning to feel as if the Battle of Waterloo had been fought on his kidneys. The dreadful ache began in his lower back and added to the pain he already had in his temples. He followed Ivy into the main control room and found a chair in the corner. There, nearly hidden by the semidarkness and the frantic hustling of the IBC staff, he could watch clearly the numerous TV monitors on the console.

On the screen that showed the actual "on-the-air" image, newsman Janssen Hennings was telling the dreadful stories of lost families and friends and ruined lives. Daniels watched him in an almost sullen mood as the pain in his head became monstrous, like a massive hangover. Only he hadn't been drinking. The stories Janssen told were like electronic surrealism, fantastic images and ghost stories, like something told by Stephen King gone berserk. He thought that even Poe, the mad poet, in his craziest fantasies would not — could not — have concocted such fabrications of reality.

A melancholy such as Daniels had never experienced settled into the marrow of his bones, a feeling he knew had to be psychosomatic. He had no doubt now that Arvella was among the missing. And Robert too. The emptiness within him was consuming. He wondered if these feelings were the preliminary stages of the acute depression that had caused Bishop Simonson to pull the trigger. The hurt he was experiencing was, he thought, similar to that now being felt by millions of others. Some great restraining hand had been lifted from the earth. The delicate veneer that kept mankind from the laws of the jungle had been jostled by an accident of cosmic proportion and the ooze of primitive man was escaping. He could feel it, smell it. There was some strange odor in the air, now that he thought about it. Something that smelled dead, dead a long time. And with the stench came a shimmering, floating image of a face into Daniels' tormented brain. The features were out of focus, so much so that he could not make out the identity right away. Some person was trying to shanghai his mind, to bring his thoughts into captivity, to influence him. He sat up, shook his head, and thought to himself, "Ye gods and little fishes — that's something of my childhood, of Dick Tracy pairing off against the evil hoodlum influence, who, with hypnotic stare, could cause a person to act against his will. And that strange, curly-haired creature of the comics can never bother anyone again because Tracy shot him through the forehead in the late '40s. All of us readers saw the bullet enter and exit his malevolent face."

Daniels snorted in quiet contempt for his suddenly irrational imagination and stood to get a better look at the control room. How often had he lectured beginning journalism students never to make snap judgments, especially when they ran contrary to logic. Now here he was, making every amateur mistake in the book all because he was tired and in panic. Not to mention unfathomable depression.

Or was it more than that? Was there some attack on his thinking processes? The image of the face grew stronger in his mind, the features resolving into sharp focus. The cry of the news executive was heard by nearly everyone in the control room, "Oh, my God! Catroux! Jacque Catroux!"

The strange and questionable behavior of the European czar less than a day before filled his mind. He relived the moments in the presence of the tall man with the golden hair. He could still hear the words: "Mr. Daniels, I cannot give you the details. But it is my opinion that an event is about to happen that will demand all of the world's free nations to band together."

Daniels recalled that he had asked the foreign leader if he was talking about war, and Catroux had responded negatively. Catroux had confessed that he did not know exactly what would happen — only that it would probably happen soon. Could he have been predicting this amazing disappearance of millions of people? Daniels' rational mind fought against such presumptive reasoning. It could not be. How could anyone, even a leader of Catroux's importance and influence, predict such an other-world experience? Unless Catroux himself were of a different world. He recalled that the European had predicted a merger between Europe and America and that he would become the leader of the free world. The newsman turned and leaned against the cool wall, his head nestled in the crook of his arm. A soft moan escaped his lips. "What's the matter with me this morning?" he asked himself. "Have I gone crazy? How can I make such incredibly stupid conclusions — or even think them?"

"Sir, are you — are you all right?"

Daniels looked up from his arm to see the inquiring face of Ivy Browning close by.

"Huh? Oh, yeah, yeah I think so. Just so terribly tired. And a little confused maybe."

"Well, that's certainly understandable, Mr. Daniels. My goodness, what with everything going on around here today."

"Ivy, ask Peter Doyle to come up and see me if he can get a break from the studio, will you? But don't tell anyone else. Just him. I want to see him right here — alone."

The secretary's eyes were questioning, but she said nothing. As he watched her go, he continued his mental gymnastics. What had made him think suddenly of Catroux — almost as if his mind had a volition of its own? "Simple," he answered himself. "Catroux made a staggering proposal to me less than a day ago, a proposal that smacks a bit of treason. It would be natural for the memory of it to still be paramount in my subconscious. Yes, that's it."

The thinking pattern continued relentlessly. "Yes, but why such a strong recollection of him now — now when I am preoccupied with the news story of the century, maybe of all time? Why think of Jacque Catroux now when I need all my faculties, all my wits about me?"

The questions piled up inside his mind. "I wonder what he is doing now? Is he still in New York? Yes, I think so, probably still at the same hotel. What would he know about all of this? Would he make a statement? Is he the answer to all this mess?

A hand on his shoulder startled him and Daniels jerked to attention. It was Peter Doyle.

"You OK, Clay? Ivy seems worried about you."

"Peter, now listen to me. What I am going to say to you sounds moronic, I know. But I don't think it is. I want you to pass on a message to Janssen as soon as he gets a break from the camera — during a commercial maybe. OK?"

"Sure, Clay. What is it? Why don't you come down and talk to him right in the studio?"

"No, no, no." Daniels' words were running together. "I don't want to be in the studio right now. Just pass the word on to him. Tell Janssen to get one or two of his staff on this right away. See if they can locate Jacque Catroux — and they need to get on it now."

The craggy-faced host stared at his boss. "Catroux? Why, Clay, he's in Europe. There was a satellite feed by him from Rome just last night."

"Last night? But that's impossible, Peter. Impossible!"

"What are you saying to me, Clay?"

"Peter, there may have been some kind of feed last night, but Catroux was not in Rome. It could have been a double, or a prerecorded tape, or some other hocus-pocus, but it was not a live Jacque Catroux on camera. Now I know this because Catroux was with me yesterday! Here, in New York!"

Doyle's face registered alarm. His voice carried the tones of a doting mother watching over her fevered child. "Oh, Clay, there must be some mistake here. Catroux could not have been in the States yesterday because —"

The soft and menacing curse from Daniels would have been enough to shut up Doyle. But even more was the stare from the executive's eyes. It was pure and undiluted anger.

"Pete, I know you think I'm nuts. But I promise you what I am saying to you is true! I was called yesterday — ask Ivy about this — to meet Jacque Catroux at the Helmsley Palace on Madison Avenue. I can even remember the suite he was in — Suite 22-A. A guy named Edmundson — Warren Edmundson — was there with him. He is a legal counsel to Catroux."

Doyle still couldn't put it together. "Well, what did — what did he want, Clay?"

"I can't tell you that right now. I wish I could, believe me, but I can't. Let me just say that I think, no — I know — that Catroux is still in Manhattan. Don't ask me how I know it, I just do. He may still be at the Helmsley. I would bet anything that he is. Now, Peter, tell Janssen that I think Catroux knows something about this whole disappearance thing."

"But how —"

"I don't know how. All I know, Peter, is that less than 24 hours ago, Catroux stood right in front of me, as close as you are right now, and predicted that something was about to happen that would shake the whole world. Well, the egomaniac was right. Whether it was pure luck on his part or a grandstand play, I don't know for sure. I only know that somebody's got to get to him and interview him. Now, please, Peter — no more questions. Get on it. If Janssen has any questions, tell him I'll try to answer them after he puts somebody on Catroux's tail."

Doyle didn't answer but looked at his boss for a few puzzled seconds and returned to the studio.

Daniels watched him depart and with a soft sigh settled back down in his corner chair to watch more of the *Wake Up* news. What he saw didn't lift his spirits. His staff was reporting stories that could have happened only in Alice in Wonderland. He wondered if maybe he wasn't the Mad Hatter.

It was only moments later that he realized — the terrible odor still had not left the control room.

14

Lee Iacocca appeared on the newsdesk monitor, extolling the virtues of the Chrysler LeBaron turbo. It was a needed break in the furious morning schedule, and Janssen Hennings watched the Detroit mogul with unseeing eyes. His thoughts were attached singularly to the news he had been reading and the remote reports from every part of the nation.

Hennings had been a newsman for only 15 years. Just 37, his rise in the business had been faster than most, due more to the passion he held for his job than for his native ability. Any lack of ability he had would have discouraged a newsman of lesser willpower. But not Hennings. Since his early schooldays, the Huntleys, Brinkleys and Cronkites had been his idols. He had determined to succeed in the business and he had done precisely that, without inside contacts and without overwhelming ability. He had worked long and hard, forfeiting many of the pleasures of life that other people seemingly needed in order to learn his trade. No one watching him today, on this horrendous occasion of suffering and loss, could have denied that they were watching a skilled TV newsman at work.

Many of the stories he had reported this day would have seemed garish and glitzy in the hands of a less-talented communicator. He had made them very real, and no viewer would have doubted their validity.

Stories such as the execution of Charley Freidman.

IBC reporter Ricky Valdez had been assigned to the story. He had covered other state executions in recent years. Such stories were no longer considered very newsworthy; however, in the case of Freidman, a convicted serial killer, it was a different matter. The prosecutor had presented an airtight case against him on a charge of murdering nine teenagers. The jury had remained out for less than an hour before returning with a unanimous verdict of guilty. Their recommendation had been death in New York's electric chair. The judge had concurred, sentence had been passed, numerous appeals filed and denied, the last by the United States Supreme Court, and the execution date had been set. New York Governor Thomas Harper had refused to halt the proceedings and at 11:59 last night Freidman had been ushered into the small 12-foot by 18-foot room.

No one had much sympathy for the killer. His slayings of nine innocent young people, with some suspicion that there had been others, had been sadistic and brutal. Although four of the victims had been girls, there had been no evidence of sexual molestation or motivation. The slayings, all by knife, had been rituals of apparent pleasure for the man to be strapped into the chair. No one would be terribly sorry to bid him farewell.

Freidman was led into the ancient room of Sing Sing's death-house, flanked by four burly guards. His arms had been secured at the wrists and elbows, and a short strap bound his ankles, requiring him to walk in a herky-jerky motion. He was wearing the clean, but faded, denims of the prison and was barefoot. His already near-bald head required no shaving preparation.

The condemned man blinked as he entered the bright room and looked about uncertainly. He did not appear to be afraid. He was not near collapse as Valdez had seen others approach the death chair. Of his own accord he sat down, having walked the last step he would ever take. The guards loosed his shackles in order to put his arms and legs in place on the chair.

Valdez took shorthand notes as quickly as he could write, looking up constantly to see every reaction of the prisoner and his guards. Freidman sat on a seat of cracked rubber secured by rows of copper tacks. He smiled faintly as one of the guards gently placed his ankles into the half-moon shaped leg cuffs, lined with worn canvas. Two straps were placed upon each arm, one at the wrist and the other at the forearm, and secured as tightly as possible. A guard asked him if the straps were too tight. Valdez could hear Freidman's soft response, "No, no, it's all right. It's all right." The reporter marvelled at the calmness displayed by the condemned man.

Now a two-inch-wide leather belt with many holes and worn grooves was secured around Freidman's waist, just above the hips. Valdez could hear the man suck in air as the belt was pulled ever so tight. Years before, when Julius Rosenberg had been executed in this very chair, witnesses reported that the current caused his body to shake violently, and his feet had tapped the floor like a Fred Astaire gone crazy. The bindings now holding Freidman would not allow that to happen again.

A momentary flicker of fear crossed the prisoner's eyes as the cool metal cone was placed on his head. He now had less than two minutes to live. The only part of the man that could still move was his eyes, and he used them to search the small room. To his right he could see the mahogany floor divider that separated him from the four brown church-like pews where the witnesses sat. He caught the glance of Valdez and held it for a moment. Freidman tried to smile bravely, and Valdez nodded in mute tribute to his courage. The prisoner broke the moment and looked up at two groups of fluorescent lights on the peeling ceiling. It looked so bright up there. So bright in a room that would be so dark.

The warden stepped in front of the chair. His name was Monty Williams. He had presided over a number of these macabre midnight affairs. He hated them. He knew he had to retain his dignity and fulfill his obligation to the justice department of the sovereign State of New York. His words were quiet.

"Mr. Freidman, I am authorized to grant you a last statement. If you wish you may speak before we proceed in the carrying out of the sentence."

The silence was stifling. Besides Valdez, 15 other state witnesses were watching the horror unfold, most of them for the first time. Several were trying hard not to be sick. A woman was weeping silently. Freidman saw her. He began to speak but his speech was restricted by the tight bindings and the knowledge of what was about to happen to his body.

"Please don't weep for me. This will be over in a moment, and I will be very thankful. I am getting what I deserve."

Valdez's fingers ached as he wrote furiously. He wanted to catch this statement word for word. Most condemned men's words could not be used on public television, but this fellow was different.

"I killed nine innocent people. I make no excuses, only my deepest apologies to the families involved. I know that doesn't count for much, but I am truly sorry about it. I was a different man then. An animal. Now I will pay the full cost of my actions."

The warden stepped forward, but the prisoner wanted to say a few more words.

"Please, Warden, just a moment longer. In recent months, I have made peace in my heart with God. I bear no one any ill will. You are just doing your job."

It was obvious that Freidman's statement had concluded. He closed his eyes, deep brown eyes that would never see another dawning.

Overhead, the air vent began to hum. The executioner turned on the fan to suck up the smell of burning flesh. The warden reached down to place a leather mask on Freidman's face. There was not much time left. Only seconds.

To the right of the chair was a waist-high, one-way mirror on the wall. Behind it stood the man who would pull the switch. Identity unknown. Before him was the panel with gauges, switches and the lethal lever.

Arrangements were now complete. The prisoner was snug. Behind him was the cable, wrapped in gray tape. It would carry the current to both feet and to the cone on Freidman's head. Five brief seconds, so quiet and eerie in this tomb, seemed like a week. Warden Williams turned and nodded toward the mirror. The executioner pulled the lever. Two thousand volts ripped through

Freidman's body. Behind the mask, his eyeballs expanded, then burst. As the second passage of electricity entered his body, his brains began to boil inside his skull. The executioner pulled the lever again, and a third time.

The sickening sweet odor wafted into the fan in the ceiling. The witnesses sat still as stone, fighting their emotions and their nauseous stomachs. The warden nodded toward the doctor in attendance, who approached the chair with his stethoscope.

A routine execution by electrocution. Until that moment. For as the doctor bent over before the dead man, the body vanished! Restraining straps sagged over empty clothes. The witnesses stood, not believing what they had just seen. The warden and the guards looked about helplessly. There was no question what had happened here. A dead man, killed by lethal jolts of electricity, strapped unmovable into the death chair, had just disappeared!

Other stories were equally bizarre. By eight a.m., they were a dime a dozen. One was the Milan Judy story.

There couldn't have been a worse place in the world to hitch a ride than Texas Highway 60 just south of Summerfield. But there was no alternative for the tall, gaunt redhead if he was to get to Clovis, New Mexico, some 50 miles away. No one could hope to walk that distance on this brutally hot night. A dry wind occasionally gusted, spewing hot sand on the man. It stuck to his sweaty face, making the evening more unbearable.

Judy looked down the highway, back toward Hereford where his last ride had dropped him some seven miles away. He had walked to Summerfield, roundly cursing every truck and car that passed him. He had to admit that he was not a likely looking candidate for a free lift. When drivers got close enough to him, they could see in the glare of their headlights the rugged, bearded face and shabby clothes of the fellow beside the road. They hurridly passed him by, ignoring his insults and obscene gestures.

As it approached midnight, Milan Judy was mad, lonely, tired, hungry and, in general, hated the whole world. He didn't want to find a place to sleep near the road for fear of snakes and Gila monsters. He didn't mind facing a rowdy in a bar, but the fangs of a sidewinder were another story. Besides, if he was not in Clovis by eight in the morning he would miss the job interview. He had to have that job — he knew that for sure.

Behind him he heard the faint hum of an engine and looked over his shoulder into the approaching headlights. He smiled and stuck out his thumb. To his surprise, the car slowed down and came to a stop about 100 feet past him. Judy picked up his duffel bag and raced toward the waiting car.

"Can you give me a lift, sir?"

The man behind the wheel was a plain-looking sort of fellow. But his face was friendly. "Why sure, Mac, hop in."

Judy threw his bag in the back seat and hopped in front. "Boy, I sure am obliged to you, friend." He stuck out a hand. "My name is Judy. Milan Judy. I'm from Oklahoma City and I'm headed for Clovis for a job interview in the morning. Man, you saved my skin on this one. I appreciate it."

The driver had taken one hand off the wheel to shake hands with his new passenger. "Nice to meet'cha. My name is George Rack. I'm going right through Clovis. Be glad to drop you off there."

"Ah, that's great." Judy leaned back to relax. The car was a late model Chevy and the cassette deck was playing some kind of music he had never heard before. He didn't much care for it, but he thought beggars couldn't be choosers. He hoped he could just drop off to sleep.

But Rack was a talker and his new passenger afforded him an audience. "What kind of work are you interested in, young fella?"

Judy swore under his breath but kept a smile on his face. Never antagonize a free ride, he said to himself. "Oh, I'm in construction. Building has really slowed down in Oklahoma but I got wind of a guy starting a shopping mall in Clovis who needed a good hand. I called him and he told me to come down. Said there was a pretty good chance he'd take me on. Hope so, 'cause I only got about 20 bucks on me and it's a long way back to OK City, you know."

George Rack was a middle-aged man, portly, with thinning hair worn short. He glanced at his passenger through rimless glasses and grinned. "Yeah? Well, I hope you get it. I'm not sure I can drive you back to your home."

Judy chuckled dutifully and closed his eyes. He needed some sleep in the worst way. But it was not to be. Rack had reached over to turn up the cassette player. The raspy voice had a certain appeal, but Judy didn't think he'd ever heard it before.

"Who's the singer?"

"Oh, he's a fella from down in Las Cruces. His name is Randy Mason. Used to sing in clubs, had a couple of hit records. Gave it all up though to sing gospel. That's what this is, a gospel song. You ever heard it?"

"Nah, don't guess so," Judy replied. "I don't know too much about music. That's pretty good country though, isn't it?"

Rack agreed. "Not too bad, not too bad. I picked up this tape the other night where this guy was appearing. Thought it might be nice to have in the car. Keep me company on these all-night drives."

The singer's voice was penetrating, and Milan Judy could not help hearing each word.

> *Tempted and tried we're oft made to wander*
> *Why it should be thus all the day long;*
> *While there are others living about us,*
> *Never molested, tho' in the wrong.*
>
> *Farther along we'll know all about it,*
> *Farther along we'll understand why;*
> *Cheer up my brother, live in the sunshine,*
> *We'll understand it all by and by.*

The young man had no comprehension of the words, but he liked the lead guitar player now doing the turnaround. "Hey, that's pretty good stuff," he said. "I like it."

The driver nodded. "Yeah, me too. Especially the words."

Judy turned toward Rack and inquired, "What do they mean? What's this 'farther along' stuff?"

The car was doing a steady 55 on the two-lane highway. They had just passed through Black, and Friona lay ahead of them about 10 miles away.

"Talkin' about the future, Mr. Judy."

The passenger groaned as he leaned toward the door. Just his luck. He had crawled into a car with a religious fanatic.

"Uh, well, listen, mister — I really ain't interested in that stuff.

That OK with you? No offense, really, it's just that I don't believe in it. Someday, maybe, I'll give an ear. But not now."

Rack took his eyes off the road for a moment to glance across the car. "That might be all right if you knew you had a whole lot of time. But then you and I don't know that, do we?"

"Of course I've got time. What are you talkin' about? I'm 22, man! Got my whole life ahead of me. Don't even have a war to worry about, no 'Nam or Korea. I'm healthy. Shoot, I'll live another 50 or 60 years."

Rack wanted to pursue the conversation, but Judy made it clear he didn't. "Sir, please, I don't want to make you mad 'cause you've been awful good to me here. But I don't want to talk. I'll listen to your music 'cause I kinda like the beat. But don't talk to me about that stuff, huh?"

The driver smiled sadly. "OK, young fella. Go to sleep. I'll let you know when we get to Clovis."

Judy flashed a smile of appreciation, leaned his head back against the window and fell asleep almost instantly.

Moments later, the Chevy hit a sharp curve, still doing 55 miles an hour. But the curve did not accommodate a car doing much over 25. The great weight of the full-sized car broke easily through the flimsy restraining cable. It began its plunge down the embankment.

Judy woke up screaming as he saw a row of trees suddenly loom before the careening car. He turned toward the driver to see what was wrong with him. But there was no driver. Rack was gone. The door was still closed, the crummy tape was still playing, but there was no one else in the car except him. "But . . . how? Where?"

Those questions were the last ones to lodge in young Judy's brain before his body was torn badly in the screaming, tearing wreck. After Judy regained consciousness he told the bizarre story to the ambulance attendants who had been called by another driver who saw the wreck.

The five-minute local cutaway was now over and Janssen Hennings' attention turned once again to matters at hand. There were still more nightmarish stories to report, more "twilight zone" disappearances. And so he began:

"Again, good morning, everyone. The world came to an abrupt halt for millions of people overnight. There is still no answer to the mystery, but these people simply vanished from our presence. Every nation on earth seems to be affected and there is international panic. For more on the story, we switch you now to Moran Kirkenwald at the United Nations . . ."

15

It was an hour earlier in Sergeant Bluff, Iowa, than New York. So when old Daniel Penning flipped on Sioux City's Channel 9 to watch the *Wake Up* show, he caught the second full hour of the presentation. Penning started each weekday with the same ritual. Alarm goes off, Penning mutters an obscenity, punches off the clock, in the same general motion sits up in bed, pushes his feet over the edge into waiting slippers and heads for the TV set. It was a habit. He wouldn't have changed it for anything.

The *Wake Up* show somehow braced the old man for the tedious day ahead. He was a building supervisor for the dilapidated airbase that had long ago seen much better times. During World War II the base had been one of the prime training grounds for pilots and navigators of the famed B-29s. Residents of Sioux City, especially on the east side in Morningside and Floyd Park, had grown accustomed to the familiar sweet music of those great bombers as they darkened the skies over the Missouri River. At the peak of the war, thousands of Air Force men were stationed at Sergeant Bluff. Most of them left for strategic sorties over Europe, others for the Pacific theatre of war. Many never returned.

Little remained now. Only twenty-four hundred or so residents. Many of the original buildings were still intact, although they were in general disrepair. The huge runways had been maintained and were used by the adjacent city airport, serviced by Ozark and Northwest Airlines. And, of course, area pilots with small planes still used two of the buildings earmarked for general aviation.

Penning hated the place. It was a ghost camp. Sometimes, while "in his cups," as the English say, he would recall the halcyon days of the base, its steady stream of air traffic, visits by top military brass, the magnificent B-29s, the friendship of airmen coming and going, the marvelous camaraderie and learning of the hard-won victories in Europe and Asia. The war was over, and Sergeant Bluff once again became a tiny town on Interstate 29 surrounded by miles and miles of corn.

The government had kept only five or six men on duty to watch over the federally owned land. Boundaried on the western side by the Missouri River and the eastern side by the Interstate, it had been written off for any future plans since no more land could be added. Besides, Sioux City was no longer expanding with the downgrading of the once-famed stockyards, which had been rivaled only by Omaha and Chicago. Occasionally a gawking tourist would snoop around to look at the mangy old museum room filled with pictures and maps — and a lot of dust. Penning never said he was a great housekeeper.

He could have cared less whether tourists showed up. In just four more months he wasn't planning to show up, either. Penning was convinced that the only thing worthwhile about civil service was the retirement policy. He was counting the weeks until the fulfillment of that dream. Then Tampa Bay bound! Fishing! He could already imagine the thrill of the snook, the singing of the line as some great fish known only to the gods of the sea smacked his lure. Ah, that was what life was all about, anyway. When all was said and done, nothing else really mattered. There hadn't been much fishing in northwestern Iowa, that was for sure.

Penning had awakened feeling rotten, which was normal, and tasting his tongue. His breath smelled of the cheap beer he had guzzled the night before. He stretched and looked up at his cracked ceiling. How dreary it all was!

Painfully, the old man sectioned himself out of the bed, into his slippers, past the TV and into the bathroom. He stared disinterestedly at his plain and blotched face in the dirty mirror and tried to decide whether the world was worth shaving for. He decided that it probably wasn't, but why break the habit?

He started the water running, hoping that sometime soon some reasonably warm water would come out of the rusty pipes. When he became convinced that it would not, he turned it off and ambled into the combination kitchen-living area. The TV was now warmed up and Channel 9 was doing its thing. Some commercial he had seen a hundred times was on and Penning showed his appreciation with a beer-induced belch. Then he started looking for the coffee pot.

The aroma of brewing coffee was the one bright spot in his morning. Doctors could tell him that the brew would cause cancer until the cows came home but it would never have concerned him. He dashed a couple of eggs in a skillet and glanced at the TV screen and the *Wake Up* show.

He was trying to recall whether he had any sausage when he became aware that something was terribly wrong with the man on the screen. Penning forgot the sausage and sat down in one of the creaky, vintage chairs in front of the set. The host, Peter Doyle, friendly, craggy-faced, usually calm Peter Doyle, looked as if he had seen a ghost. His news reporter Janssen Hennings didn't look any better. Both men ushered Penning into a new age from which he could never emerge.

It was the top of the hour, so the show sounded like a near rerun of the first hour. Doyle was seated in a dark blue, upholstered chair. Next to him was a coffee table, a slim lamp, and a sheaf of papers. The backdrop behind him was simple, a couple of clocks showing times in various parts of the world. Jackie Quinland, the co-host, was not on the set, which looked like something from home. Doyle began his ominous report.

"Ladies and gentleman, good morning. But then again, it may not be after all. For while the nations of the world slept on this historic day, an event occurred which may one day be recorded as the most frightening day in the history of man. For more on that story, here is Janssen Hennings."

Now Penning's screen was lighted with the news set, a terribly expensive bit of carpentry.

"Peter, Jackie, as impossible as it seems to all of us, apparently millions of people disappeared during the night from homes, places of business, cars, factories, the streets of our cities and — yes, even from airplanes.

"Very early this morning, IBC began receiving calls from distraught people who could not locate missing family members. Apparently most of those who were gone were children.

"Local law enforcement agencies around the world have called in every available officer, including reserves, as people by the thousands are coming to the stations to report the strange disappearances. Several of our cities, Miami, Florida, and Los Angeles, have verged on panic and martial law has already been declared in those metropolitan areas.

"This strange phenomenon is not peculiar to the United States or this hemisphere. It seems that Europe, Africa, Australia, and even the Far East are reeling under the impact of this simply staggering occurence.

"The question, of course, is: where did these people go? What caused their disappearances?"

Penning shook his head and grinned in black amusement as he turned off the stove that was about to incinerate his eggs, if not his whole shack. He poured a cup of coffee and sat down to watch more of this intriguing detour from his morning routine.

Even on his bad-vintage Sony color set, the co-hostess looked as white as a ghost. Her hands were visibly shaking and her voice cracked as she attempted to read the bulletin in her hand. Penning listened intently as she began to speak.

"Several moments ago, we received word from the White House that President and Mrs. John Forman are apparently among the missing. None of their children can be found at the various colleges they attend. Covering the story from the White House is IBC's Sheila MacKenzie."

Penning was no longer grinning. Something really terrible had happened; he could feel it. The old man found himself very frightened, more frightened than he had ever been in his life. A long forgotten scenario was playing out in his mind. All the pieces were not together yet, but the mixture promised to be terrifying, he was sure.

The cameras at the White House revealed the young black reporter, standing under the East Portico.

"Jackie, there is no doubt about it any longer. The President and his family cannot be found. It has been assumed that they are among the missing. The facts, as we know them, are these: The president's valet, John Worthington, attempted to awaken the first family at five this morning, as word of the tragic disappearances began to arrive. The valet knocked on the door of the Forman's master bedroom repeatedly and received no answer. Attempts were made to call into the room with the same negative response. The Secret Service was notified of this and agents broke into the room immediately. There was no one there. There were no signs of any struggles, no forced entry. The sheets and blankets on the beds had barely been disturbed, just enough to show that someone had obviously slept there during the night. Guards posted all around the family quarters have been questioned thoroughly, and all of them report the same thing — no one left the quarters all night long. No one came in and on one went out. And yet — yet the family is missing. I can assure you, ladies and gentlemen, there is panic inside this historic building. It is controlled panic, to be sure, but still it IS panic. This is Shelia MacKenzie for IBC news at the White House."

Once again Janssen Hennings' eager face filled the screen. "And we have another report in that Vice President Barry Cane has been alerted to accept the oath of office should the president not be found today. It is an unbelievable chain of circumstances, unparalleled in history. Outside our IBC studios this morning several thousands of people have gathered, some attempting to learn the whereabouts of their loved ones, others simply to get some kind of assurance that none of this is really happening. Unfortunately, it does, indeed, seem to be happening. Uh, Sheila, are you still there at the East Portico?"

The question triggered the action that caused the White House correspondent's face to appear. "Yes, I am, Janssen."

"Sheila, do you know if President Forman is still considered technically the head of the government? If so, how many hours can transpire before legal change of government is required?"

"Well, in answer to your first question, Janssen, yes, the president, that is John Forman, is still considered alive. So there has been no official changeover. However, in President Forman's absence, I believe that any major situation would be brought to the vice president's attention. As to the exact length of time in which the current president can remain in office, even though he cannot be found, that I will have to check. I am just not sure on that matter. But it is a precedent-making moment in U.S. history."

The screen again showed Hennings, now seated next to Peter Doyle. "Thank you, Shelia. Peter, this is the most bizarre happening that I can remember."

The countenance of the host showed deep pain and concern. "And so we are going to devote all of our show to this story, and, I am sure, we will remain on the air the rest of the day — or as long as it takes to get some resolution of what has occurred. Janssen, you have an update, I believe, on the fiery crash of the 747 near Paducah today."

The old man, Daniel Penning, was no longer listening to the various reports of tragedy. When he heard the president was missing, his mind began racing into his long-lost childhood. Now the pieces were clicking together. He believed he knew why multitudes of people had disappeared, where they had gone, and what had triggered the fact. But, and he shook as he considered this part, the disappearances were only a small part of the story. If his calculations were correct, and his memory had not failed him, he knew there was now a danger so horrible that nothing else in mankind's history could be compared to it.

But how could he tell it? And to whom? Any idea of calling IBC was out of the question. But he could call the local Sioux City Channel! Channel 9! He took the dog-eared phone directory from the top of the refrigerator and began thumbing through its pages. As he looked frantically for the number, the reporters continued telling the world of one disaster after another.

16

Jacque Catroux was unhappy. He had been in that dark mood since his abortive meeting with Clay Daniels in his suite at the Helmsley Palace. It was a rare thing to hear someone turn down one of his offers. Daniels had not only turned him down but promised him virtually no news coverage — certainly no good coverage — on IBC. Catroux could not afford that.

His anger toward Daniels had abated somewhat as he realized he had come on too strong, especially concerning the merger of Europe and the United States. He knew such a joint venture was going to happen and that he would lead it. How he knew it, he was not sure. But he would stake his life on its coming to pass. Daniels did not share such a dream; in fact, the whole scheme had come across to the American as treason. The advance resume' Catroux had gathered on Daniels had not shown the newsman to be so sensitive and tough. He had come across as both, and Catroux knew it was not a bluff. This only made the European want Daniels on his staff more than ever.

He had told Daniels that something was going to happen, some cataclysmic wonder that would change the world as they knew it, forcing a merger among the free nations of the world. In retrospect, Catroux knew the prophecy must have come across to Daniels as obnoxious pomposity. He would have to find some way to rectify his bungling of the whole affair. The prospect did not make the evening any happier for the would-be world leader.

At six that evening, Catroux had a meeting at the posh Cyranno's Supper Club. After the sumptious dinner, he and his guests, six representatives of the European Economic Community and two of the major bankers in New York, tackled some sticky matters of import quotas. Nothing really was resolved at that meeting, either. Nothing was working out well for Catroux this day. At 9:30 he went back to his suite to entertain an outlandishly expensive callgirl. Afterward, Catroux did not want her around; her conversation was gauche and boringly predictable. He dismissed her well before midnight, mixed himself a drink and sat alone in the mammoth bedroom.

He had never married and, actually, never wanted to. His love affair was with power, with the machinations of world government, with the rolling of the dice of humanity. There was no room for a woman in his life, other than the brief liaisons as he had just experienced, pleasurable but of no meaning. Nothing meant a thing to Catroux except his dream, his passion of world conquest and total authoritarian power. All of his life he had been a driven man. Indeed, his mother, who had died nearly eight years before, had been excessively secretive about the existence of his father. He knew only that he had been born prematurely in Bern, Switzerland, on April 30, 1945. His mother, Cassandra, had access to vast wealth, inherited from his father's side of the family. She had kept her maiden name, Catroux. Jacque did not even know his real last name. His mother had told him that his father had never revealed his last name to anyone.

Jacque had inquired of her many times if his father was dead. She always answered negatively, while looking at him with wonderful tenderness. Once she smiled and answered him, "Someday, little one, someday you will meet him. He is not dead. He lives now and he always will. He will come to you one day. And in that moment you will cease to wonder about your destiny. As your father wills it, and empowers you to do so, you will be great, and will govern a kingdom without end."

Her words had always sounded a bit like something from the Wizard of Oz to him and he had not paid too much attention. Yet Cassandra's prophecy had buried deep into his subconscious, and he knew somehow that she was not lying. Perhaps someday he would meet the father who had given him physical life and monetary treasure. However, the years, the decades, had passed and such an event had not happened, and the possibilities of it now in his later life hardly ever passed through his busy mind. He had tended to consider the juvenile remembrances as fantasy, especially since Cassandra had died.

But now there had grown a new and pressing awareness of his beginnings, a sensation of his father, whoever in hell that had been, and a deep and abiding concern for a relationship to develop between them.

Catroux swirled his drink in the glass, looking without seeing into the amber liquid. There was still another strange phenomenon of later years that troubled him. Lately he seemed to be doing and saying things that originated from some other power source than himself. Yesterday with Daniels was a key example. In his normal thinking, he could never have said to this newsman something to the effect that an event would happen worldwide that would ultimately cause Europe and America, as well as the rest of the free world, to unite under one banner — his banner, Catroux's! He believed that, yes, with all of the fervor he could muster; but to tell such a thing to a rank outsider at a first meeting was tantamount to insanity. It was a wonder, Catroux mused, that Daniels had not called a mental home to come quickly with ambulance and net! No, under normal circumstances he would never have made such a preposterous advance. So why now? Why did he say those things to Daniels — almost as if something, or someone inside him, were stimulating the words. And why did he call the prostitute tonight? In days gone by, he had done his share, and more, of bedding strange girls, and even a few men when the mood had struck him.

He preferred the women, to be sure, but the men had held strange and exotic quirks for him that the found quite amusing for the moment. But a long, long interlude had passed between such explicit nocturnal passions and the present, when those illicit desires had welled within him again. Why? Catroux smiled wanly to himself as he considered that he must be going through some monstrous and much-belated midlife crisis.

He prepared to get ready for bed. Tomorrow he would try to reach Daniels by phone to apologize for the strange come-on of their first meeting. The newsman had promised him a rough go at any future network coverage, at least as far as IBC was concerned, and Catroux believed the ruddy fellow might have the guts to do precisely that.

He stripped off his clothes and stepped into the shower. The stinging beads of hot water eased away some of his anxiety and he luxuriated in its therapy for nearly a half-hour. When he had towelled off and dried his golden hair, he donned pajama bottoms, left word at the front desk for a five a.m. wake-up call, and turned off the light. There was a slim crack of light coming from beyond the velvet draperies, and, on a whim, Catroux walked to the window and pulled them apart to overlook the myriad lights of the crown jewels of Manhattan. New York City at night remained one of the greatest views in the whole world, and again he was enthralled by the beauty and sheer power of the city. Even at night it throbbed with might, might that could be unleashed and used for any purpose whatsoever if one could gain the secret of its mastery. The concept caused the European more erotic stimulation than all the ministrations of the callgirl, and he began breathing heavily. "Oh," he moaned softly to himself, "what this world could be if one powerful man could control everything! If every nation and giant corporation and union and power station and army could be used for one single interest, rather than for the hodgepodge vested self-uses of nearly 300 completely separated countries!"

He was so enamored with his visions of power that it took a moment for his brain to register the whiff of a terrible odor, that of something long-since dead. Then he heard a brittle chuckle directly behind him. The hair on the back of his hands stood up and he began to turn slowly, like Scrooge of old reluctantly meeting one of his ghosts. What Catroux saw filled him with more horror than anything Dickens' strange little man had envisioned.

It had not been his imagination. Someone was there. The figure was nearly seven feet tall and bathed in a strange light, an other-world luminescence. It lit up the figure himself, but nothing else in the room was touched by it. Everything else remained in the blackness. The figure had the face of a leading-man motion picture star, handsome and oozing charm. His hair fell in glistening folds well below the ears. The garment was like something from an expensive Broadway musical, a period piece, like something you would expect on an angel — seamless, dazzling white and costly. The feet were bare, and the figure's arms hung quietly at his sides. He stood less than 10 feet away. It was the eyes that caused the terror in Catroux. They were not human eyes at all, but rather small cauldrons of blazing fire.

Catroux was unable to speak as he fell against the drapes at his back. His vocal chords had frozen in his throat. He could not have moved had it meant his very life. With all his might he wished it would go away, but it didn't; instead it took a step forward and opened its mouth to speak. The voice was not human, it was deep as a bottomless cavern, and yet as piercing as a spear.

"Fear not, Jacque, my son. Fear not!"

The figure made no move to come closer. One hand stretched forward in greeting. The fiery stare remained and the words continued.

You have waited for me a long, long time, my son. And I have come. Just as your mother told you long ago I would. I have come to you, Jacque, in the fullness of time I have appeared to you."

"Who — who a-are you?"

Oh, the gaze, the stare! Those eyes that unravel the soul! That read every thought in your mind! The lips of the creature began to move slowly. And the eyes burned a little brighter.

"I am your father!"

Catroux's body began to sink toward the floor. Never in his life had he known fear so pitiless, so ruthless and unending as this. He knew the creature was awaiting some response, some answer from him. But he could not speak. He did not dare attempt to form the words that were in his heart. His eyes bulged from their sockets as the figure took another step toward him and the outstretched hand came closer and closer.

"You have no need to fear, Jacque! You need never fear me at all. I truly am your father. It was from my loins that your mother Cassandra received the seed for you. It is I who have guided you through life, who have sustained you from my unseen vantage point. It was my inestimable fortune — a fortune beyond any other known to the history of man — that has sponsored you and which sustains you now. I have watched over you every day of your life, from your premature birth in Bern in 1945 until this very moment. And I have come to tell you of my love for you and share with you my plans which will give you rulership over all the world. You will have power such as you have never dreamed!"

Catroux tried to speak. "I — I don't believe you. You are not real. This is some kind of mental breakdown. You are not really here, and you are not my father. My mother would never have allowed you to touch her!"

"Oh, but he is, Jacque! He is indeed your father!"

It was the voice of Cassandra, his mother, his mother who had been dead for years. Jacque could not see her, but he had absolutely no doubt that she too was in this room somewhere.

"Mother, Mother, are you here? I can't see you!"

A faint touch of something soft and warm caressed his cheek. "Yes, my dearest son, I am right here beside you. You cannot see me, nor can you touch me in this spirit form; but I will join you soon when you sit on the throne of your father and rule this earth."

Cassandra's soothing voice had taken the edge off Jacque's fear and he turned again to stare into the face of the creature directly before him, now a step closer. But somehow at this moment it did not seem so menacing or evil.

"I believe my mother. I know she is here with us in this room. I accept her word that you are my father. But if you are, then who are you? Tell me your name!"

The creature shrank back and stood to full height, apparently growing ever larger even as it stood there. "You ask my name, my son? My own flesh and blood does not know the name of his father?" There was a thunderous explosion and the bedroom was split by dazzling light. The heavy brass light fixture that hung from the center ceiling crashed to the marble floor. Fragments of wood and plaster soared through the air like miniature rockets gone out of control. The figure had grown until its head now touched the broken plaster of the ceiling. "You dare to ask my name," it repeated. "I am Lucifer, Star of the Morning! I am the god of this whole earth!"

"No!" Jacque screamed. "You are an illusion, nothing more! I deny you!"

But if it was an illusion, the heat coming from it was not. A chair nearby burst into flames and was consumed in an instant, leaving nothing but a smouldering set of springs. Out of the corner of his eye, Jacque saw the small aquarium on the night chest that had been filled with sparkling water and an assortment of charming cichlids now overflowing with blood and bile.

The voice rolled across the room. "I am your father! And you will repeat that to my face. You will say that I am your father! I, Lucifer! Now I command you Jacque, repeat it to me!"

Catroux felt a rolling in his stomach and a horrid sensation in his mouth. It felt like fur caressing the inside of his cheeks. When he opened his lips to speak, a small, dark, slippery creature that looked like a rat came out of his mouth, ran down the front of his shirt and across the room. Catroux tried to scream, but he could not open his mouth.

"Say it!" thundered Lucifer. "Say it, or by hell I will leave you and find another, just as I left the *Obermensch* of Germany decades ago. Now say my name and acknowledge that I am your father!"

Catroux could hear the delicate voice of his mother imploring him to obey. Again, he had no doubt that she was somewhere in the room. If only he could see her. He felt a hand gently touch his shoulder; it was an unseen hand. "Rise, Jacque. This is your mother. The one who stands before me is my lover, the one who impregnated me with your very life. You have an earthly mother and a supernatural father, just as the earlier pretender to the messiah's throne. You have been born of a union of power and you will not fail as all the others have done. I am flesh and blood as you are, even though you cannot see me now. But the seed from which you sprang flowed from him who stands before you now — Lucifer, who is true god and lord of this earth."

The gorge which had filled Catroux's belly seemed to have

dissipated. A sweet sense of security began to satisfy him. His mother was there somewhere. So all was well. Yes, he could stand and face his father now, he, Jacque Catroux — the son of Lucifer.

Still trembling, but now more from excitement than from fear, Catroux stood before Lucifer who had once again revealed himself as the gentle angel of light. He knelt at the naked feet and stooped to kiss them. "Yes, Father, I acknowledge you this day, not only as my actual earthly father, you who gave me my physical life, but as my very lord and master. I am here to serve you at your pleasure." And with his confession, springs of tears broke within the European and fell from his eyes onto the naked feet of his father.

The hand from hell, now somehow cool as September rain, took hold of the sobbing man and lifted him up. He held him close and lifted his eyes to some target in the heavens that only he could see. His cry was a wail in the night: "This is my beloved son, in whom I am well pleased! You will hear from him, Galilean! And you will never come back!"

Taking him by the elbow, his father steered him to the large window of the penthouse suite and pulled aside the draperies revealing once again the majesties of Manhattan. "My son, this is only a part of the world I give you. You have bowed before me to worship me. You have made your confession. And your reward is this whole world. I tried one other time to give it to one I thought worthy. He refused me. He rebuked me to my face. He turned his back on me and walked away. But I had my revenge. In several years I had nailed his frail body like raw meat on a Roman cross. His pathetic followers buried him in a tiny grave outside the city walls, where his bones lie moldering to this very hour!"

It was then that Catroux made a near-fatal mistake. "But, Father, didn't he — and I take it you are speaking of the Galilean — did he not rise from the dead?"

Lucifer released his hold on the man and pushed him aside. His eyes were intense points of fire blue. There was a noise in the room that sounded like a million Niagara Falls, like a runaway loco-motive crashing through the building, like a thousand Phantom jets breaking the sound barrier all at the same time. The room had turned intensely black and Jacque could see only the burning eyes and face of his father, his great mouth agape and his chest heaving in an attempt to get air. From his throat came a wail that could have stopped the stars in their courses: "NOOOOOOOO–O–0–OHHHHHH!"

Across the room, the stone fireplace turned to pulpy dust and collapsed on the hearthstones. The projection TV screen burst into life with the flickering faces of demons hissing and clawing. From somewhere in the darkness Jacque could hear his mother softly crying and pleading for him to have mercy. Then there was a silence, dark and ominous and from some unknown origin a gust of ice-cold air swept through the room.

When he was able to lift his eyes again, Catroux looked up, hoping that his father had gone. His heart skipped a beat as he opened his eyelids to behold Lucifer's face only inches away from his. But the fire was cooled down in his eyes, and the countenance was once again beautiful and alive with light. "My son, you did not know, so I forgive you. Never mention the myth of the resurrection of the pretender. He is dead. But you, my beloved son, are very much alive. And this is your hour. I have this night filled you with spirits of centuries past (Catroux shivered as he remembered the rat escaping from his mouth). No mortal has ever lived with the power you now possess. Now rise up, my son!"

With legs that had grown steady and a body no longer churning with mindless fear, Catroux stood before his father. He began to feel the pride he had always longed to know. There could be no question to whom he belonged and his heart was filled with gratitude. He felt within himself the power of a million demons of hell awaiting his least initiative and command. He turned in adoration to the one who had given him life. "Father, I pledge to you my love and devotion. I now know without question whose son I am. Give me any mission and I will obey."

The father beamed at his earthly son, now filled with his spirit, and placed his hands upon the broad shoulders. "Now listen to me very carefully, Jacque. The moment you were born in Bern in 1945, another son of mine died. Your birth and his death took place at the same precise instant. His name was Adolf. Adolf Hitler. You have two parts of his body — his pale blue eyes; yes, son, those are the very eyes of Hitler, and you have his heart. The things that Hitler did, even greater things you shall do. Hitler did not succeed because, beginning in 1939, he ceased listening to me. Pride filled his heart. And I took my hand from him. His kingdom began to fall with Dunkirk and his insane early invasion of Russia. I had warned him against full treaty with Japan. He did not listen and Japan brought the United States against him a full year before I was ready. Before he blew his brains out, Hitler had claimed the lives of nearly 50 million men, women and children through wars, death camps, pogroms and other persecutions. He came close, but he failed in his quest for world domination. But you, my son, you will do much, much more. My pet name for Adolf was Wolf. But he was only a cub. You, my dear, Jacque, will be a full grown beast, yes, A BEAST! And there will be no one on earth or in the skies to stop you. No one! This is my legacy to you."

Catroux felt the pride of family and mission. He could not have been more fulfilled. But he had a nagging question that would not go away; it had to be asked. "Father, will there be no one from the other side, you know, the followers of the dead Nazarene, who will attempt to stop me?"

Lucifer threw back his head and laughed silently. "Hardly, Wolf! Every believer and follower of the Nazarene has vanished from the face of the earth. God, whom I have sworn to destroy through you, my son, overplayed his hand. He foolishly lifted every force he had from this arena of life. It now belongs to me — to us, father and son. And from this time on you may do anything you wish. Now let me tell you a little trick you can play. The Nazarene, it was rumored, healed the sick. You now have the power to do the same thing. If you touch a cancer patient, the disease will be gone at your will. Lame feet will walk. Deaf ears will hear. And the world will see your miracles and behold their new messiah. You will become the leader of peace for which these poor wretches have long cried. So promise them peace, Wolf, my son — peace on earth, good will toward men!" The fire in Lucifer's eyes grew intensely hotter and brighter as he laughed uproariously at his good joke.

Jacque looked up questioningly: "Peace, my father?"

"Only for a short time, Wolf! Then you will live up to your name and bare your fangs and the world will hear your savage snarl. It will feel the pain of your fatal bite. And everyone will know that

Lucifer and his family have taken control of this earth and dared God to do anything about it! This is our realm now, just as it should have been in the beginning of eons past."

Catroux bathed in the love he had longed for. For the first time in his strange life he knew he had a mission that far exceeded Europe. Oh yes, far, far beyond Europe.

Lucifer read his thoughts and chuckled. "Oh, yes, Wolf, you will govern more than Europe. The world is yours to conquer and to govern. Everyone who has been left here will have to bow to you and subscribe to your new title."

Catroux reacted sharply. "Title? What title, father?"

His laugh could have made marble shiver. "Why, Wolf, you are the messiah, the savior! The Wolf! You are the long-awaited christ."

17

By nine a.m. there was not a hamlet or village in the western hemisphere that did not know the story of the disappearances. All hell was breaking loose everywhere. There seemed to be no restraint left.

Despite the horrors unfolding before his eyes on the dancing monitors, Clay Daniels could not help being moved once again by the marvel of live television. He wondered if he could ever get over it. He had moved into the audio control room where he had pulled up a steel folding chair to sit behind the main console. The *Wake Up* show had now evolved for the day or whatever duration into one continuous news operation trying to figure out the tangles and knots of a world gone berserk. He knew it would be days before regular television could be restored.

A normal TV viewer would not appreciate the fact that sound was equally as important to a good show as the picture. IBC had some of the finest engineers in the business, including Sonny Vanderberg, boy genius. Like many geniuses, as mad as a hatter. Clay's mind was taken off some of the night's insanities as he watched Sonny and his staff mixing the sound that was in that instant being heard by millions. The room looked like the cockpit of a space ship. It was therapeutical for Daniels to watch his staff work the sliding pots and equalization controls on the mammoth sound boards.

The main video control system was in an adjacent control room. Marilyn Garrett had assembled a team of masterminds who had added the computers and other technical gadgetry that could bring the world effectively into a living room. They all somehow reminded Daniels of electronic Gepettos creating life in their strange little Pinocchios.

His people were pushing buttons, pulling levers and duplicating scenes of today's events in millions of houses in a single instant — in Clever, Missouri, in Denton, Texas, in some little shack in the cotton fields of eastern Arkansas, in the home of a multimillionaire in Palm Springs, into Alaska, Hawaii, Puerto Rico. Instantly! It was the wonder of the world. Perhaps it was his never-dying awe of the medium that kept Daniels so fresh. He had never lost the sense of majesty that TV really possessed. Watching it all on this fateful day, he mused that the great medium of television in the wrong hands — say, the hands of a dictator — could mold the world into any shape or form he wanted. Daniels shuddered at the thought.

But the staff was not as sharp today. Daniels understood. The news was too shocking, too overwhelming, too other-worldly. Particularly, the news of the president's disappearance had hit everyone hard. Some of the staff members were crying. One was attempting a crude prayer. Every available worker was on duty; no one was exempt from working during this emergency. The IBC parking lots were jammed as workers from all shifts had converged on the place at the same time. The switchboard was overloaded and other operators were called from home to assist, but the electronics could still accommodate just so much saturation. Daniels knew that nearly everyone connected with IBC fully understood the magnitude of the crisis. He wondered for a moment if it had been like this in various radio newsrooms in 1941 when the Japanese attacked Pearl Harbor.

Oh, there had been other serious situations — terrible ones, as a matter of fact. He could remember the killings of the Kennedy brothers and Martin Luther King, the terrors of various groups holding hostages, the bombings of American embassies. But nothing like this. Certainly nothing of this scope. Only God knew how many millions of people were involved in the disappearance.

His staff had been monitoring other network shows as well — NBC's *Today Show,* ABC's *Good Morning America* and the CBS *Morning News.* None of the guests or analysts had come up with a reason for the missing people.

Daniels had wanted to shake off that bizarre episode with the bishop but he couldn't. Some inner sense kept telling him that this was the right track — stay on it and he would find the answer. He really didn't believe the bishop. Yet he couldn't ward off that inner voice that kept warning him.

Another disturbing thought continued to occur to him. He kept wondering what Jacque Catroux was doing this morning. No world leader had ever shocked him as much as the European had the day before. His thoughts about merger of nations and his own ascension to world power would have been laughable coming from any other source. But he wasn't laughing. He was deeply disturbed. He made a mental note to see if Peter Doyle had gotten any response from Janssen Hennings regarding Catroux's present whereabouts.

"Clay, Clay, can you come here, please?"

He was shaken out of his mental gymnastics by the voice of a frantic associate producer. "Clay, come back to the video tape room with me, please. There is something here you have to see for yourself."

The young associate was Kathy Noren, a bright hope for IBC's future. Daniels leaped from his folding chair and followed the vibrant girl into the adjacent screening room.

"What is it, Kathy?"

"This tape was sent to us from our affiliate in Sioux City, Iowa — Channel 9. You really need to see it, but please withhold any judgment until you've seen the whole thing, OK?"

"Yeah, yeah, sure. Play it. Sioux City? That's near my old territory."

"You'll understand — I think — after you see the tape. The guy being interviewed is named Daniel Penning. Clay, he's a weird-looking old guy, but there is something about what he says that is compelling. It's stuff we haven't heard from any other source.

Maybe we should use it, but Marilyn wants you to see it first."

"OK, roll it."

The visage of the strange man filled the monitor. The fact that he was clean-shaven and probably wearing his best did not change the fact that he was a lifelong "scruffy." He had deep-set, intelligent eyes, a bulbous nose and jowly face. Clay could not imagine what this unknown fellow could say that would be worthwhile but he listened intently, and heard a strange story.

". . . and I saw the story a few minutes after I got up in my old house in Sergeant Bluff. When it first came on, I laughed. I thought someone was playing a joke. But the more I heard — like President Forman and his family missing and the UN thing, I realized you people were telling us a real story, a terrible story."

Daniels gave Kathy an annoyed look, but she shrugged and said, "Please, Clay, there's more. You need to hear this."

". . . and it awakened something deep in my brain. I couldn't figure it out for a few minutes. But then it hit me. I knew why those people were gone, and I knew where they went. And besides that, I knew something so terrible that would happen next, that I knew I had to tell someone."

A flash of understanding flared in Daniels' eyes and he leaned forward for this warning of things to come. He sensed it would be something he could somehow understand.

". . . quite a few years ago, I attended some church services at the Fellowship church — out on Myrtle Street on the west side of Sioux City. Nice church, some good people in it. But I thought they were kinda fanatic in what they said. But you know, I never saw one of them do anything to hurt another human being. They seemed to really love each other, you know?"

Daniels uttered a choice curse and stood up. "Kathy, I don't have time to listen to this lame-brain preach."

She blocked his path as he tried to leave. "Please, Clay, please listen to this whole thing. I know there's a lot of junk on here you aren't interested in, but there's a purpose behind all of it." She laid a hand on his arm. "Please?"

He sat back down, still angry and afraid. It had been his fear of what Penning would say that had caused his outburst.

The visage on the screen continued.

"Well, the preacher there — and I can't remember his name 'cause it's been such a long time ago — used to get up and tell us about a time when millions and millions of people would vanish. He quoted a lot of Bible verses. I don't remember any of them, 'though I've sure tried hard this morning to. But I didn't pay much attention to them then, so I just can't recall one single verse. But the gist of them was that God was supposed to appear to his believers in the clouds and give a loud shout or something — and there would be a trumpet blast. But nobody would see it or hear anything except those people who were looking for him. And his followers would then disappear.

"Well, not everyone, they said. Depended upon what you called a follower, I think. The preacher said that only those people who deeply loved God and were sincerely lookin' for him would be taken when he appeared. And he said that when it happened, it would take place real fast. I think the phrase he used to say was 'in the twinkling of an eye.' In fact, the people there had a song about it. They sang it all the time.

"Anyway, everything that's happened here today makes me think that what the preacher said came true. I tried to call his house and there sure wasn't any answer there. And I tried to call a lot of people in that church but I couldn't turn up a single one that believed like the preacher did that's still around here.

"But the clincher to me was when our president disappeared too. And his family. I know a lot of folks, some of you TV reporters, used to laugh at him, kinda. You gave him a hard time of it. But he hung right in there. And now he's gone. And you ain't.

"And I ain't gone neither. See, I told the preacher back there I thought he was nuts and didn't want to have anything to do with that bunch. So I dropped out of it and never gave it another thought until now. And I'm still here. And so are you. And so's the man who is coming next."

Daniels gave a soft cry and stood up. "What? What's he saying here, Kathy?"

She put a finger to her lips. "Shhh, this is the part I want you to hear, Clay. I think this might be the most important thing he says."

The camera had zoomed in tight on the old man now. There was a trace of a tear coming from one eye.

"I remember the preacher sayin' that after God took all his people outta here, that there was another man comin'. That he would bring war and death. That this world would be a terrible place to live for seven years. The preacher said the one who would come next would be the Antichrist and that the whole world would follow him. And he would lead 'em straight into hell. Yeah, that's what he said. And I figure that's what's gonna happen. None of us disappeared, folks. And now the man is comin'. And we're all gonna end up in hell, sure as anything."

The video went to black and the only sound was the static. Kathy got up and shut the monitor off. She looked at her boss. "Well, Clay?"

Daniels stood and put his hands in his pockets. His eyes were looking at the floor. Finally he managed to look at his associate producer. "What do you mean, 'Well?' "

"Clay, that's a rough piece of tape. What do we do with it?"

Another moment passed while Daniels put some things together in his mind. "Tell Marilyn that we run it. As soon as possible. Tell Hennings not to cut it. I want him to run the whole blasted tape from start to finish."

"The whole thing, Clay? Every word of it?"

He nodded grimly. "Every word of it, Kathy. See, I think the guy's right. I think God really did take those people. And I think what's coming next is going to be pure hell."

18

His head throbbing and the pain in his back burning like fire, Daniels threaded his way through the maze of IBC corridors to his office and shut the door. He had poured himself a fresh cup of coffee on his way in and he gratefully sipped the hot, black brew. He eased himself into the chair behind his desk. Even more distressing than the physical pain was the mental pain of knowing that Arvella and Robert were gone — forever, as far as he could tell. He would never see his son again. It shocked him when he realized how much he would miss Arvella. A terrible fear gnawed at his insides. He somehow knew that old man from Iowa was telling the truth. Something was coming. He could feel it. And it scared him beyond any fear he had ever known.

It had long been a journalist's gag that such and such a story would be "bigger than the coming of Christ." He realized now that no story could be that big. If what he surmised was true, if Christ had been responsible for the taking away of all the people, this was, indeed, the biggest news story in the history of man. Out of habit he reached for a cigarette and flicked his lighter, drawing the smoke deeply into his lungs. He put one foot on the desk pullout shelf and idly watched the smoke curl toward the ceiling. Everything gone in an instant, he mused. Everything except Marsha.

Marsha! With a start he remembered that he had failed to call her and she would be getting frantic. He reached for the phone, dialed his number and breathed a little easier when he heard the phone click at the other end of the line.

"Hello." The voice was tentative and frightened.

"Yeah, it's Clay. Are you all right, baby?"

"Well, I am just so relieved that you called. I have wanted to talk to you all morning, but I didn't call because I knew how busy you must be."

"Busy is not the word. Have you been watching the news at all?"

"Sure. Ever since you left the apartment. It's all really quite horrible, isn't it? Do you know what's caused it?"

"Yes, I think I do, Marsha. I think I do. And if I'm right, you haven't heard anything yet. Are you feeling all right? How's the baby?"

She laughed appreciatively. "Oh, just fine, Clay. I'm missing you, that's all. I'm a little scared about all this."

"Me too, to tell you the truth. Listen, honey, I'd feel a whole lot better if I knew you were down here with me. Can you pack a little bag of your stuff and mine — all my necessary toiletries and so forth and come on down? We may be here for quite some time."

"Oh, that would be a relief to me, dear. I know I can't take any of your time down there, but just to be near you and know what's going on firsthand would settle me down, I think."

"OK, grab a cab and get here as soon as you can. How long do you think it will be?"

"Well, I need to clean up a little and pack the bag. Let's say at least an hour or two, huh? You know me, Clay — slow as molasses."

"Yes, well, you're my molasses, so get on down here. You sure you feel OK?"

Her laugh was comfortable now. "Of course. I'm fine and so is Junior. I've already told you so many times that it's going to be a healthy baby boy and then you'll have two sons."

There was silence on the line.

"Clay? Are you still there?"

"Yes, I'm still here, Marsha. I heard you."

"Oh, I thought maybe we had a disconnect."

He breathed in deeply and said, "Marsha, you take very good care of that baby inside you. Because when he's born, then I'll have one son."

Marsha giggled nervously. "Clay, what are you talking about? One son? What about Robert?"

"I thought maybe you would have figured it out from our newscasts. Robert is gone. So is Arvella. They're among the missing."

Marsha caught her breath. "Oh, Clay! I never put two and two together. But why did they go? Where did they go? Do you know?"

"I'm not sure where they went but I think I might. I'll explain it to you when you get here."

"OK, darling."

"Now, Marsha, when you come down here today, get the cabbie to bring you to the back entrance of IBC. Got that? You'll never get near the front door."

"How come?"

"Because there are large crowds gathered outside. We put up a big monitor screen and some speakers so people could keep up with the happenings. We're staying on this story all day or as long as necessary. All other programming has been suspended at IBC and the other nets too, for that matter. Anyway, you can't get near the front entrance. But the people don't know about the back gate so you come there."

"All right, darling. Are you sure you're all right? You sound tired."

"Well, I've felt a lot better, I guess. Physically, I'll be OK. But mentally and emotionally, that's another story. And the loss of Robert — and even Arvella — are extremely difficult for me to take. There's just no way I can get out of here for a long time."

"Try to get some rest."

"That's just not possible. Now don't forget to bring me some clothes — just casuals and the toiletries. It may be a couple of days before I can leave here."

"I will, Clay."

"And, Marsha — "

"Yes?"

"Please come as soon as you can. I need you desperately. I love you. I'm awfully glad you're still here."

He hung up the phone. Opening a desk drawer, Clay found a bottle of Excedrin and took out three of the tablets, downing them with some of the cooling coffee. His headache was growing steadily worse. He sat back in his chair, rubbed his pounding temples with his fingertips and began to think about his brief time with Marsha.

He had met her about a year after his separation from Arvella. He had not been looking for another involvement and certainly not an affair. It just happened. He had gone to Chicago for an NAB convention, always a main gathering among broadcasters. In previous years he had enjoyed the activity and the sessions which he found profitable and enlightening. But the hassle with Arvella had tainted any enjoyment that might have come from the convention. Even the normal camaraderie with his fellow executives was boring. So he had slipped away alone to a small Italian bistro where they served marvelous cuisine and imported wines. It was a neat little place, tucked between two larger buildings. Soft, indirect lighting and gentle, live continental music combined to soothe the troubled heart. Service was expert and friendly and he had gone there often on his trips to the Windy City.

He had already ordered his food and was daydreaming over a cigarette when he noticed the girl sitting several tables away. It would have been impossible to have missed her. She was extraordinarily beautiful. She wore her ash-blonde hair long and over her shoulders. Even in her sitting position he could tell that the gods had spared no material in her design. But it was her eyes that riveted his attention; they were the darkest he had ever seen, like forbidden violets. She was, in a word, gorgeous.

She smiled at him, not a flirtatious one — just friendly. He grinned back nervously, a little annoyed that she had caught him looking at her so openly.

"Hello," he said lamely.

"Hello, yourself," she responded.

"We seem to be the only two lost souls in this establishment," he said. "I would be delighted if you would join me."

She looked at him for a moment and nodded. "OK. But this will be on separate tabs, of course."

"Of course."

Their conversation had been unforced and light. She said she had recently moved to Chicago from Wisconsin where her father owned a department store. She was entertaining thoughts of going to the University of Illinois to finish a degree in English.

"No kidding," Clay responded. "I work with the language myself in a manner of speaking. I run the news department for IBC in New York."

If he expected her to be impressed or excited he was disappointed. She showed no emotion one way or the other. "That must be an important position," she said.

He smiled at her. "Sometimes I like to think so. When things get hectic though, I often dream of becoming an undertaker." She chuckled quietly.

They had a long and quiet evening together, which ended when she allowed him to take care of her bill and to escort her home by cab. They had not touched or kissed, but both knew there would be other times. They had stayed in touch by telephone and letter until the weekend he flew to Chicago solely to be with her. This time the date ended with a passionate rendezvous in her apartment. And he knew he had to have her permanently.

He had taken her back to New York. At first she maintained a separate apartment. But their need for each other was so great that they abandoned all efforts of hiding their relationship and Marsha moved in with him.

Several months later, she told Clay she was pregnant. For some reason, which she had never completely figured out, he was delighted and they had decided to keep the baby. If his divorce finalized within a reasonable length of time, perhaps they would marry to make the child legitimate. But if not — so what? They were enjoying each other and nothing else seemed to matter. No one at IBC took much note of the relationship which was becoming more and more common in the business.

Daniels stubbed out a cigarette in the overflowing ashtray and silently urged Marsha to hurry to the studio. She would be the one bastion of sanity in a day that had already declared out-and-out war on logic and believability. Then his reverie was jarred rudely by the buzzing of the intercom. Still a little lost in his thoughts, he responded.

"Yes?"

"Sir, Janssen would like to see you," Ivy said.

"Surely."

The news director, who was on a short break during a local 15-minute cutaway, entered the office and collapsed in a chair near Daniels' desk.

"Well, Clay, we have really tied into a monster here, haven't we?"

"Have you been able to locate Jacque Catroux yet?"

"He is in New York. You were right about that. His staff at the Helmsley promised that he would call within the hour. Want me to put him through to you?"

"I think so. I'd like to have him come down here if he would." Daniels looked at his news director with a steady stare. "Janssen, what would you say if I told you that Catroux predicted something like this was going to happen?"

Hennings shook his head slowly from side to side. "Peter told me that you had intimated something like this earlier. Do you mean Catroux actually predicted these disappearances?"

"No, not in so many words. But he did say that something was about to happen that would change civilization as we know it. So much so, Janssen, that he said Europe and the United States would merge governments!"

"My god, Clay! Why did he tell you such a thing?"

"Because he wanted my assistance. He actually wanted me to leave here and join his staff. He really believes, you know! He really thinks there is going to be such a merger."

There was a short silence between them.

"Well, Clay, everything is awfully shaky around the world this morning. I guess nothing would surprise me a whole lot. I guess you know that the governor has called in the National Guard."

"No, I didn't. Is it that bad?"

"Yeah, it's that bad. The people have gone nuts. The looting has been incredible during the last half-hour and there is rioting in the streets. Quite a few have already been killed.

"Can't really say for sure, Clay. It's almost as if there's no restraint left. Do you remember that terrible riot at the New Mexico penitentiary a few years go? Well, guys were hacked to pieces in those cell blocks. There was even a couple of cases of cannibalism. It was like a bad horror movie."

"Sure I remember it."

"Well, that prison riot was like a big vacuum of insanity. No restraints. All actions suddenly became rational, no matter how irrational they would have been before. I think that's what we have here, Clay, only on a much larger scale. There are absolutely no holds barred. People have gone berserk. Maybe from fear. I don't know."

"What about other cities?"

"Same thing, Clay. On various scales, of course. And in other countries, as far as that's concerned. It's everywhere. The world has just blown up, that's all. And without even one bomb being dropped."

Daniels put another cigarette between his lips. The smoke cradled his head. "Well, I think the veneer of civilization doesn't go so deep, after all, my old friend."

"No, guess you're right about that. Well, I just wanted you to know about Catroux. We'll let you know as soon as he makes contact. I need to get back to the studio."

Daniels stood to let the newsman out of his office. "Thanks, Janssen. You're all doing a fantastic job. I'll be down myself in a few minutes."

Hennings disappeared down the hall as Daniels turned back to his desk. He refilled his coffee cup, thinking disconnected thoughts about his horrid diet of nicotine and caffeine. With his cup in one hand and the lighted cigarette in the other, he walked through the main newsroom. Everyone was working so hard that nobody noticed him. He watched them for a few minutes. Typewriters and word processors were going like crazy. Writers surrounded the wire service machines. Others were gripping telephones. He thought the scene looked like a man keeping a diary on the deck of the *Titanic* with the iceberg emerging from the darkness just ahead.

The only thing was that Daniels didn't know how close the iceberg really was.

19

Marsha Lavin finished her shower and began making her face. Preparing herself for the day was always a long process for her. After she had done extensive aerobics in front of her video machine, she enjoyed a lengthy and luxuriant bath. Even in her pregnancy she was determined to keep her figure as trim as possible. She felt pangs of morning sickness and her eyes were a little bloodshot. She used some Visine and began applying eye makeup. She was really quite accomplished at the art and never overdid it. Her face shone with natural beauty rather than something that looked as if it had come out of a can or bottle. Marsha was 24-years-old and reaching the peak of her beauty.

She stood in front of her full-length mirror and carefully studied her pregnant body. She looked good and she knew it. It was not arrogant pride, just a fact of life.

Daniels had insisted that she have the clothes she wanted at any cost. But she had not abused the privilege. Other women had a more extensive wardrobe, but few had one as tasteful. She selected a pair of tan slacks and a deep brown blouse that accentuated her magnificent ash-blond hair. She hummed a disjointed tune as she dressed. She wanted to look so good for Clay today. She understood that he would be hurting from the loss of Arvella and his son. She could accept his retained love for them, but she didn't want their disappearances to pose any threat to their own relationship. She didn't think it would.

Marsha used a minimum of jewelry. She didn't particularly like the stuff, not even gems, although she had her share. She was striking enough without the gaudiness of metals. A simple pair of fragile hoop earrings and a mere touch of lipstick and her face would have been a suitable model for a great painter.

She dialed a taxi service, was told it would take a little longer than usual, packed a few things for herself and Clay should they not be able to return to the Marguerry for a while, and did a little touchup on her housecleaning. She had a maid but, like some other women, hated to have the maid find her house very messy.

Finally, the doorman downstairs rang to tell her the cab was waiting. She slipped into a leather coat and walked to the elevator. The descent to the main floor was made quietly and quickly. She murmured a morning greeting to the doorman and entered the waiting car — a quite old and dilapidated cab, she noted.

"Where to, lady?"

"The IBC studios, please. The back entrance, if you will. I'll show you how to get back there when we arrive."

"You got it. I hope."

"Excuse me? What did you say?"

The driver pulled the machine into the line of traffic as he set the meter on the dash.

"I said that I hope we get there. It ain't all that sure a thing today."

A tiny alarm began to buzz in Marsha's brain. "Why? Is there trouble between here and the studio?"

"Lady, there's trouble everywhere today. Ain't you heard the news? This town has gone crazy. It's like there's a war goin' on. The truth is that nobody in his right mind will go near upper Broadway right now. There must be about a 10-square block area up there with people actually shooting at each other and burning buildings and —"

The young lady was growing increasingly nervous.

"But why?"

"Well, it's all them disappearances. It's like I said before. This town is nuts. Like yesterday people went to bed as human beings and woke up today as animals. It's as simple as that. You do know about all the disappearances, I guess?"

Marsha looked at the rearview mirror, trying to see the face of the scared little man driving the cab. "Yes, I know about them. I have a friend who is the executive news producer at IBC."

He turned off the main boulevard which was jammed with cars and pedestrians and headed down a side road. It was not as crowded as the main streets and the old car was shooting down the man-made canyons at breakneck speed.

Marsha leaned forward and touched the driver's shoulder. She was growing extremely nervous. "Do you have to drive this fast?"

"Yeah, lady, I do! I think if we want to get to your studio in one piece we gotta go very fast. By the way, you better lock your doors in case I have to slow down or something."

Marsha quickly locked the doors on both sides of the cab. The driver did the same thing in the front seat. She leaned back to watch the macabre drama on the streets. It looked as if nearly every door of every building was open and occupants had spilled into the streets. Something was terribly wrong with them. She had made this trip many times in other cabs; yet she had never seen New York so resemble a jungle. People were screaming — at no one in particular, just screaming. Many were sitting on curbs, looking into space as if they were on heavy narcotics. Some were drinking and waving the bottles around foolishly. Others were fighting. Marsha could not believe what she saw — the people hitting each other with fists, bottles, sticks — anything they could get their hands on. A rock came from nowhere and splattered the left rear window. Marsha cried out in sudden fear, but the safety glass held and she was not harmed.

They had traveled several miles before she realized that she had not seen any children. There were teenagers and adults, but not a single child to be seen anywhere. Marsha couldn't understand it. She knew that little Robert had also disappeared. She stared at the spectacle of parents running from building to building, crying out the names of their youngsters. There was panic written across their faces and they seemed to have lost all rationale.

She could see cars overturned and on fire. Trash littered the streets. Shop windows had been smashed and the merchandise inside stolen. It was like a scene from hell, she thought to herself. There didn't seem to be any restraint left anywhere.

The driver turned to talk to her over his shoulder. "Now, lady, somewhere along here I have to cross through the roughest part of this mob. I'm not positive there'll be an opening, so I'll just have to make one. Get down in the seat and hang on and maybe we'll be all right."

Marsha was afraid to move. She stared ahead at the glut of cars and people blocking the streets. There was no way to get through. She voiced her fears to the driver.

"I don't think you can get across there. Look at those people! They look like they might attack this car! Please be careful!"

"Lady, you don't have to tell me that. I'm as worried as you are. You're gonna be my last passenger today, I'll tell you that right now. Get down now, please — get down on the floor of the car. I have to cross here if you want to get to IBC today."

Marsha crammed her body as low to the floorboard as she could. She could hear and feel the car accelerate wildly as the driver began his assault on the human wave ahead of him.

The bullet came from a high building to their left. It had been fired from the third or fourth floor and had a sharp downward trajectory. The lead projectile pierced the side window of the cab and exploded into the driver's head, leaving a relatively small hole near his left temple, but blowing away most of the right side of his face. It splattered against the other door. He was dead instantly.

The cab veered to the right as the driver's body slammed against the steering wheel. The machine climbed the curb and smashed against the front of a clothing store, the hood resting on the naked mannequins in the display. Their clothing had long since been stolen by the mob. Marsha's body was heaved against the front seat and she felt as if her baby were being smashed within her womb. The pain was excruciating.

The door of the cab was jarred open and Marsha, unrestrained by a seat belt, fell against the pavement, the rough surface scratching her beautiful face. It took a few moments for her to regain enough strength to stand. She looked inside the car at the dead man sprawled against the steering column and she cried for help. None was forthcoming. She began to stagger down the busy avenue to find someone to help her.

Someone jumped her from behind and wrenched her arm behind her back. She twisted her head to try and see who was there but a fist rammed against her cheek pushing her face back toward the front. She could smell the whiskey breath of the man who held her.

"Well now, baby, welcome to our little party. My friends and I are glad you could come."

She was quickly surrounded by a half-dozen or so drunken men who began pulling at her clothes.

"Hey! Look at that coat!"

"You look at what you want to, stupid, I've got other things in mind!"

Marsha realized that her clothes were being ripped from her body and several men were tugging at her slacks.

"Ah, look at that! This broad's pregnant!"

"So what! She's still a doll!"

Marsha hoped she could somehow pass out as she was gang-raped repeatedly. Pain tore at her and she could hear her screams being wrenched from her throat. A huge hand came from nowhere and slapped the side of her head. It was then that she mercifully passed out.

That was fortunate. She never felt the knife that cut her neck open from ear to ear.

20

Jacque Catroux had not slept for nearly 48 hours, yet he felt fresh and strong. He could not remember feeling such vibrancy of youth. His mother and newly found father had left about five that morning, leaving behind a delighted and dazzled son. A volcano of resolve and determination seethed inside him. He felt as if he could speak but a word and any wish he had would be fulfilled on earth.

He flipped on the light of his bathroom and prepared to get dressed for the busy day's activities. He caught sight of himself in the mirror and stepped closer to get a better look. The first thing he noticed was his eyes. What was it his father Lucifer had said? Oh yes, that he had the heart and eyes of Adolf Hitler. Were these really the eyes of Hitler, he wondered? They were pale blue and could turn mean in a split second. If they were the Fuhrer's, they were now over 100-years-old yet their keenness of sight was never better. Catroux remembered seeing pictures of Hitler wearing reading glasses. But these eyes did not need them now. What sights had been mirrored through those irises? They had seen the abortive November *putsh* of 1923, the death of Hindenburg, the frightened countenance of Neville Chamberlain, the glories of conquered Paris and the nightmare years of the Berlin bunker. But those eyes would never behold defeat again! Hitler was an amateur, the joker in the deck. The false messiah! The true superman had arrived, empowered by Lucifer himself. No, there would be no defeat this time. Nietzche's mighty words strummed a chord in his heart:

"Behold, I teach you the Superman. The Superman is the meaning of the earth . . ."

Unlike the fake *Ubermensch* of the 1930s and '40s, Catroux would need no mescalin, no shot by a witch doctor to keep his resolve. His father had rejected his predecessor, but he would not reject him! He would see to that! His obedience would be unquestioned! Lucifer had come to him in the night and bestowed upon him the coveted name of Wolf. And the world was his. He would not only tighten his rule in Europe, but he would now conquer the western hemisphere as well, then the Middle East, and on and on until the world was under one grand banner. He would never be denied.

A mental image of Clayton Daniels flashed through his mind. He had unfinished business with the newsman. He needed this man to fulfill his plans in America. He needed the strength of a major news network declaring his glory. So he would wine and dine the stocky and belligerent news executive until he had become putty in his hands. There had to be a way. He knew his father would provide it.

So much had happened during the night. Not only had he been crowned as prince of hell, but the Galilean had "air-lifted" every bit of his earthly following from mankind's existence. Lucifer had been shocked at this bit of foolhardy bravado by the enemy. Catroux could not believe it, either. He remembered the words of his father: ". . . every believer and follower of the Nazarene vanished from the earth. The world belongs to me. And from this time on you may do anything you wish. . . ." Catroux grinned at his visage in the mirror. "You hear that, Wolf? Anything at all! To whomever I want! For whatever reason I choose! I am god, next to my father, the greatest god of them all."

A quick thought of the Galilean entered his dark mind and an enraged snarl slipped from his throat. It was not a human sound, but deep and deadly menacing. The Galilean, if he were alive, had better not cross his path now! He, the Wolf, would kill the Lamb! He would nail the Galilean to another cross and then another and still another until there was not enough flesh left of him to nail to anything. And anyone else who dared breathe the Galilean's name in Catroux's presence would pay the same fatal price. Every church and every synagogue — especially the synagogues — would be burned, and anyone found inside them would be burned right along with the pews and pulpits. When he finished there would be no trace of the followers of the Galilean. Where there were churches he would build whorehouses. Where there were synagogues he would construct death camps. A hatred rose up within him that he knew he had inherited from his father, a temper that could explode at any slight, any imagined insult. He would carry out his work with daring and dispatch!

Catroux slid his fingers through his golden tresses and stretched. A quick shave, shower, and a good breakfast and he would be on his way. He lathered his face and took out a straight razor, the one he had used all his adult life. He was an expert with it, and not only for shaving, he thought maliciously. The sudden remembrances of former covert activities caused his hand to jerk and the sharp blade cut his cheek. Drops of blood splotched down his face. It was a deep wound and would not stop bleeding. Catroux cursed and fished around in the drawer for a styptic pencil. Looking intently in the mirror, he took one finger to wipe away some lather from the cut. But the moment his finger touched his cheek, the cut healed! The skin shut back together as if there had never been a wound. It was instantaneous. Even the blood was gone. His face appeared to have never been marred. Catroux blinked and stared at his reflection in the mirror. Then he grinned, a cruel and malicious turn of his lips. His father was right. Of course, he was right. He had promised him that he would have the power to heal — just like the power the Galilean was rumored to have had 2,000 years ago! Catroux threw back his head and laughed. What a marvelous gift! "Thank you, Father!" There would surely be a way to use his new-found power. He had little question of that!

He quickly showered, dried his hair and began dressing in his elegant and tasteful clothes. The shirt had just a touch of tan in the silk fabric. His expensive two-piece tailored suit had been made for him by the finest tailor in Rome. A matching tie and dark leather loafers augmented his finest feature, his golden hair. He looked in the mirror with proper appreciation, eyeing once again the place on his cheek that had been cut. He whistled softly as he considered his newly acquired powers and realized that he was very hungry. Considering having breakfast sent up, he remembered suddenly the devastation of his angry father a few hours ago — the burned chair, the ruined aquarium, the smashed fireplace and scarred ceiling. He would not want any of the hotel help to see what was left of the once-smart penthouse. The fires and winds of hell had demolished its beauty to the tune of thousands of dollars, none of which Catroux had any intention of paying. Who cares, let them pay, he thought.

He called the hotel kitchen to have two poached eggs, tomato juice, one slice of rye toast and coffee sent to his room. He wondered if he could have simply willed the food into existence rather than ordering it as a normal human being. He somehow knew he could not, that his father's gifts were not to be abused. And he settled down to wait for the breakfast to arrive.

His thoughts turned to the missing American President John Forman. Now Vice President Barry Cane would be sworn into office. The new American leader would be much easier to sway than the former one. Forman had been a follower of the Nazarene whom his father had slain on the cross. Cane had no use for faith and was believed to be an agnostic. He would be much more susceptible to the intense pressure that Catroux had every thought of exerting. It would be necessary to see the new American leader as soon as possible. He laughed to himself as he considered that no official invitation would be necessary or perhaps even desirable. Perhaps the best thing would be to drop in on Cane uninvited and explain to him the new rules of leadership on this planet. Yes, that would have to be done right away, before the week was out.

Clay Daniels too! The hole in the fence would have to be mended even today. He had a busy time ahead and could not waste a moment. Thus it was that Catroux was in an edgy frame of mind when the bellhop knocked at his door with the breakfast order.

21

The descent into hell was in full motion.

Activity at IBC and other news bureaus was unbelievably hectic. More and more details of worldwide tragedy and shock were swamping the airwaves of radio and television. The newspaper people in every corner of the globe were bringing in reserves, part-timers, anyone who could write, edit, do manual labor and, in general, make themselves useful.

By 10 that morning, all the IBC personnel were fatigued. Had they been able to stop for even a moment, they probably couldn't have gotten themselves going again. Daniels had no time to worry about Marsha's late arrival. In fact, he had temporarily forgotten that she was coming. He was fully occupied with the dismemberment of civilization before his eyes and ears. Without exception, the missing people were in some way tied in with the Galilean.

IBC had already confirmed the story on the air, Daniels insisting that they do so. He felt their analysis was right. The other networks were still hedging on the explanations. News sources in communist nations were finally admitting, under extreme pressure, that their part of the world had been affected by the missing people, but they emphatically denied that there could be any supernatural explanation for it. *Pravda* had assured its readers that while it was true that millions had vanished they would soon have a valid reason for the strange happening.

An interesting story was breaking in East Berlin. Police there were undergoing severe interrogation from the KGB and other strongmen. The government was embarrassed by the fact that so many East Germans had apparently escaped into West Germany. What good was their vaunted Berlin Wall if it could not hold the fortunate citizenry inside the country?

By midmorning, every church in New York City was open. The doors that had been kept locked by confused vestrymen had been smashed by panicked mobs. Every sanctuary was packed. But what strange services! No order or service, no litany, usually no minister — although some, strangely enough were still around to continue their work. One enraged congregation had hanged a clergyman that morning from a beam directly over the pulpit; his dangling feet were only inches above his Book of Prayers. The only thing that was common to all the churches, regardless of the faith, was the dreadful mourning, the silent weeping, the occasional cursing of sullen-faced parishioners. Church had never been like this before.

Law enforcement officials were hard-pressed to keep up with the rash of suicides. Over 19,000 had been reported in Manhattan alone since seven a.m. — thousands overdosing, or leaping from tall buildings or shooting themselves. The day so far had made Viet Nam and Corregidor look like picnics in the park.

The New York Times had issued a special edition with the bold headlines: MILLIONS DISAPPEAR WORLDWIDE — JESUS CHRIST SAID TO BE RESPONSIBLE.

One of the most macabre details of the day came to light in the fifth paragraph of the front-page story:

Apparently there are more than live bodies that have been taken from the earth. Cemetery attendants have reported from coast-to-coast that the graveyards have been vandalized on an unprecedented scale. Virtually every cemetery in the world has torn-up graves with the corpses missing. It is reported that the missing had religious backgrounds.

Law enforcement officials could not keep up with the outbreak of crime. Many of the towering skyscrapers already had been turned into feudal estates, much like those of the Dark Ages, with the inhabitants inside withdrawing for mutual protection and consolation. All that was missing were the drawbridges and knights in armor. Instead of using spears and bows and arrows, these knights in polyester armor were using high-velocity guns.

Daniels took a short break from his wearying duties to withdraw into the sanctuary of his office. He turned on only his desk light, so the room was nearly dark. He sat behind the desk and cradled his head in his arms just beneath the light. He felt like crying, but he knew he didn't have the time. Never in his whole life had he felt so weary. Over and over he told himself that this was all a crazy nightmare and that, in a few more minutes, he would awaken, holding Marsha in his arms, her warm, full body tucked against his. He sat up with a quick sudden movement. Marsha! Where was she? She had not come to the IBC building or he would have known about it. Perhaps she was delayed in getting a cab. He picked up the phone and dialed the number of their apartment. He let it ring a long, long time before he reluctantly cradled it again. She was not there. She must be somewhere between the Marguery and IBC. And that was a jungle now! Suddenly, he was frightened.

Janssen Hennings knocked on his door and looked into his office. "Clay, you OK?"

"Oh, come in, Janssen. No, I'm not really OK; in fact, I'm a little unnerved if you want to know the truth. I called Marsha several hours ago and told her she better get over here. But she hasn't shown up and I am more than a little worried about her."

The newsman mirrored his boss's concern. "Anything I can do?"

"No, I don't want to unduly burden the police anymore than they already are. I just wish I knew where she was. Oh, was there something you wanted?"

"Yeah, Clay, I thought you should know that Vice President Cane will be sworn in as President at 11 o'clock. Our crew is already there. The swearing-in will be in the portico of the Capitol. I thought you would probably want to watch."

"Janssen, that means they have no hope of finding President

Forman."

"Uh, yeah, that's right, Clay. There is no sign of him or his family anywhere. So this is not even going to be a provisional swearing-in. This is the real thing. And we are told Cane is going to make a major statement."

"God," breathed Daniels softly. "All right, thanks, I'll be down in a few minutes. OK?"

Alone again in his office, he looked blankly at the ceiling. Just 24 hours ago life had seemed relatively normal. Nothing more serious than an assassination, world peace, the super-heated economy, the Middle East and a few other day-by-day realities. Then, in the space of one shot around the sun, everything was different. Arvella and Robert! He would never see their faces again. The strange overture from the European Jacque Catroux. What a bizarre offer! Now the worldwide panic as millions have gone somewhere. Now a new president to be sworn in. Had anyone predicted such things the day before, he would now be committed to a lovely home with mattresses on the ceilings and walls!

His intercom buzzed and he reluctantly responded. "Yes, Ivy?"

Her voice sounded tight and frightened. "Sir, there is a policeman out here who has asked to see you. Says it's personal and urgent."

"Ivy, everything today is personal and urgent. What's it about?"

There was a pause while his secretary checked out his caller more thoroughly. Again he was on the line. "Sir, he said it was about your family and that he really had to see you."

Alarm raced through Daniels' brain as he asked her to show the officer into his office. He had hurriedly run his fingers through his tangled sandy hair in an attempt to look presentable when the door opened and the officer entered. Daniels walked over to meet him.

"I'm Clay Daniels. How may I help you?"

The officer was built like a fireplug. Daniels thought he would never want to tangle with the man. They shook hands. "Sorry to bother you today of all days, Mr. Daniels. I understand you are very busy."

Daniels laughed quietly. "Well, this is not a typical day for us, but then I'm sure you're not having a picnic, either. Pretty bad out there, isn't it? At least, from the reports we're getting, it sounds bad."

"Mr. Daniels, you probably don't know the half of it. But what I want to see you about is far more personal. Sir, there has been a car accident and a murder. Do you know a girl named Marsha Levin?"

A soft cry escaped from Daniels' throat as he grasped the officer's shoulders. "What has happened to Marsha? Where is she?"

"Mr. Daniels, please — try to be as calm as you can." The executive had not noticed the appearance behind him of Ivy Browning, Marilyn Garrett and several other staff members, all looking at him with pale faces. The officer continued, looking directly into Daniels' eyes. "Sir, Marsha has been killed — "

An animal scream filled the room as Daniels began shaking the burly officer. Staff members reached for him and tried to pull him away. "Clay, Clay — easy, man!" Marilyn, who was powerless to tear her boss away from the policeman, said "Clay, get hold of yourself! Stop — let go of him."

Something released inside of Daniels. He dropped his hands to his sides and leaned against his desk. "Marsha's dead? How? When did it happen? Where?"

"Mr. Daniels, it happened about an hour ago. Miss Lavin was in a cab, apparently headed here —"

"That's right," Daniels interrupted. "I told her she needed to be here for safety reasons."

The officer kept speaking. "Crossing a boulevard, the cabbie was shot through the head and killed instantly by an unknown sniper. He lost control of his cab and it smashed into a store window. Miss Lavin was apparently thrown out."

"Oh, God," Daniels moaned. "Is that what killed her? A lousy car accident?"

"No, sir. The crash didn't kill her, although we think she must have been hurt somewhat. She was trying to get help when she was attacked by a gang of men. She was raped and killed."

Daniels slumped to a sitting position on the floor and stared up at the officer. "Killed her? But why? Why would they kill her?"

"Who knows, Mr. Daniels? The city has gone crazy. Miss Lavin is only one of hundreds who have been killed in similar fashion.

You know that. And today it's far, far worse than usual. It's brutal!"

"You say brutal. How was she killed, officer?"

The lawman looked away and tried not to answer. Daniels leaped to his feet and reached for him, screaming, "I asked you a question! How was she killed?"

The officer stared at the floor and his words were soft and barely audible. "With a knife, sir. They cut her throat."

Perhaps a deer feels the same way when an arrow pierces its body. First the shock of the blow, then the terrible awareness of the fatal wound. Then the fear of dying. Daniels was bleeding inside. He fought for his breath and maintained his balance by hanging onto his desk. Several of the staff tried to help him, to take his arms, but he shrugged them off.

"No, leave me alone. I can stand up."

It embarrassed his people to see him like that, to know there was nothing they could do at that moment to ease his pain. They had never seen Clay Daniels in such a mortal position. Tears washed his face and he made no attempt to flick them away. His chest was heaving. He turned to the officer again.

"What about the baby?"

The policeman simply shook his head and began walking out of the office. As he passed Ivy Browning he said, "Call this number and you can get the details on claiming the body." And he left.

Daniels suddenly whirled and grabbed his coffee cup from the desk and hurled it against the wall. It smashed and little rivulets of coffee spilled down the expensive wallpaper. His curses ran together in a jumble of rage and his face was red and covered with tears and sweat. "God is responsible for all of this! He did it! First Arvella, then Robert. Now Marsha and the baby. God did it! I would kill him if I could! He did it!"

No one could control him. He threw materials from his desk, turned over his chair, and was reaching for one of the table lamps when the IBC security men entered the office. It took four of them to wrestle him to the carpet and hold him there. The company physician had been summoned and he ran into the room with a small black bag. From it he took a syringe and emptied its contents into the struggling executive's arm. In a few minutes Daniels passed out.

22

It was a frightened and strangely subdued contingency of the party leadership that filled the historic Great Rotunda of the Capitol for the swearing-in of the new president. On only a few occasions had this high-ceilinged room been used for such an auspicious ceremony, the last time in 1985 when Second Inauguration services for President Ronald Reagan had to be moved inside because of subzero weather. Although not many could view the proceedings live, the Rotunda made a much more aesthetic locale than did the steps of the Capitol. Well before the 11 o'clock starting time, the cathedral in miniature was packed.

Staff members and ardent followers of the missing president — and there were many across the nation — were still in shock over the strange loss of their beloved first family. Still others who, under other circumstances, would have tried to get near the Capitol building for this swearing-in, were not present now because of the loss of their own family members. Even Secretary of State Dean Wildenmank was not present because of his grief at the disappearance during the night of his wife Margaret. Outside the Capitol building, huge crowds wedged tightly near the barricades. Many were weeping. Others appeared to be stunned. No one seemed to be moving very fast, as if the horrors of the preceding night had somehow stunted their motor skills. Their collective attitudes seemed to form the unasked and moot question, "How could such a thing happen in America?"

The citizens were not strangers to such emergency oath-takings. There had been a number of them throughout the history of the Republic. A few in the crowd could still remember the swearing-in of Harry Truman in April of 1945 following the unexpected death of Franklin D. Roosevelt. Many others could recall Lyndon Johnson's incredibly macabre ceremony in Air Force One with his predecessor's widow standing nearby in her bloodstained pink suit. But as sad as those occasions had been, they were caused by natural forces that could be understood if not readily accepted. However, the swearing-in of Barry Cane was different. The crowds knew, yet could not quite adequately grasp, that the day had been ordered by the gods and they were dealing in the political "Twilight Zone."

In the small anteroom just off the Rotunda, built especially for the privacy of any chief executive who had business on Capitol Hill and really very rarely used, stood Vice President Barry Cane. In a few moments he would place his hand upon a Bible and be sworn in as president, a moment for which he had waited all his political life. Cane had begun long ago as the mayor of Phoenix, Arizona, a position he held for two elected terms, after which he ran successfully for the Senate. He had built a prestigious reputation in that capacity for enacting legislation aimed at peace. It had been Arizona, ironically a state long controlled by the highly conservative Goldwater family, that had led the way toward a national platform of nuclear disarmament. Cane led that initiative and thus had become a controversial senator. His acquisition of superb television skills had helped him to overcome many natural barriers. Few men since John Kennedy had his expertise at communication. He was nearly 6 feet 5 inches tall, slim, and of sleek looks and charm. His wife, Anne, filled her role in the social necessities with equal grace. The two made a formidable-appearing couple. Their panic and fears caused by the disappearances put aside, many Americans would warmly welcome the change from

Forman to Cane.

The conservative Forman had insisted upon balancing the ticket with his old foe Cane, despite the outcries from the right-wing element of the party. But those cries were soon quieted when the political "odd couple" scored a smashing victory over the incumbents in the national election. The two men had gotten along well, at least in public, despite their outrageous differences of opinion. Forman, deeply religious and conservative — Cane, an agnostic and very liberal; Forman, committed to arms buildup and carrying a big defense stick and Cane equally committed to *de'tente*; Forman, in the political image of Reagan's *laissez faire* doctrine and Cane a militant for letting government be the "big brother."

Cane had understood the principles of being a proper vice president and had remained discreetly in Forman's shadow. Now that the shadow was lifted, Cane had every intention of vaulting into the sunlight of promotion and power. He just wasn't sure he knew how to do it. Somehow he would have to find a person with visionary ideas and the promotional capacities to sell them to the public. He intended to begin looking for such an advisor as soon as he was safely in the White House and had allowed Forman's memory to pass away.

He had been notified officially less than an hour before that the presidency was declared vacant. The head of the FBI and a representative of the Secret Service, along with members of the majority party, had called a news conference to state for the record that President Forman and his family were irrevocably missing and that Cane would be sworn in. In the press give and take, the inevitable question had come right away: "You say the president is missing. Missing from what? Or—for what? Why is he missing?" No one knew for sure. Only IBC, goaded by Clayton Daniels, and *The New York Times* had proposed the solution to the disappearances as related to religion. No one else was yet willing to take that stand.

Most of the reporters were fully aware of President Forman's religious stand, a position that had frankly rankled more Americans than it pleased. In earlier years, Ronald Reagan's religious commitment was accepted. But the mood of the nation had turned steadily to the left since his administration. The only reason

Forman had gotten away with it was because of his artful leadership of the nation as a whole. Now that Forman was gone, the reporters no longer felt any need to continue paying homage to his whims and Dark Ages beliefs. So neither of the government spokesmen mentioned religion as the reason for the president's apparently permanent absence. It would be, in fact, some time before the name of the ancient Galilean would be officially mentioned again in Washington, D.C. Cane would see to that.

The IBC news coverage of the swearing-in was being directed by Washington-based Simon Carrington. He had just been told that Clayton Daniels had been hospitalized for at least 24 hours due to the tremendous shock of learning of Marsha's death. Carrington hoped he could do an outstanding job on this assignment, void of any of his private feelings for the president-to-be. He hated him. Carrington had been based in Phoenix during the years of Cane's tenure as senator. The two often clashed, and Cane had gone out of his way to torpedo any hopes Carrington might have for advancement.

Carrington had watched his senator become a powerful figure both at home and abroad. He had covered Cane's establishment of the Citizens' Free Fulfillment Committee, an incredibly powerful organization that had directed the economic policies of the previous administration. Under this group, free enterprise had been severely threatened and Cane had nearly gotten through the Congress a government-controlled earning and purchasing amendment that would have ended free enterprise forever. The bill had received early advancement due to the poor economy. Under President Forman, however, the nation had reawakened, the dollar had come alive, and the public was no longer in any mood for such proposed government interference. Cane had never put his desires to rest in this matter, however, and Carrington could still remember hearing his senator address the issue—that the Federal government should have the power to set irrevocable prices and interest rates, that it alone should dictate the economy and not the marketplace. Cane had authored the much-ballyhooed theme, "More Is Not Better," and had done everything he could to squash any economic rising expectations of the working class.

But it was in the field of international politics that Cane had swung his biggest stick. More than any other American, he had been instrumental in the economic and military buildup of the European Federation. He had been a fervent supporter of the continental policies of Jacque Catroux and he believed that it was only a matter of time before there would be a political amalgamation uniting the United States, England, France, Belgium, Luxembourg, Italy, West Germany, Greece, Switzerland, Denmark and Sweden. Forman had not been vehemently opposed to such a plan. It had always been Cane's "baby" and he had exerted tireless legwork on its behalf in the diplomatic arena.

The only thing Carrington admired about Cane was that he shared Forman's consuming hatred of the Soviet bloc. Although they never were really friends, and never allies, they had still given the nation workable political leadership that had once again put the United States at the forefront of conceptual politics.

Watching from his control room, Carrington saw his cameras pass over the visage of leaders from many parts of the world, those who were already scheduled to be in Washington or who had just shuttled in from the United Nations. The dramatics of the previous night, the riot situations in many of the major cities, and the trauma of knowing that a good percentage of the world's people was suddenly gone had caused most of the major international airports to be shut down. However, the European embassies in Washington had ordered their diplomats to be present for the swearing-in of a man they considered their friend.

"Are you frightened, darling?"

Cane was startled by the soft words and turned to see his wife Anne. "Oh! No, not frightened, really. Apprehensive. Very much so. I can hardly believe all this has happened. I shall miss John Forman very, very much — hard as that may be to believe."

The lovely woman smiled. "I believe you, dear. You two made quite a strange pair of bedfellows. But now you will be able to implement all those cherished hopes you have held for so long."

"Well, not for some time, Anne. I am going to be quite alone for a while. But I really believe that something marvelous will happen if I can just put together a good team, one of my own choosing, not John's. I am going to allude to that briefly in my acceptance speech."

"Good luck, Barry. I am very proud of you. You will be the best president this country has ever had."

"One thing I know for sure — I will have the loveliest first lady the White House has ever known," he said.

The door to the Rotunda opened, the band began to play, and the crowded audience in the small chamber stood to acknowledge the new leader. It was the proudest moment of Cane's life when, moments later, he repeated the new presidential pledge: "I do solemnly swear to uphold the Constitution of the United States and to properly fulfill my role as President of this Republic, in accordance with national and international law and humanitarian principles."

The new president then walked before the battery of microphones and TV cameras and made his first address to the nation as Chief Executive.

"My fellow Americans: this has been one of the darkest days in the history of mankind. Millions of our country's citizens have vanished — and we do not yet have a sufficient explanation. They left in their wake the sorrow and mourning of broken-hearted family members. And America has lost a great president today. President Forman and his entire family were among those millions who have somehow left this dimension of existence.

"At the very outset, may I express my deepest admiration for our late president as a man and as a leader. It is no secret that his policies were somewhat removed from my dreams and visions for our nation's future. But President Forman was a man of principle and courage. He will be greatly missed.

"There is perhaps not a family in our nation, and perhaps on the earth, which has not been affected by the phenomenon of the early morning. We have no explanation or rationale for the disappearances. Yes, I am aware of some of the attempted explanations, especially by one of our great TV networks and a New York newspaper, an explanation that has to do with the supernatural and a religious leader who was executed in the Middle East over 2,000 years ago.

"But I want to caution all Americans in this desperate and searching hour not to revert to superstition and old wives' tales. I

believe that I can assure you there has been no religious docu-
mentation that this has a supernatural meaning, and there has
certainly been no appearance of the historic figure of yesteryear of
whom I just spoke. Let us not accept fairy tales simply because we
do not fully understand this incredible happening today. There is
no question in my mind that our scientists and scholars will find the
reason for the disappearances within the next few hours or days.
And I believe they will have uncovered something that will prove
to be of the utmost benefit to mankind's continued existence on this
planet.

"Have faith, my fellow Americans — faith in the genius of
mankind to solve its own problems, to find a path to new levels of
cooperation and fellowship among nations. There is nothing that
man cannot do, no problem so great, no mystery so deep, that the
genius of the human mind cannot overcome."

There was warm applause from the spectators, craning their
necks to see their new president.

He continued.

"Now, on a negative note, I must say to my fellow citizens that
since the strange occurrence of the morning, a wave of lawlessness
and disorder has broken out among people overcome with fear. It
should be made very clear at the outset of this administration that
we will not tolerate any breaking of the law by anyone for any
reason at anytime. I have given directives to the proper authorities
that at the moment of my swearing-in a few moments ago, a state of
martial law is in effect for the entire nation until further notice.
Curfew for all citizens, regardless of age, will be eight p.m. Anyone
failing to comply with this official directive will face the fullest
penalty of the law. I can promise you that this is only a temporary
cessation of freedom and your full rights will be returned to you as
soon as the emergency is over.

"We must all work together and pay whatever price is necessary
during this time of crisis to restore America to her normal lifestyle.
Let us remember that individual rights must never take precedence
over the national good. Our motherland and her sanctity will be
uppermost in every mind. We are entering a new time of peace and
prosperity in the world. America is joining ranks with our sister
nations of Europe to work together to defeat every foe that would

pose a threat to our tranquility and stability.

"Anne and I thank you for the many calls and wires we have already received in the last hour indicating support and best wishes. We are your servants and will therefore serve you with all our hearts. Ladies and gentleman, a new age has begun!"

The reaction nationwide was overwhelmingly positive. It was as if a mother had taken her hungry infant to her breast. Some of the pain of the morning's loss of loved ones had somehow been lifted. No one could really explain why. It had just happened. A new day of plenty, a new era of peace had begun. Oh yes, there were some detractors who cried aloud about the cessation of any number of human rights snatched away in the first few moments of the new president's reign. But those cries were drowned out by the majority who knew that a few rights couldn't mean much if together the nation could forge ahead in a warless and poverty-free society!

The friends of President Barry Cane stood in the Rotunda for a long time applauding the new national hero. The media cameras whirred and clicked to capture the amazing response. Cane beamed and waved, quickly at home with his new-found acceptance. In just a few brief minutes, Cane had made a nation forget, for the most part, the missing former chief executive and his family, put aside their own individual losses and grief and look to the future. Reporters were caught up in the euphoria and briefed their listeners and viewers around the world. Rarely had any of them been so excited.

One by one, President Cane shook hands with the dignitaries who came to greet him. Some embraced him, others simply shook hands. It appeared that the same lack of restraint that had earlier in the day sunk humanity to new depths of hopelessness was now raising others to new heights of ecstasy and joy.

Two hundred thirty-seven miles away in New York City, a solitary figure in a gleaming penthouse room watched the proceedings on the giant projection screen. His blue eyes had watched every gesture and his keen ears had heard every vocal inflection. His lips were smiling, although his eyes rarely reflected mirth. Jacque Catroux was delighted with Cane's effort. It had exceeded his best hopes. His father had come through again. He had no doubt about it. Sometime that morning the spirit of his father had entered into the new president of the United States. The old Cane could never have pulled off such a public relations coup! It had been an effort from another world. Catroux knew he and Cane would have much, much in common from that moment on.

Everything was on "go" for Jacque Catroux.

23

Clayton Daniels lay in the heat of the Death Valley desert, slowly dying of dehydration. His tongue had swollen to several times its normal size and it kept gagging him as he tried to manufacture enough saliva to moisten his mouth. He was on fire — he was sure of it. Calling for help had proven to be impossible. There was no one near and he could not generate enough sound from his parched throat to be heard if help *was* nearby. He had no idea how long he had lain there or even how he had gotten there. The brutal sun would not stop its lethal ascent, and when it, at last, reached its perigee, Daniels knew he would be burned to a painful cinder.

He wanted desperately to reach up with his hands to ward off the rays. But the desperadoes who had left him here to die had made sure of their work by tying his hands firmly to stakes driven deeply into the sand. He could not move so he had no way to protect himself from the sun's rays. He finally stopped pulling against his restraints or trying to call out. Once or twice he thought he heard approaching voices, but when he waited for them to materialize in this ghastly furnace, they had never approached near enough to see him in his plight. All he could do was lie there as patiently and comfortably as possible — until he died.

Something fuzzy in his thinking processes made it impossible for him to figure out exactly what had happened to him, or why the vicious men had left him in such a precarious state. Several times the shadows appeared to lift momentarily and he thought he could make out figures lurking in the distance, one of them tall and with golden hair. But like shimmering rays rising from a scalding pavement they too turned out to be nothing more than illusions and then were gone.

Daniels blinked his swollen eyes several times in the general direction of the rising sun. He knew somehow that he must not look right into the ball of fire or certain blindness would result. But the blazing sphere had become a fixation to him and the more he looked in its direction the stranger it appeared, certainly unlike the old sun he had watched as a boy sinking into the plains behind Omaha, Nebraska. There was something unique about this light, something downright weird, but he could not figure it out. It remained a mystery in his burning, tormented brain.

Suddenly — there it was again! The voices! No question about it this time! They were human voices, far, far away, but real! And one of them sounded familiar. Daniels tried to push himself up to a sitting position, but the restraints held firm and he could not move his arm any better now than before. Nor could he cry out. A paralyzing restriction bound up his vocal chords. It was maddening to have help this close and be unable to call out to them.

He could not remember ever being so afraid. It must be the final fantasy in the death process, when all hope is abandoned and no salvation is possible, he thought. He gazed in the direction of the sun again and he could see the shape of a man's face in it. His thinking processes rejected such a vision for it was the moon that was supposed to have a face, not the sun. But there was no question there was a visage in this sphere and it was looking down on him, the lips forming his name. And now he could hear the words being spoken, "Clay, Clay, can you hear me? Clay?" The words were spoken with gentleness. And a hand reached out of the atmosphere to touch him lightly on the shoulder.

Some vestige of rationale began to infiltrate the newsman's brain and he began to comprehend what had really happened and where he was and that it was not the sun overhead at all, but rather the very bright light of the nurses' office in the IBC building shining into his face. The voices he had heard, somewhere in space, were not ethereal but were the medical people in the room conversing about his condition. The face in the light was not some god from Olympus but rather the kindly smiling countenance of Jacque Catroux.

Daniels blinked stupidly at the bending figure and tried to smile back at him.

"Daniels! Welcome back, old boy. This is Jacque. Can you hear me? Do you understand what I am saying to you?"

Daniels attempted to reach out a hand but his arms were still paralyzed at his sides, held tightly in place, he now realized, by restraining straps that bound him to a gurney. He looked blankly at the bonds and then back toward the face of Catroux and tried to ask the question, "Why?"

"No, no, it's quite all right, Daniels. The nurses will remove the straps just as soon as the sedative wears off. The doctor gave you a shot back there in your office. That's why you've been off in dreamland for such a long time." The voice was quiet and encouraging.

Daniels urgently wanted to speak but his throat seemed full of bitter cotton. He gave it his best shot and his voice emitted a dull, croaking question. "What — what am I doing here? What happened?"

Alice Renner, the head nurse at IBC, slipped to his side. She pressed a cool cloth against his face. "Would you like to sip on a piece of ice, sir? Yes?" He nodded and she spooned the marvelous cold nectar to his lips. "Mr. Daniels, you are in the dispensary here at IBC. You had a bit of a shock in your office this morning, I'm afraid and, and —"

Catroux broke in. "It was right after you heard the terrible news about Marsha and her accident."

Daniels spit the ice on his chest and his eyes took on that frightened look of a chased deer.

Catroux's hand rested firmly on Daniels' chest. There was something about his touch. Even in his near-delirious condition, the frantic man could notice it. That touch had some kind of healing virtue to it. It emitted peace, tranquility. It was so soothing, like a mother gently tucking in her little boy. He could feel something inside him, something good and very gentle. As long as Catroux's hand was upon him, Daniels felt that he would be OK, that everything would work out, that Marsha would come any moment.

"Clay, do you recognize me? It's Jacque Catroux."

The newsman nodded thankfully, nearly weeping in gratitude for the European's presence. Catroux bent toward him, still smiling sweetly. "That's fine, Clay, just fine. Now listen to me: there was a bad accident. The deputy told you about it. The taxi in which Marsha was riding was ambushed enroute to IBC. Do you remember?"

Like a vexing nightmare, the reality of it began to seep into Daniels' memory. Oh yes, he remembered! He remembered! Tears spilled down his cheeks.

"Yes, Clay, the driver was shot and the taxi rammed into a building. Marsha was injured and she left the car to summon help. She was attacked by a wild mob and they killed her. You recall that now, don't you?"

"Yes," he said.

Catroux continued. "When the deputy informed you of Marsha's death, you were overcome with emotion. You blacked out finally, after the doctor was called. There was some damage done to your office. You threw a few things around in your emotional reaction. You had to be sedated. And you were brought into this infirmary. You'll be all right physically in a couple of hours, we believe. But you have been hurt inside very, very deeply."

"Oh, yes, " Daniels wept. "God, I've lost everything in life that's close to me — my wife, my son. And Marsha."

A knowing look crept into Catroux's eyes, but he kept his gaze steady and gentle. Without looking away from Daniels, he asked the nurse and her attendant to leave the room for a few moments. Without a word of protest, they melted away into the hall and the European and the newsman were alone in the infirmary. The strong hand pressed against the heaving chest a bit firmer. He then reached down and unloosed the straps which bound Daniels to the gurney.

Daniels painfully pulled himself up to a sitting position, his legs dangling from the table.

Catroux was watching Daniels closely, never taking his eyes off the newsman's face.

After he settled down some, Daniels attempted to apologize to Catroux for his actions but the tall foreigner said, "None of that, Clay. You don't have to apologize for anything. I don't know how you have taken all the pressure you've been saddled with, anyway. I need to fill you in on some things that have happened while you've been 'resting.' " Catroux smiled as he said the last word, and Daniels grinned back at him.

"Such as what, sir?"

"Well, of course, the big story is that you are now covering a new administration in Washington."

"What?"

"Late this morning, the government made it official that President Forman and his family vanished with the rest of the Nazarene's followers. And the leaders of the administration felt it in the best interest of the nation that Barry Cane be sworn in right away, that there be no gap in leadership, even under a temporary leader. So the ceremony was called very quickly and it was held in the Capitol Building Rotunda. And Mr. Barry Cane is now your exalted leader."

Daniels sat in disbelief. "How could the administration do something like that so quickly? What are they gonna do if Forman shows up tomorrow?"

The smile on Catroux's face was not pleasant. "Oh, come on, Clay, dear boy, you know that Forman is not coming back. And neither are any of the others. They are long, long gone. And they are never going to return to my — to this earth again."

Any temporary feelings of jocularity had now faded from Daniels' heart. Catroux's words were piercing and cruel: "They are long, long gone. And they are never going to return to my — to this earth again." First it meant that Arvella and Robert were gone forever. The pain of that loss was still excruciating. The second part of Catroux's statement caused some fear in the newsman. He ventured his thoughts. "Sir, was that a 'slip' there when you said they would never come back to 'your' earth again?"

The European's facial expression did not change. "No, not really, if you must know. And I suspect that you do know. Remember, Clay, what was it now — a little over 24 hours ago that you visited me at the hotel? I offered you a position with me in the future development of the Western world. I told you then, didn't I, that something very, very big was about to happen that would change life as we know it."

Daniels nodded feebly.

"I admit to you that I didn't know the happening would occur this soon, nor that it would result in the disappearance of millions of people. My father had not yet revealed these things to me. I knew only that the event would be colossal and that it would open doors for me and others who believe as I do to conquer the world."

"Mr. Catroux, I know you have some strange powers and incredible charisma, but you don't really think that our new president and the Congress and our armed forces are just going to roll over now and play dead, do you? How do you think you're going to take over the world? The truth is that most Americans don't even know who you are."

Catroux chuckled. "Well, you're right about most of your assumptions. But let me give you another little prediction here, my friend. Within 48 hours, every person on this earth will know who I am, who I really am, and what my powers encompass. And if you think there's been a change, a wild and drastic change, I might say, in these past 24 hours, well hang on to your hat and watch what's going to happen. Even you news people are going to be shocked."

Catroux's voice dropped to a near whisper now as he squeezed Clay's hand in his, "And, Clay, I want you at my side. I have plans for you. You feel right now that you are a dead man. Yet I will restore you and bring your life to full fruition once more. And out of your innermost being will flow rivers, yes, rivers, of living waters."

Clay withdrew his hands and painfully stepped away from the guerney. He opened the door in preparation to leave. Once more he turned to face the tall golden figure. "Mr. Catroux, my life has been blown all to bloody hell. I really have nothing left. My one chance at survival is to continue excelling in my work, which I still love. I want to stay at the helm of IBC news. I don't have a chance outside of that work release. To leave it now, and to join you on whatever quest you are pursuing, would be fatal to me. The truth is, sir, that I am quite afraid of you. I have respect for who you are and for the dreams you have for a united world. But I don't really believe in you. I hope you can understand that. It was great of you to come here today. And I thank you for it. But I really don't want to get involved. OK?"

"Clay, you are very weary. You've been through a tough ordeal. I don't know if you're even aware of the fact that you've been under a sedative here for nearly seven hours. But you're going to be fine. Tomorrow will be another tough day; the Lavins are coming in from Wisconsin to assist with burial plans for Marsha. The services will be held the day after tomorrow at their request. All right? And I will be right here to assist you in any way I can."

It was all becoming too much for Daniels. "Please, Mr. Catroux, I don't expect these personal favors from you. You are a world figure with many more important things to worry about than my problems. I have already told you how I feel about any future involvement with you."

The tall man patiently watched the stricken newsman in his anguish of spirit and body. Finally, he responded. "Clay, you need to know this from me. I mean these words with all my heart. You can count on me. I want you to understand that. I will never leave you. I would stay with you in your need to the end of the world."

Daniels looked up at this self-appointed benefactor. "Sir, my life was going along pretty well until yesterday. The downward slide began with your phone call to my office. I don't want to be rude, but I've really had all I can take for one day. So I'll just say goodbye."

"Of course, Clay. Of course. Why don't you get some rest now? Why don't you just go home?"

Tears glistened in Daniels eyes and he didn't really care if Catroux saw them or not. "Home?" You want me to go home? To what? Marsha's dead, my son is gone, my wife too. So what is home, Mr. Catroux? You tell me — you with all the snappy answers! Just what is home, anyway?"

24

About 33 hours had passed since the world had undergone its strange and magical transition, when men, women and children from every walk of life suddenly were no more. With no warning, no inclination of the trauma to come, a veritable army of humanity had mysteriously vanished. Their losses were felt with stabbing senses of pain by many while others summarized the transformation with such phrases as, "Good riddance!"

The drama was played out in every nation: in the Berner Oberlan region of Switzerland, carefully guarded by the brooding Jungfrau peaks, an old farmer named Otto now tended his small farm alone — his wife was among the missing; in Taormina, Sicily, where the frantic children of a fishing boat operator seached diligently for their missing parents; in Quebec City, where a maintenance supervisor at the Chateau Frontenac could no longer be found; in Killarney, Ireland, where the owner of the buggy concessions that operated in the Gap of Dunloe, had vanished along with his entire family. No state in America, no province of Canada, no burgeoning state in the Third World, no island of the sea was immune to this strange and terrifying phenomenon. The reactions by those left behind were as numerous as the individual personalities they represented: fear, rage, grief, nonchalance, sarcasm, drunkenness, suicide, hopelessness, revenge, and on and on.

The realities of this brooding new world he had inherited hit Barry Cane on his first morning in the White House. Under almost any other circumstances he would not have moved his family into the mansion quite so soon. However, his predecessor, John Forman and all his family, were not to be found anywhere. And during the swearing-in ceremonies the previous afternoon, a large cadre of hard-working movers had taken the Forman goods to an unnamed warehouse even as another crew moved the Cane belongings in. So Cane and his wife had slept their first night in the White House in the room where Forman and his wife had vanished the night before. It was all a bit disconcerting to the new Chief Executive, but he was determined not to let it show. He and Anne had a hard time sleeping in this great house with its ghosts and memories. John and Abigail Adams had become the first residents of the White House in November, 1800, while the mansion was still under construction. Mrs. Adams had not been all that fond of the new domicile. In candid letters to her daughter, she complained about some of the inconveniences such as not a single bell to summon a servant, no firewood in this region of forests. There were only six rooms in the entire building, she said, which were at all comfortable, and none of the six were hers. People passing nearby could see the Adams' laundry hung up to dry in the East Room, flapping in the winter winds which invaded the open windows.

The Canes discussed many of the innovations and renovations that had occurred under recent first families. During the Kennedy years, great pains had been taken to acquire fine paintings. A Fine Arts Committee for the White House had been created and museum experts and a curatorial staff had assisted in the search. President Lyndon Johnson issued the directive to hire a permanent curator for the White House whose duties would include ". . . making recommendations as to the articles of furniture which shall be used or displayed and as to the decor and arrangements best suited to enhance the historic and artistic values of the White House." Mrs. Richard Nixon undertook a major renovation program in 1969 and much of the building was redecorated. The Jimmy Carters and

Ronald Reagans had also contributed greatly to the stately elegance of the mansion.

Cane gently held Anne in his arms as they neared sleep. "Darling, we have three years left of my predecessor's term to enjoy this marvelous place. And, who knows, your old Barry may even win a term here himself. Seven years to make our mark on this world."

Anne kissed his cheek and murmured, "Barry, you'll be such a fine president. I just know that you will. And I will always be at your side. You know that, don't you?"

There was a long pause before Cane spoke again. "Anne, I entertain my first official guest at nine o'clock in the morning. I learned he was in the country — no one seemed to know about it except a reporter from IBC. He got word of it and leaked it to my staff. And more than anyone on this earth, I need this man!"

Anne opened her sleepy eyes. "And who might that be, darling?"

"Jacque Catroux."

Any thoughts of imminent sleep immediately vanished. His wife rose up on a supporting elbow to look at her husband.

"Catroux? What is he doing in the country?"

"You know, that's the funny thing, Anne. I don't have any idea. Only that he was here for some personal reason. But no matter. He is here. And one of my first major concerns is a new unity pact between the United States and Europe. It could not have been better! Catroux will be with me in the Oval Office in the morning."

The day's proceedings had worn them out. Approaching their sixties, neither of the Canes had the stamina of their youth. Sleep finally came.

The new president arrived at his official office at dawn the next day to meet with his closest advisors: Bertrand Tally of the State Department, Alice Sydney Evans from the Fed and Philip Hawthorne from the Pentagon. Cane was briefed by each of the three separately and then met with the trio for nearly an hour to discuss other major concerns. At eight o'clock he met with staff supervisors of the White House. They briefed him on what he could expect from the large crew of servants, maintenance people and chefs. He was impressed with their professionalism and how quickly they had passed their allegiance from Forman to him. He hoped

Congress would do the same.

When the last of the house staff left he still had a quarter of an hour to collect his thoughts before the arrival of Jacque Catroux. He had been in the Oval Office many times before as a member of Congress going as far back as the Nixon years. Deep in his heart he constantly entertained thoughts and hopes of the presidency, but the suddenness with which it was thrust upon him was still a bit more than he could handle emotionally. Thus it was that he looked about with the awe of a tourist at the room that was now his and his alone.

At Cane's request, a historic desk had been secured, one built from the oak timbers of the *H. M. S. Resolute* which Queen Victoria had presented to President Rutherford B. Hayes in 1878. The desk had been in the Smithsonian since the Carter Administration and Cane thought it was about the most impressive piece of furniture he had ever seen. The large and unbelievably heavy desk sat on the oval rug of pale gold, highlighted by turquoise rosettes and the Savonnerie-style border. Sitting at the desk, Cane looked straight ahead to the quaint fireplace where matching antique Chinese covered vases sat on the marble mantel. Directly over the fireplace hung a portrait of George Washington in dress uniform, painted by Charles Willson Peale. Other equally marvelous paintings were present, some depicting scenes of 19th-century America and other American leaders. Behind Cane were the tall bow windows giving him visual access to the Rose Garden where he would meet many important presidental guests, including Catroux in a few moments. What a setting for the meeting that could change the course of the Western world!

Cane already had given orders that he wanted to greet Catroux in the Rose Garden and that the press would be allowed to photograph the historic meeting. The two world leaders would meet in the colorful garden where there were tulips bred in the hothouse and placed in the garden for just such a historic day and hedges of holly and boxwood under the crab apple trees. During the summer months the greatest colors came from the roses, anemones and other hot-weather flowers. Cane loved it and knew that he would use the area perhaps more frequently than any other president. He also had some ideas for the Rose Garden that he wanted to develop with the chief gardener.

At nine o'clock sharp Catroux was led to the portico entrance where he was warmly greeted by America's new president. The constant click of cameras and occasional questions by reporters broke the morning silence. Finally Cane made a motion and he and Catroux stood before the waiting microphones. The president issued a statement:

"It is a rare pleasure to meet with my dear old friend Jacque Catroux. Far too long the destinies of Europe and the United States have wandered along on separate courses. And yet it is the dream of us all that we can join forces toward world peace and prosperity. I know that Mr. Catroux shares that vision, and I too raise my voice with him in a call for mutual understanding and labor. Our session this morning will be a preliminary one only. I cannot surmise that there will be any statement of import to give you upon its conclusion. But do not give up on us. We believe we can change the world. In fact, you watch us!"

Polite applause greeted the ebullient speech and Catroux took his place behind the podium.

"I share today the dreams of your new leader. While in recent months we have had much reason for common understanding, no man in your history has better understood the potential for common sharing than your new president Barry Cane. All of Europe mourns the loss of your former leader as we mourn the loss of all those human beings no longer with us. But we cannot remain in such valleys of dark shadows. We must come into the sunshine of new dreams and visions. And President Cane, by his marvelous acceptance speech yesterday in your Capitol, has shown his comprehension of this truth. Today he and I will speak together of our mutual concerns, our shared goals. And I have no doubt that in these years ahead, years in which we will not be encumbered by superstition and those still chained to dark history, yes, in these brilliant paths of brightness still ahead of us, America and Europe will rewrite the history books. Mr. President, thank you for your hospitality here today and for your strength, compassion and courage for the future!"

Again there was polite applause, several perfunctory questions from the reporters and answers which had little substance, then the two men disappeared into the West Wing of the White House. When they arrived at the Oval Office, President Cane made it clear that he was not to be interrupted for 45 minutes. Each of the men ordered a light drink, which was delivered immediately and the doors were closed. Rather than taking the auspicious position behind the massive desk, Cane walked to the fireplace and offered his guest one of the high wingbacked chairs by the coffee table, then sat down in the other one.

"Mr. Catroux, I —"

The European raised a hand in protest. "Please, sir, in a place such as this, I am just Jacque to you. Or, as my closest friends call me, Wolf."

The president raised an eyebrow. "Wolf?"

Catroux laughed gently. "Oh, just an affectation, I am afraid. It is a name my father calls me quite often. I rather like it."

"I was not aware that your father was still living. How fortunate you are, Jacque — uh, Wolf. May I ask where your father resides?"

Catroux smiled at the president and answered, "Oh, I think it could be said that he resides everywhere, Mr. President."

Now it was the American's turn to demur. "Please, now. Just call me Barry."

Both men laughed at their almost childish efforts to bend over backwards in friendliness.

"You know, this reminds me of Henry Kissinger's classic statement after he was named Secretary of State," Cane said, "At the news conference immediately after his swearing-in, one of the reporters asked him, 'Mr. Kissinger, we have known you and covered you for so long. How would you like us to address you now?' And Mr. Kissenger answered, 'Oh, a simple Your Majesty will suffice!' "

Catroux laughed heartily. "Ah, Barry, perhaps we all take ourselves too seriously. These little moments put everything in proper perspective, I think. Now please let me thank you sincerely for the invitation to be your first guest here today — the first of your administration, as a matter of fact."

"Well, Jacque, I meant it when I said there was no one I more wanted to speak to than you. We have far, far to go, you and I, and much to accomplish. I never thought I would have this chance, you know. If you would have asked me about this 48 hours ago, I would have said there was no way. Forman was a good man, but he really was not one of your biggest fans."

A scowl crossed Catroux's face. "Yes. We clashed on a number of occasions. I don't wish anyone harm, but his disappearance is a rather fortuitious blessing."

The president set his drink on the mahogany table near a vase of daffodils. He leaned forward, his arms resting on his knees. He stared at his guest intently. "Tell me, friend — tell me the truth! What do you think really happened to Forman and all the rest of those people?"

The European swirled his drink a moment and then answered, "I think, no, I know, that they all disappeared with the Nazarene. Somewhere! Somehow!"

Cane paled. "You really believe that, Jacque?"

"I know that, my friend. There isn't any doubt about where they went or who took them. I don't know how it was done, only that is was, indeed, done."

The president stiffened, his face now a study in stone. "How can you be so sure of that? What on earth would make a thinking man such as yourself believe such a fairy tale?"

Something happened to Catroux's eyes. The friendliness was suddenly gone. The blue had turned to ice. Cane blinked a moment. He had never seen a look quite like that one before.

"Barry, I believe that the Nazarene took all those people because my father told me so."

"Your father?" Cane bit savagely. "Just who in hell is your father?"

Catroux lifted his head and laughed. "Well put, Mr. President. Well put! For that is exactly where my father comes from. My father is Lucifer. I am his only begotten son, Mr. President. And from this moment on, he is god of this world."

Cane began to shake. The frightening thing was that he somehow believed there was truth in what Catroux had just said. As ridiculous, as superstitious and outlandish as his words had sounded, Cane knew he believed them. He sputtered, "But, but how? How could —"

"And not only is my physical father Lucifer himself, but my

heart and eyes have lived on this earth once before, sir. Look into my eyes very deeply. That's it! Look at them, sir, and then try to remember someone else in fairly recent history who had eyes like mine and who also was known as 'Wolf.' Well? What name comes to your mind, Mr. President?"

Cane suddenly understood total fear. His heart pounded madly and sweat beaded his face. "My God, Catroux! My God! Hitler was know as 'Wolf.' And he had pale blue eyes like yours —"

"No!" Catroux pounded the coffee table and the drinks spilled onto the elegant carpet. "No, Mr. President, not *like* mine! These *were* his eyes! And through the eyes of a man you can look into his very soul! Look into my soul, sir, and tell me what you see!"

Cane could not speak. He was cowering in his chair like a child cringing from a brutal father.

"Not only do I have his eyes, but his soul, his heart and his mind. And his ambition, Mr. President. His ambition. His desires for world supremacy! And I will have it!"

Cane tried to get up to ring for help. But he could not move. Catroux, whom he thought to be one of earth's greatest ambassadors of peace, was really a madman. But even more than that, he had some kind of power that caused mere mortals to want to become invisible, to disappear. Catroux stood up and reached for the terrified American. Grasping his arm he lifted him to a standing position. "You don't doubt my words, Cane, I know that. You know I am exactly what I say I am. But just so you will know and never doubt again in these years that you will work closely with me, I will demonstrate to you the will and power of my father."

The president could not resist him. He had no strength left. He could not even cry out for help. His first morning in the Oval Office and he was a prisoner of a madman, of a man who believed his father was the devil. He shivered in Catroux's one-handed clutch and watched in fascinated horror at what ensued.

Catroux's face was contorted with triumph. The pale blue eyes appeared to have an inner burning light. Cane could not look at him any longer. He turned his eyes away toward the direction of his desk — or where his desk had been. It was no longer there. Nor were the tall bow windows, nor behind them the graceful lawns of the White House or the needle of the Washington Monument piercing the sky. All of these things were gone, and what Cane saw now was a vast open space. Overhead was open sky that was rapidly filling with a dull, wailing sound. Flying at them at supersonic speed were masses of Air Force bombers, first two or three, then behind them a hundred or so, and yet behind them so many bombers that the sky was black. They were flying low, perhaps a hundred feet above the ground, and they were laying a crosswork of nuclear bombs in a death pattern. But the bombs did not detonate. Behind the planes came rows of equally low-flying missiles, coming at such dazzling speed that Cane could not make out their exact identification. He knew each one was tipped with a lethal warhead that could wipe out Washington, D.C., or New York, or Chicago. He was trembling more than ever now, not just from fear, but from the vibration, the movement of air around him.

Next in the macabre parade came hordes of people — red ones, yellow, black, white. No children, just adults, hobbling, crawling, stumbling. Cane peered at them cautiously, trying to make out their faces. When he did, he cried out in horror. They looked like walking skeletons, human beings dying from hunger. Sunken eyes, hollow cheeks, arms that looked like animated sticks, teethless mouths groaning and crying. These were the starving of Ethiopia, of Bangladesh, of Chad? But no, Cane could see that most of these were Americans. Even in their emaciated, dying condition, there was no question that they were citizens of his own country. But how? How could these Americans be dying of famine when there was so much food all around them?

The parade was not yet completed. Behind the starving millions came an even greater mass of humanity, each one dying from some putrid, flesh-defiling disease like the ancient plagues of Europe. Cane could see lepers, some with faces missing, others with huge blotches of flesh missing from their torsos and they were wailing and weeping.

Then suddenly, all the horror was gone and the space was being filled with a brilliant light, as if the sun had been crammed into the Oval Office. It was so bright that Cane could not look at it. Turning his face away he caught a glimpse of Catroux, now on his knees, his face rapturous with delight, his arms extended as if in worship. Cane turned back toward the brightness, and emerging from it was a tall figure. It was walking slowly and resolutely to Catroux and Cane, closer and closer. It was obviously a man, but a man such as had never walked on this earth. He was beautiful beyond all measure, with such perfection of facial symmetry and bodily form that Cane was caught up in it. His magnetism was beyond a sexual desire; it was rather a yearning for him that came from the spirit, from the soul. Cane, who had never been religious, who had never given his spiritual adoration to anyone other than the human race, knew he could love and serve this magnificent creature without reservation. And at that moment the president of the United States knew he was in the presence of Lucifer. But he would not bend his knees, he would not acquiesce, not just yet. Moved, yes. Stirred more deeply than at any time in his life, yes. But converted? No.

Lucifer moved to his kneeling son and touched his forehead with a forefinger. "You have done well today, Wolf! You have pleased me. I have never been summoned into this house before. And I come eagerly to meet this man who will serve us and our cause." With Catroux at his side, Lucifer moved forward until he was right in front of the stunned Cane.

"Do not be frightened, Mr. President." Lucifer's voice was resonant, rich, deep, reassuring, altogether pleasant and lovely. "Do not be afraid," he repeated. "I come in peace. Let me explain the manifestation you have just seen. For over 200 years, the masters of this great White House have given genuine service or at least lip service to their God. They have made a shrine of his memory, of his laws. They have even had purveyors of the Nazarene, my nemesis, whom I long ago crucified and buried." He extended his arm as if he were embracing the world. "And what has it brought back to them — all this childish bowing and scraping to the God who cared nothing for them? It brought those tragedies I have shown you, Mr. President — wars, famines, pestilences and untold death. 'A God of love,' they have preached. Well, where is that God of love? Where was he when the wars disemboweled their youths? Where was he when the famines struck the land and millions died as writhing skeletal frames in the stinking desert? Where was he during the plagues when bodies were stacked like cordwood each night in the narrow streets? Where was he two nights ago when he arbitrarily destroyed the lives of millions of families by causing their loved ones to disappear?" He swept his arms in a dramatic gesture of contempt and Cane could hear the winds howling viciously above the White House. Bringing his face now closer to the trembling president's, he whispered, "I am the god of peace, President Cane. Only *I* can bring this world the tranquility it has sought so long. And I will bring it through my beloved son Wolf! Behold, Mr. President? Behold my son! I give you the *Ubermensch!* Behold, I teach you the Superman. It is he who is the meaning of the earth!"

Cane felt Lucifer's hands upon his head and knew he was receiving some form of blessing. He wanted to resist. Yet there was nothing within him to make him do so. It was as if there were no longer any restraints to unfulfilled desires within the man. That any whim or thought that passed through the human brain was no longer a temptation but a command. Cane, to his shock — and yet to his eager relief — found himself kneeling beside Catroux at the feet of Lucifer. The rich, marvelous voice began caressing his spirit, even as the great hands stroked his body.

"So it seems I now have two sons, eager to do my will on earth, my supernatural and only begotten son Wolf, and my adopted son in the spirit, Barry Cane." Lucifer looked up as if to address some great personage above him. "I have defeated you, Galilean! Look on me and despair. The Earth is forbidden to you from this hour on. Look at these kneeling at my feet: the messiah! And the president of the United States!" His eyes now spewed fire as his anger began to boil. "I offered you the world once, Galilean! You were hungry, broken, destitute and alone. There on the mountain I showed you the kingdoms of the world and offered them to you. All you had to do is what these two sons do now, kneel at my feet and acknowledge me as god. But you would not do that! You turned on your heel and walked away from me. And I drove the nails into your burning flesh. I dropped the stone over your pathetic, unmarked tomb! And now I have banished you and all who are called by your name from this earth. You are finished, Nazarene! We are one and we have defeated all your forces!"

Lucifer's demeanor calmed once again and he stooped to raise the two men to their feet. Even the tall Catroux was dwarfed by his size and majesty. Cane had never felt so small, yet so fulfilled. He knew that what he had just experienced was not a vision, but something very tangible, and he knew Lucifer was expecting some kind of response from him. It was not difficult to give. The president of the United States reached up his hands and, with face adoring and reverent, he said, "My father, I too give you my life. I will be your servant and the faithful helper to your son. I thank you for calling me into your service and for giving me the strength, the will, and the vision to do your work among men. I shall not fail you. I promise you my service and I pledge you my undying devotion."

Drawing on all his strength, Barry Cane reached up on tiptoes to reach Lucifer's face with his hands, pulling it down to him. He then kissed him fully on the mouth after which his new father held him tightly to himself. Now drawing back, Lucifer looked at his family, smiled benignly and spoke. "This has been the greatest hour of my long, long life. I shall return soon to give you instructions, to give you plans for peace. You shall bring peace to the world. Wolf, my son, you are the messiah of the earth. And you, Barry Cane, my other son, will supply Wolf with the power and prestige in America that he already has in Europe. I tell you now that our first target will be the Middle East, there to bring about peace on our terms, and to suit our purpose. Then we shall deal with Russia."

Lucifer began backing away, shafts of sunlift shrouding his face and body until they began to disappear. Still the men could hear his voice. "May my love and mercy attend you, my sons. Farewell for now."

He was gone. Once again Barry Cane found himself in the familiar Oval Office. Jacque Catroux was looking at him with a pleased expression. He extended his hand. "Well, my brother, you have met my father. I am glad you accepted him. As you please him, he will honor you beyond any expectations you have ever known. And together we will bring peace to this battered old world."

Cane looked at his watch. It was not quite 9:30. All of this had happened in less than a half-hour. In a 30-minute period of time, his whole life had come together. Yesterday he had found his mission — president of the United States. And today he had found his god — Lucifer, Star of the Morning.

"I don't know what all has happened here, Jacque. I only know that it pleases me very much. You have much to teach me. I will be a good student."

Catroux drew him close and embraced him. "I know you will, my brother! I know you will."

Now holding the tall European at arm's length, the president asked him, "When will we meet again?"

Catroux smiled. "Soon. Very soon. Within several days. But you will know where I am. The whole world will become aware of me and our mission in the next few hours."

"How? Where are you going?"

"Mr. President, I am going to a funeral!"

25

Clayton Daniels awoke before sunrise with a maniac beating a savage tom-tom in his head. He flipped on his bed light and stumbled into the bathroom to try to find some Excedrin. He took three and went back to bed where he lay awake until his alarm buzzed at six. While less emotionally unstable than several days ago in his office when he was informed of Marsha's death, he was still far from normal. He knew he could not push himself too hard or he might break up again.

It was lonely in this king-sized bed where he had lain so many nights with his beautiful Marsha. She had known vistas of love-making that Arvella had never dreamed existed. She was a creative, volcanic torrent of motion, who caused the many years of age difference between herself and Clay to dissipate with the first touch and kiss. There were many things about Arvella that Daniels truly missed, but the noctural trysts were not among them. She went about her conjugal obligations with all the warmth of the Ku Klux Klan embracing Martin Luther King. In a fit of pique, he had once told his wife that if they had a water bed, they would call it the Dead Sea. Marsha was different. She had made him live again.

Together they had begun a new life in her womb. The doctors shocked him when they said they could find no evidence of Marsha's pregnancy. Did she miscarry? Daniels wondered. Or did the little unborn baby also disappear with the others.

He turned on his side toward the pillow where his lover had placed her head every night. He reached out his hand to stroke the linen covering and realized he was weeping. Not uncontrollably, but without any reservation or shame. There would never be another Marsha. He knew that, and her loss was incalculable. It would be his devotion to his work that would keep him going for a long, long time — he knew that. Only it would never be the same again. Life would now be perfunctory and obligatory, the magic moments of momentum gone forever.

A clap of thunder far away piqued the newsman's curiosity and he rose from the bed and walked to the window. He drew back the heavy drapes and looked outside. The weather was as bleak as his spirit. It was raining softly and the dark skies promised a day of more of the same. He turned from the window and walked over to the stereo. The tape in the deck had not been changed from the last night he had lain with his lover. It was the Bob James album. He turned on the system, punched the auto-search for his favorite song on the tape, Joe Cocker's haunting "You Are So Beautiful." From its simple opening to its fading conclusion, the song had become their favorite. Holding each other close, they would listen to the saxophone lead, gently pursuing the theme while the background singers gave the elegant and soft counterpoint, "You . . . are . . . so . . . beautiful to me . . . can'cha see . . ." Clay pushed the repeat switch so the song would play over and over. It was all he wanted to hear this grim, gray morning. Tears spilled over his face as he listened. He could almost smell Marsha's musty, sensual fragrance, feel her full body thrust against his, hear her soft, low voice saying the most delightfully outrageous things in his ear. He lay back on the bed, arms and legs in spread-eagle surrender to his most treasured memories. "You . . . are . . . so . . . beautiful to me . . . can'cha see . . ." Now she was gone. By nightfall her body would be nothing more than ashes in a sculptured vase at Graceland Gardens.

The discordant jar of his alarm ripped him from his reverie and he sat up to turn it off. There was no more time for pity. He had a tired old body to shower, a worn and wretched face to shave, a black mourning suit to don and a funeral to attend.

He was not looking forward to meeting Mr. and Mrs. Lavin, Marsha's parents. They could be foreboding people under the best of circumstances and this day surely didn't fit that ethereal category. Her parents had arrived the previous night and stayed in a hotel near La Guardia Airport. They had not wanted to see the man who had "maliciously ravaged" their daughter's body and deranged her mind. As far as the Lavins were concerned, Clayton Daniels was as much responsible for the fatal mayhem orchestrated on their daughter as those thugs in the street. It had been Raymond McClure who had called them with the news. He had reached them at their Kenosha department store where they had been frantically attempting to find enough employees to open business after the previous night's disappearances. The word of Marsha's murder had crushed them. McClure had not informed Daniels of the extent of their grief because he knew it would further devastate his already emotionally unstable boss. He had told him only that the parents were deeply wounded and would be present for the memorial service and cremation ceremony. But Daniels knew it would not be easy and that there would be hell to pay before the day was done.

By 6:30 he had finished his shower and shave and was dressing for the grim task of the morning. The memorial service had been scheduled for 10 o'clock. An IBC limousine would transport him to and from the proceedings so he wouldn't have to worry about driving. He donned a robe and walked into the kitchen to make some coffee. He turned on the small kitchen television set to see what new developments had transpired during the night, especially those concerning the disappearances.

The *Wake Up* show was now back on its normal programing schedule, so it would still be nearly an hour before Peter Doyle was on camera. But the early news with Janssen Hennings was on, and this was what Daniels really wanted to see.

Hennings looked very tired, despite the super lighting and make-up available to him. Daniels could sympathize with his news anchor because Hennings had hardly left the IBC Building since the crisis began three days earlier. The newsman had not complained; the truth was that he relished his assignment and physical weariness would not be a deterrent to his reporting capacities.

"Seventy-eight hours have now passed since the story of the century broke, that of the missing millions. Estimates now put the figure over the 400-million mark, and predictions are that it will rise still higher. The ramifications of this catastrophe — or phenomenon, if you prefer — are beginning to unfold. Such things, for example, as future redistricting in the political arena, the lowering of the unemployment rate as many who had been without work will now pursue those jobs vacated by the missing employees. The joker in the deck, however, is that many of the missing were themselves employers, and the question remains as to whether the businesses they left behind can function without their leadership. Law enforcement is a major concern. The situation has evolved beyond the normal human reaction of some to stress situations, such as looting, rioting and general nuisance-making. Here is New York City Chief of Police Henry Morrison with an observation."

Daniels looked at the familiar black face of the city's chief law enforcement officer. He had known Morrison for a number of years. On several occasions he and Marsha had dined with Morrison and his wife Tess in some of the city's supper clubs. Morrison was a solid thinker and his observation would be of more than passing interest to him.

"The thing we are battling in New York City — and I understand this is happening in other major metro areas as well — is that there seems to be an unhinging of reasoning among the people. As if they are not thinking properly, as if they cannot seem to come to terms with what has happened here. Someone once said that the veneer of civilization has always been very thin. If so, I think the veneer has been stripped. We are in a jungle here. So our martial law will continue in the city, and I understand the governor has requested our new president to send some of the reserves into the state."

Morrison then listed some of the travesties that had occurred during the night. Daniels thought the lawman's observation about reverting to the laws of the jungle was quite proper. Then Hennings appeared on the screen again.

"This story just in from Washington: President Barry Cane, in an unprecedented move, has ordered federal troops into Miami, Los Angeles, Atlanta, Baltimore, Philadelphia and St. Louis. Crime in the streets has gone beyond the capacity of local law enforcement personnel to handle. All of the networks have been alerted to stand by for a special announcement from the White House, we believe by the president, concerning this new crisis." Hennings paused to listen and Daniels knew he was receiving quick and frantic signals through the small piece in his ear. "Yes, and now, ladies and gentlemen, to the White House."

Daniels was struck immediately by Cane's appearance. He wasn't sure what it was, but there was something different about his countenance, a look in his eyes, the jut of his jaw, the set of his body. Although always a go-getter, there had been a timidity in Cane. But not now. This man was the epitome of confidence. How could a simple swearing-in ceremony do that to him, Daniels wondered. The president began to speak.

"My fellow Americans, this is my first opportunity to speak to you since I became your president several days ago. I have a simple announcement to make to you, one of major importance. And since it is unprecedented, I thought it best to make it to you in person.

"We all know of the many tragedies of the week, of the hundreds of millions of our friends and families missing around the world. This mass exodus has caused untold grief and heartache to those of us who remain. Many have proven to be unable to cope and have resorted to activities that are both unfortunate and against the law. While we want to be understanding toward the plight of humanity in this dark hour, it is also necessary to maintain law and order in our streets and neighborhoods. Therefore, we will continue the temporary national martial law throughout the United States. Jacque Catroux has done the same for Western Europe. Until further notice, all citizens must continue to be off the streets by seven p.m., your local time. There will be no gatherings of any kind in churches, in schools, in stadiums, in auditoriums. No more than four people may congregate at any place for any period of time. I know this is a severe order; but it will not last very long. In a few days, I believe we will be able to rescind this order. But to put some importance to the directive, it should be known that anyone violating the martial law ordinance will be subject to the fullest punishment by law, including death. Anyone found looting, breaking and entering, or causing another bodily harm will be shot. The only exceptions to the ordinance against congregating together are those involving necessary meetings and they will be covered by obtaining a 'meeting permit' at your local police department. There will, of course, be no charge for such a permit.

"Shopping will now be done on alternate days. Those persons whose last names begin with the letters A through N may shop Mondays, Tuesdays and Wednesdays. Those whose last names begin with O through Z will shop Thursdays, Fridays and Saturdays. There will be absolutely nothing open on Sundays, this includes the churches for which there no longer seems to be a need. To expedite this order, the IRS has been directed to send to each family a shopping permit. Such permits will be issued only to those whose taxes have been paid up-to-date and they will be known by an IRS number issued to each individual. This number will have to be shown in order to buy and sell.

"My fellow citizens, I know these directives sound harsh. And, to be very truthful, they are indeed difficult. But these days of turmoil require extraordinary measures in order to preserve the peace. Mr. Jacque Catroux of Europe has joined me in these efforts and we are dedicated to peace, peace not only on our own continents, but throughout the world. Please bear with us during these trying days. They will not last long. In the next few days I will come to you again with a progress report. It is my belief that you will be pleased by the results. Let us work together for the common good of us all. Thank you, and good day."

The presidential statement had been carried by all four major news networks, as well as the independent ones. For once, no newsman had an analysis of the speech. There were no conjectures, no synopses, no editorializing. Even in his mental depression, Daniels noted the strange silence and wondered why. Even his own Hennings made no comments, though it was in all likelihood the strangest presidential proclamation in history. Daniels reached for the phone to call and ask about it, then replaced the receiver and shrugged his shoulders. Today he did not care. Let someone else worry. But he could not help being troubled by the freedom-restricting directives of the declaration and of the strange absence of any network response. Had any other president ever issued such a proclamation there would have been all hell to pay. What was different now, Clay wondered.

He turned off the TV, not wanting to hear any more of the depressing news, and went back to his bedroom to dress. He set his steaming coffee cup on the dresser and looked at himself in the mirror. He looked like an old man, one who had lived an entire lifetime in three days — no, four, he reconsidered, counting the day he met Catroux at the Helmsley. "God, what has happened to us all?" he whispered. "And what is yet to come?"

26

The plans for Marsha Lavin's funeral had been carefully prepared by Ivy Browning on behalf of Daniels and after receiving suggestions from her parents. Fogerty's Funeral Home at Eighty-second Street on Madison Avenue had been chosen for the service, which would be followed immediately by cremation with burial of the ashes at the famed Ferncliff Cemetery in Westchester County. Daniels had chosen that resting place because of Marsha's love for the legendary Judy Garland who had been buried there in 1969 following her tragic and premature death. He had authorized Marsha's ashes to be placed in a crypt within the massive mausoleum. The building gave one almost a *deja vu* feeling with its Egyptian tomb-like appearance featuring its imported white marble and the drawers for the dead that looked like a macabre filing cabinet.

The friends and family began arriving at 9:45 that morning, about a quarter-hour before the service was to have begun. No minister had been employed to guide the memorial, only a spokesman from the funeral home along with Ray McClure of Daniels' staff who would give the eulogy. McClure was really gifted at that sort of thing. By the time Daniels had arrived at Fogerty's, he had had several drinks to ease his mental anguish and make it possible, hopefully, to face the wrathful stares of Mr. and Mrs. Lavin. The IBC limousine brought him to the canopied front door of the elaborate funeral home and an usher assisted him into the lobby where he was met by McClure, Peter Doyle, Ivy Browning and Jackie Quinland who had arrived considerably earlier to expedite the funeral plans. Peter and Jackie called Daniels aside to talk to him about something they both considered important enough to break into his reverie.

"Clay," Jackie said, "we know how deeply hurt you are, and how sensitive this whole arrangement is. There are several things we believe you should know. First of all, just so you can relax about it, we were able to get a waiver on that idiotic directive of President Cane regarding more than four people congregating at a time. I tell you, Clay, that man is a moron if he thinks he can get away with that kind of fascist directive!"

A dark look from Doyle quickly brought the producer off her soapbox and she apologized to her boss. "Sorry, Clay, I just get mad thinking about that nincompoop being in the White House. I've never liked him."

Daniels had heard the president's speech but didn't want to discuss it — not now, anyway.

She continued. "Well, the thing that we — that is, Peter and I — really wanted to check with you is that we brought a cameraman along."

"But why?" he protested.

"Because, Clay, because of your stature in the news business, this really is a story. You know that! There is great news value in this service this morning. We don't plan to exploit it in any way, but we hope you won't mind if the cameraman takes some footage. Is it all right with you?"

Daniels stared at his producer dully. "Frankly, Jackie, today I don't care what anyone does about anything. Just tell the fellow — uh — what's his name —"

"Tom Heidleman," Doyle said.

"Uh, yeah, tell Heidleman to stay as unseen as possible. I don't mind his being here, but Marsha's parents might be upset about it and I wouldn't want that to happen. I guess you're aware that it's a closed coffin service, so I don't think there's anything that should be off limits to him. OK?"

"Thanks, Clay," Jackie said. "You're a real trooper."

"And we're all with you, Clay," responded Doyle. "You know that, I hope. Anything you want or need, please let us know."

Daniels hugged both of them, the tears starting again in eyes that he thought were long since bone dry from his early morning weeping. He whispered something unintelligible that both of his friends took as a murmured thanks. They went into the main lobby where friends of the families were congregating.

The Lavins were also waiting there. The moment he had dreaded most was upon him and there was no way to avoid running into the parents now. He swallowed and approached them.

"Uh, Mr. and Mrs. Lavin," he began lamely.

But Daniels was in for a surprise, a rather pleasant one. Marsha's father approached him with an outstretched hand. He was much taller than his daughter's lover and he wore a large mustache which he hoped would draw people's attention from his balding scalp. "Clayton, I know you are hurting today as much as we are. This is a terrible time for us all and both Marsha's mother and I hope you are not blaming yourself for our daughter's tragic death. It was not your fault."

Mrs. Lavin came closer. She reached an arm around Clay's waist and tried to hug him gently. She had never done that before, under any circumstances. "That's right, Clay. You never did anything for our daughter that was not kind and loving. We know that she just adored you and we would not want this horrible week to cause any barrier between us. We appreciate you and, before this unfortunate service gets started, we just wanted you to know that."

Daniels looked curiously at the elderly couple. He could not understand their attitude. "Well, uh, thank you. Thank you a lot. I appreciate your kindness to me. Quite frankly, I didn't expect it. I, uh, I loved your daughter very much. I hope you know that. I miss her more than I can begin to express to you."

In that tender moment the three were held close by their shared love of Marsha Lavin — the cold, dead girl who lay in the coffin in the next room.

Mrs. Lavin tightened her grip on the newsman a bit and looked into his face. "Clay, do you think they will ever apprehend the men who did this to our poor daughter?"

"No, I really don't. New York City, like any other city in the world now, I suppose, has become one great big mental ward. This tragedy is very close to our hearts, but it's being repeated again and again every hour. No, I don't think there's a chance at all that the men will be apprehended."

Mr. Lavin nodded. "I suppose you're right about that. I hate it, but that's probably the way it is." The older man gripped Clay's hand again and said, "Well, there's nothing we can do to change what has happened, young man, but Mrs. Lavin and I think it would be just wonderful if you would sit with us during the service today. Do you think you could see your way clear to do that?"

Daniels choked back a little sob. "Yes, sir! Yes, ma'am. I think that would be wonderful. It would be my honor. Yes, thank you."

A somber-faced usher led Daniels and the Lavins to a pew within the chapel. Mrs. Lavin sat between the two men on the third row and they waited for the service to begin.

The coffin was white, covered with some kind of ornate fabric. It was flanked by rows of yellow roses and yellow and white mums. Ivy had wisely suggested that the decor be as cheerful as possible. The organist was hidden from view somewhere behind all the flowers and she played softly on the Rogers Organ some innocuous song that Daniels didn't know. The room seated about 300 persons and it was comfortably filled when the spokesman for the Fogerty Funeral Home stood behind the podium to begin the proceedings. The man was very fat, dressed in black, and quite nervous to be speaking in front of the IBC news staff and other gathered dignitaries. With an oily voice he began reading from a small, dark book which he held in his pudgy, trembling hands.

"We have come to this place today in memory of Marsha Lavin, who was taken tragically from us several days ago —"

Daniels swore savagely to himself under his breath. This pathetic mound of quaking Jell-O in the pulpit never knew the gorgeous woman whose ravaged body lay in the casket beneath him. How dare he even mention her name! He hoped he could just get through the service without exploding, or crying so loudly that everyone there would hear.

"—forasmuch as it has pleased Nature to receive back to herself the soul of our departed sister, we will soon commit her body to the unknown future, earth to earth, ashes to ashes, dust to dust. And we bear up each other this morning in the spirit of humanity, knowing that our affliction which is grievous worketh for us a far more exceeding and lasting weight of glory . . ." The man droned on for what seemed like forever to Daniels, although it was really only for a few moments.

When the plump man finally sat down, he was replaced in the podium by Ray McClure, who would give the eulogy. McClure was not a professional speaker, but he at least exuded sincerity.

"The life of Marsha Lavin was short but its duration was filled with joy and life. Those who knew her well knew that she was so very much in love with life. Her spontaneity and joy were contagious, spilling out upon everyone she contacted."

Mrs. Lavin reached over to grip Daniel's hand and squeeze it tightly. He turned his head her way and gave her an understanding smile. McClure's words had touched all of the mourners, particularly the three sitting together in the third pew. Daniels knew that he would probably never again have any woman, certainly not one like Marsha. She had been his brief sojourn in Camelot. For those few brief months together, he would ever be thankful to whatever power it had been that had brought them together. Her magnificent velvet eyes, her ash-blonde hair that spilled across his pillow each night, her laugh that rang like purest crystal, her figure that would have shamed most film actresses, and her giving and gracious personality all poured like fine wine across his memory. He could no longer hold back the tears, but his crying was soft and gentle, just as his Marsha had been.

McClure continued. "Today we take the opportunity to be thankful that our paths crossed and that —"

But that was as far as he got. Ever! Suddenly his eulogy was interrupted. The mourning trio became aware of commotion toward the back of the chapel, of people around them turning and craning their necks to see someone near the vestibule. Daniels was outraged at the interference and stood to locate the interloper who dared do such a thing. But as he focused his eyes on the back of the little auditorium, he froze! Jacque Catroux was striding down the center aisle!

Like a conquering Alexander the Great, the tall golden-haired European strode toward Marsha's coffin. Ray McClure had shrunk away from the podium and silence filled the room. In a small alcove, unseen by the crowd below, Tom Heidleman aimed his IBC minicam at the drama unfolding below him. He had one of those premonitions that he was taking videotape of a history-making event. Carefully and expertly he brought the focus in on Catroux. His powerful microphone easily recorded everything of audio substance within the chapel.

Catroux stopped directly in front of the white coffin and turned toward the mourners. His pale blue eyes caught Daniels and he looked directly at the newsman. Then he smiled and nodded, bowed slightly toward Marsha's parents in friendly acknowledgement and then surveyed the crowd. After a few moments — that seemed like forever — he lifted his hands and began to speak, playing his voice like a superbly-crafted musical instrument.

"Mr. Daniels, Mr. and Mrs. Lavin, honored guests of this solemn and tragic occasion; please excuse what must seem to you an intolerable breach of manners and decorum. My interruption of the proceedings here has come as a shock to you all. But in a few moments, I believe you will be thankful that I have come. We are here to commemorate the memory of a beautiful young lady, Marsha Lavin. But, as I am about to show you, you have come in vain."

Anger was rapidly approaching the boil-over point in Daniels and he stood to publicly rebuke this arrogant man who had so brazenly interrupted the memorial service. Catroux saw him, as he seemed to see everything, and lifted his hand in a gentle rebuke. Against his will, Daniels found himself sitting down, unable to speak or move, gripped by some sort of temporary paralysis. Catroux continued.

"As I have said, you are here in vain, for Miss Lavin is not dead. She is only sleeping."

A collective gasp could be heard throughout the room, easily picked up by Heidleman's powerful shotgun mike. What effrontery! What arrogance! Even those who barely knew her knew Marsha Lavin was very dead, a sharp knife had slit her lovely throat, and she was only an hour or so away from the fires of the crematorium. Her ravaged, broken and lifeless body lay in that white coffin. How could this strange man utter such a thoughtless and cloddish assumption!

"My name is Jacque Catroux!"

It was more than a statement of fact or identification; it was a command, a command to be silent. The spoken name was like water on fire. Everyone became quiet again.

"I say to you again that Miss Lavin only sleeps." He reached inside his suit jacket to produce a small, black, leather-bound book. "This book in my hand is known as the New Testament. It is the mythical story of a man named Jesus Christ, a fellow who was executed by the Romans some two thousand years ago. In the section of this volume, a section known as the Gospel of Mark, there is a fairy tale about Jesus that has been repeated in churches of old many times. It bears repeating here today because it has a direct correlation with what occurs here. I want to read you this story. Please listen carefully to these words:

"When Jesus had gone across by boat to the other side (of the Sea of Galilee), a vast crowd gathered around him on the shore. The leader of the local synagogue, whose name was Jairus, came and fell down before him, pleading with him to heal his little daughter.

" 'She is at the point of death,' he said in desperation. 'Please come and place your hands on her and make her live.'

"Jesus went with him, and the crowd thronged behind. Messengers arrived from Jairus' home with the news that it was too late — his daughter was dead and there was no point in Jesus' coming now. But Jesus ignored their comments and said to Jairus, 'Don't be afraid. Just trust me.'

"Then Jesus halted the crowd and wouldn't let anyone go with him to Jairus' home except Peter and John. When they arrived, Jesus saw that all was in great confusion with unrestrained weeping and wailing. He went inside and spoke to the people.

" 'Why all this weeping and commotion?" he asked. 'The child isn't dead; she is only asleep!'

"They laughed at him in bitter derision, but he told them all to leave, and taking the little girl's father and mother and his three disciples, he went into the room where she was lying.

"Taking her by the hand he said to her, 'Get up, little girl!' (She was 12-years-old). And she jumped up and walked around! Her parents just couldn't get over it. Jesus instructed them very earnestly not to tell what had happened, and told them to give her something to eat."

The tension in the chapel was now stifling. Hardly anyone dared blink. Heidleman kept his camera trained on Catroux, occasionally opening the wide-angle lens to include Daniels and the parents of the slain girl. Their faces mirrored shock and incredible fear. But Catroux's face was calm and kind, as placid as a lake. He closed the little black book, tucked it inside his coat pocket and turned once again to the audience. He was smiling, but his pale blue eyes danced with light that did not seem to be reflected, but created inside the sockets somewhere. Later, several people in the crowd would say that they had smelled a rancid odor, just faintly, but had not mentioned it then for sake of propriety. After all, they had heard that the body had not been embalmed. Catroux began again.

"The story I have just read you is, of course, a myth. It did not happen, at least not the way the followers of the Nazarene, who happily are no longer with us, preached and believed. If you will recall, Mark, the writer of this fable said that when Jesus entered the room of the dead girl, he made everyone but the parents leave. How convenient! It is possible to conjure all sorts of marvelous miracles if there is no one to behold them but grieving loved ones who cannot be objective and your choice three henchmen to assist you! He could no more have raised a dead person than cattle can fly. But," and Catroux paused dramatically, "today you are looking at one who is greater than the mythical and mystical Jewish Messiah. Today you behold Jacque Catroux, son of Lucifer, Wolf the *Ubermensch*, and the one you have long awaited. I am your true messiah. The departed Christians used to call me Antichrist!"

Several audible cries could be heard from the quaking audience.

Daniels no longer had any urge to stop the interloper because deep inside he had some kind of premonition, some inner voice, telling him what was about to happen. It was all he could do to breathe!

"Yes," Catroux shouted, "yes, I am your long-awaited messiah, redeemer and lord! I need no cloaks of darkness, no luxuries of privacy, to conjure mythical miracles. And what I will show you today will convince you, and the watching world — for we have a network news cameraman among us today."

Heidleman nearly dropped his camera! How did the European know he was there?

"I will prove to you that I am exactly who I say. What I do now, I do not in my power, but in the power and name of him who sent me, my blessed father, Lucifer, Star of the Morning!"

Catroux stepped into the center aisle and walked to the third row of pews. With extended arms he beckoned to Daniels and the Lavins. "Come with me. You, Mr. and Mrs. Lavin, parents of the girl in the coffin, you come! I bid you come just as Jesus called the parents of the dead girl long ago. And you, Mr. Clayton Daniels of IBC news, you who adored this girl and lived with her and who fathered the dead infant taken from her womb, you come, too." The frightened trio could do nothing except obey the royal bidding. They stepped into the aisle to follow Catroux to the coffin. At the bier, they stopped and Catroux spoke to them in a voice that could be clearly heard by everyone.

"The mythical Jesus summoned Jairus and his wife into the room of their little girl. They thought she was dead. And I now bring you to the coffin of your little girl, Mr. and Mrs. Lavin, and that of your sweetheart, Mr. Daniels. And I say to you again, she is not dead; she only sleeps."

This repeated outrage was more than the manager of the mortuary could take. He stood at the back of the chapel and cried out, "Stop this! Stop this outrage in the name of everything that is decent, sir! This young woman is dead, certified so by the coroner of this county!" The little man did not notice a group of tall uniformed men — Catroux's men — forming a semicircle around him.

Catroux stared at the mortician and in a voice dripping with acid, asked, "Then, sir, you can tell me exactly the time she was embalmed!"

The official from Fogerty's fumbled for words for a moment and finally stammered, "Well, uh, she has not been embalmed. This is not proper to speak about now, sir. You know that she is to be cremated and so the embalming process was not necessary."

Catroux threw back his golden head and laughed. "I beg to differ with you! She is not dead. We do not embalm the living. Marsha Lavin is alive. And to show you that I am who I claim to be, and that my father Lucifer is now the king of the world, I show you his glory. You, sir," he commanded to the now-terrified Fogerty manager, "come here quickly!"

Afraid for his life, especially when he turned to see the tall guards behind him, the little man bolted to the aisle and stood at Catroux's feet. The tall man spoke quietly now, almost in a friendly tone, "Open the coffin."

"But, but, I dare not — this is a closed coffin service!"

"Open it. Now." The words remained softly spoken, but Catroux's baleful blue eyes pierced the mortician's mind like a hot knife pierces butter. Without a further look at Daniels or the girl's parents, the official obeyed instantly, turning the locks on the three sides of the casket, removing a floral spray from its lid and then slowly opening it. Daniels and the Lavins stared in mute horror as the body of Marsha came into view.

The last time Daniels had seen her alive was the night he was called in the early morning hours to meet Chris Sergeant at IBC. Marsha had been so beautiful standing by the nightstand as he left their bedroom, her eyes glistening, lips moist and forming a kiss. That is how he remembered her, how he wanted the memory to remain — not this pale, cold as marble, corpse in the box. Catroux was wrong! She was killed! Look at her! She is dead!

The Lavins were now weeping audibly. They turned their heads after they saw the long scar on Marsha's neck, a ragged wound that ran just under her chin, the fatal gouge inflicted by some psychopath in the riotous streets of Manhattan. The cosmetologist had not taken much time to cover the hideous incision, knowing that the service was a closed-coffin funeral. Daniels stared in choking horror at the violated body of his lover. He turned to Catroux, the paralysis of movement gone, and reached for the tall man's throat, screaming, "You lie, Catroux! You are a devil! Marsha is dead!

You lied to us, you lied!''

Catroux did not react strongly to the outburst. He gently took Daniels' hands from his neck with powerful movement and held them at the newsman's sides. "Clayton, look at me! And you, Mr. and Mrs. Lavin, look at me. I do not lie to you. I am your messiah. I will now show you the power of my father."

Releasing Daniels, Catroux turned toward the coffin and bent over the battered corpse. Even though he continued to speak quietly, everyone in the chapel could hear him clearly. "I say to this body, 'Arise! Arise in the name of the king of this earth. Arise!' "

He stepped back with Daniels and the Lavins to watch. Those in the audience were standing, leaning forward to look into the coffin. In the alcove above, the cameraman zoomed in so that the entire TV screen would be illuminated with the corpse of Marsha Lavin. Everyone waited, watched, listened — hardly breathing.

The movement began almost imperceptibly. Marsha's right eyelid twitched ever so gently. Then it was still, then twitched once more. There was a trembling of one of the crossed hands. A soft moan came from her body. Mrs. Lavin fainted, her husband barely catching her body before it fell to the carpet. Even in the act of saving his wife from bodily injury from her fall, he never took his eyes off Marsha's body. Now another moan was heard, louder this time. Her mouth opened — not a mouth that had been filled with some terrible substance and then sewn shut, but a lovely, wet, glistening mouth. It framed the soft exclamation, "Oh-h-h . . ." The jagged scar on the neck was fading and in a few brief seconds it disappeared. The lovely chest heaved once, then again and her whole body shuddered. Marsha's eyes batted once, then again, then opened! Those deep violet, gorgeous eyes looked up. The head on the satin pillow turned and the face was magnificent, framed by soft ash-blonde hair that shone and sparkled with life. Marsha Lavin was alive! And she was calling softly, "Clayton, Clayton, please — Clayton!"

But Daniels could not move. As much as he wanted to, he could not make his hands and feet do his bidding. His face was a study of panic, joy, fear, love, surprise and unbelief.

Catroux watched him with amusement. "It's quite all right, Clay. Marsha is just fine, just as I told you she was. And I think she would like your assistance in getting out of that wretched box."

Daniels stared at the European, then at Marsha, and finally summoned the strength and courage to go to the coffin where he embraced her. She was warm, soft, breathing, smiling, fresh, alive! As he bent over, her arms went around his neck once again, just as they had done so many times before. He helped her from the coffin and held her close to him. "Marsha—!" But no more words would come. Only the grateful sobs of delight and unbridled emotions.

The clapping began somewhere near the back of the chapel. In an instant the entire crowd was cheering, clapping, whistling. They were showing their unrestrained joy. No one could doubt what they had just witnessed. They had beheld a miracle! A girl who had been savagely murdered several days before, declared and certified dead by the county coroner, prepared for cremation and burial, was now standing before them alive and well! All because of Jacque Catroux!

Word of the miracle spread across America and around the world on television and radio stations. Pictures of the laughing Marsha Lavin appeared on the front page of every major newspaper that afternoon. The IBC tape was shown again and again on the network newscasts that evening. A person who was dead had been made to live! America had beheld a miracle! The world had seen it. "Behold, I teach you the Superman." *Ubermensch!* The nations had seen and they believed.

Quickly forgotten were those who had disappeared earlier in the week. Good riddance! The new martial law proclamations no longer seemed important. The citizens could get along without some of those unnecessary freedoms of the past. There was now a world leader who could master death and the grave, one who could finally — after all the centuries of fighting and death — bring the world the peace it had so diligently sought.

Tom Heidleman had let his camera run, taking in reel after reel of the marvelous, miraculous morning.

Daniels thanked Catroux and pledged his service to him. Marsha also gave him her allegiance.

At long last, the messiah had come!

EPILOGUE

The midnight stars shone brightly over the island in the middle of the sea. Normally, this little dot of land on the map was uninhabited by anything other than wild animals and exotic birds. On this night two figures were silhouetted against the moonlight. One was exceptionally tall; his name was Lucifer. The other, also tall for mortal man, was Jacque Catroux.

"The world took note of us today, my son," Lucifer said. "And your fame has spread to nearly every land. No one can doubt your identity now."

Catroux gazed up at his father with adoring eyes. "Tell me something, Father. Was the girl really dead?"

Lucifer chuckled and squeezed his son's hand. "Of course not. You told the people that yourself, didn't you? She was not dead. I caused the coroner to fill out the false affidavit. The young lady was severely wounded on the street the day of her attack and would have died had I not intervened. I touched her, at once healing her and putting her into a deep catatonic sleep. It was so convincing that even the morticians believed. You see, Wolf, and remember this because it is vital — people want to believe. They want to see

— 215 —

miracles. And if you plant the seed of a miracle in their hearts, they will make that seed grow into anything they want. We will capitalize on that. Now had Miss Lavin really been killed that day, she would have stayed dead no matter what I did."

Catroux was alarmed. "Do you mean that you could not have brought her back to life?"

"Of course not. I have no life-giving powers. I can take life, but I cannot give it. This is what separates me from my nemesis, the Galilean. We can spread our story that the Galilean is still dead. But we both know different, don't we?"

Catroux stared into the eyes of his father. "But if the Galilean still lives, will he not come against us? Against me?"

Lucifer put his hands on his son's shoulders and said, "Oh yes, he will come against both of us. Our time is limited — seven years, and no more. We will insure that your puppet Barry Cane stays in the White House for the remainder of Forman's term which will be three more years, and then get re-elected on his own to another full four-year term. That will be the seven years, not just for America, but for the world. He will lead America and you will lead Europe, amalgamating the two continents into the world's premier powerhouse. You will have the most formidable army in the history of the world."

"But what about Russia?"

"Russia will fall on some hard times. Very soon now, she will attack Israel. She needs that land to insure her dominance in the Middle East. You will surreptitiously assist the Bear in that quest. Because in Israel, Russia will meet her Waterloo. There will be unbelievable devastation. Over a billion people are going to be killed in just a few weeks time. But after Russia has collapsed, there will be no power left on earth to question you or to defy your authority."

The island was as quiet as a grave. Catroux had another question that must be asked. "Father, for how long? How long do we have?"

Lucifer breathed deeply, and replied, " Until the time of the end, until the end of the seven years. Then there will be war. Terrible war. You will unite with the kings of the Far East to fight the Galilean. We will meet him on that field that my servant Napoleon once called the greatest natural battlefield on earth. Armageddon!"

"And will we win, Father? Will we conquer the Galilean there?"

A look of defeat crossed Lucifer's handsome face. "I don't know. I truly don't know. It is written in the book that we will fall, and that we will be forever condemned to the fires of hell by our eternal nemesis. But I haven't given up. I still wonder. There must be a way to change the outcome. That will be your task for the next seven years. You will have unchallenged authority. You will have all my mighty powers to assist you. Any miracle, any wonder, just call upon me and I will help you. Just as today, the image on television catapulted you to international acceptance, so you will use the image throughout these years. Make it say anything you want. Use your powers to do anything you need. All things are possible to you now."

"You mean, anything except the giving of life?"

Lucifer jerked his arm from his son's shoulder. "We take life, Wolf. We don't give it. Remember that!"

The two figures walked together into the darkness.

"Come, my son, we must go now. We have much to do. And so very, very far to go."

ONLY THE BEGINNING